FERAL

SHADOW BRED BOOK 3

GRACE MCGINTY

Editing by Aubergine Editing

Cover by DAZED Designs

ALSO BY GRACE MCGINTY

Hell's Redemption Series: The Redeemable/The Unrepentant/The Fallen

Damnation MC Duet: Serendipity/Providence

The Azar Nazemi Trilogy : Smoke and Smolder/Burn and Blaze/Rage and Ruin

Dark River Days Series: Newly Undead In Dark River/Happily Undead In Dark River/Pleasantly Undead in Dark River

Black Mountain Mates: Hunting Isla

Eden Academy Series: The Lost and the Hunted (Prequel)/Heart of the Hounded (Prequel)/ Rebels and Runaways (Book 1)/Sweethearts and Savages (Book 2)

Shadow Bred Series: Manix/Frenzy/Feral

Stand Alone Novels and Novellas: Bright Lights From A Hurricane/The Last Note/ Inside The Maelstrom Part 1 and 2

For my Family
Always xo

FERAL

PREFACE

This book runs concurrently with the end of Frenzy, so there are some overlapping events. If you haven't read the emotional rollercoaster that is Frenzy (Shadow Bred Book 2), now would be the time!

PROLOGUE

CORVIN

Before

I f the Alpha General caught us out here hunting with guns instead of claws, he'd kick our asses. You were only meant to hunt in your Beast form; the weapons of humans were only good against other humans. The Legion soldiers still used them though, even if most of them sucked. Couldn't hit the side of a barn from five feet away.

Not that Beckett or me needed to train to be Legion. We didn't want to be soldiers, whipping boys for the Alpha General, that old cocksucker.

"Corvin, I'm starving," Beckett grumbled. "Can we just go home now?"

Beckett wasn't much of a hunter, but he was so

fucking smart. That was worth more than being able to throw a punch, in my opinion.

It was because of Beckett that I hated the Alpha General. Beckett's mama was a Legion Widow, and the Alpha General had come around when his dad hadn't even been in the ground a year, trying to insist that Beckett's mother remarry as soon as possible and produce more offspring. Preferably with him.

One day, he didn't take no for an answer. It was only by sheer luck that we'd arrived home when we did, with the Omega Raiden—forcing the Alpha General to finally accept her vehement rejection. Because while he might've been able to brush our concerns aside, Raiden's dad was a fucking Legion General, and Raiden was his pride and joy. Raiden would have told too; he was a good guy like that. Believed in doing the right thing, and didn't expect to be treated like a crown jewel because of his Omega status.

"You think we should try and court Raiden?" I whispered to Beckett, who just frowned.

"What the hell does that have to do with food?" I gave him a pointed look, and he sighed. "He's nice. I like him. But my Beast doesn't think he's right."

I hummed in the back of my throat. Yeah, neither did my Beast, but... "There aren't many left, and Raiden *is* nice. He's pretty cool, plus not too bad to look at," I argued with a grin.

My gaze traveled back to the trap we'd set in the woods. Even though we were hunting for deer, it wouldn't hurt to catch a few rabbits for Beckett's mom. It wasn't a particularly clever trap, just some grain spread over the ground with a net held above it. I just needed one or two rabbits stupid enough to set it off.

"I dunno, Corvin. Do we need an Omega so bad that we'd settle?"

I shrugged. "It's what we're supposed to want. It's the 'Manix Dream.'" I did air quotes around the words.

Beck snorted. "The Manix Dream is an Omega pair and a whole house full of cubs, but that's never gonna happen. Why don't we settle on a Beta or two?"

Fucking hell, now I wished I'd never brought it up. This conversation was too heavy for a hunting trip. "We're only seventeen, I guess. We got time."

Beckett seemed relieved I was letting it drop, so I went back to focusing on the trap, ignoring him sifting through my pack for more food. The dude was always hungry—I wasn't surprised, because he was ridiculously tall. I'd swear he had hollow legs, because he ate like a pig and never got any bulkier. I'd met his dad though, so I knew he'd eventually grow out instead of up. Then I'd catch up to his height, and I couldn't fucking wait. He gave me so much shit about being three inches shorter than him.

Until then, he'd probably continue to eat everything in sight.

An odd scent on the wind had me stilling. "Shh," I hissed, the Alpha in my voice coming to the fore. Beckett just rolled his eyes, since he was an Alpha too, but he stilled completely.

My nose twitched. The scent was another Manix. Fuck, I hoped it wasn't the Legion—or worse, the Alpha General.

Out of the trees stepped another Manix alright. A half-blood at most, and a fucking girl. A Beta. But not one I recognized, and I knew everyone.

I looked over at Beckett, whose eyes were wide with surprise. "Who the fuck is that?" he mouthed.

I shrugged, hyper focused as she wandered straight into our rabbit trap. Reacting more than thinking, I loosed the ropes so the net fell down around her. The noise she made as she got tangled up was ear-piercing, almost animalistic as she flailed about furiously.

I jumped down from our perch, Beckett right behind me. When we made it to the net, she was thrashing around like a stuck pig.

"Jesus, fuck, calm the hell down. We'll let you out."

She didn't say anything, just growling and hissing, more beast than girl. She looked like she was only about ten, and she smelled bad. But under that was the unmistakable scent of Manix.

"Still," I growled, throwing out my Alpha voice. I wasn't as powerful as I would be one day, but I wasn't a weakling either. The girl stopped throwing herself about. "We're gonna let you out, okay? Don't run away."

She was saying something unintelligible, and as I cut the ropes away, she was already trying to run.

"Stop!"

This time I put more Alpha in my voice than I'd ever used, and the girl fell to her knees with a pitiful whine. Beckett gave me a scolding look, before walking over to squat down in front of her. She lashed out with her human hands, and I wondered if she even had a Beast form. Surely if she had, she'd have turned by now, right?

Beckett held up his hands. "Easy now, Kitten."

I laughed. "Kitten?"

He shrugged. "She's tiny, angry, and hisses. I think it's fitting." He looked at the girl. "Hey, kid. Do you have a name?"

More garbled words.

"You think she's, you know, not all there? In the head?"

I wasn't sure she understood my words, but she must have understood my tone, because she hissed at me again.

Beckett watched her, his head tilted to the side. "I don't think so? I think..." He frowned. "Name?" He pointed to himself. "Beckett." Then he pointed to me. "Corvin." Then he pointed back to the girl.

She said something in a mumbling slur, and

Beckett shook his head. "I think she's saying 'girl.' In Latin."

"Her name is Girl? And why the hell do you speak Latin? Who the fuck speaks Latin?" I didn't need to see Beckett's face to know he was rolling his eyes. "Fine, so she doesn't speak English, but she speaks Latin. A dead, ancient language. How does that make... Holy shit."

Beckett looked up at me, his eyes wide. "Lorso."

"Lorso."

The girl stopped her struggle at the name. Oh god. I began to hyperventilate on the inside, despite the fact I was trying my best to be a calm Alpha on the outside. "Wasn't it said that he lived on the border?"

Beckett shrugged. "I thought he was dead. Or like, a rumor."

Lorso was the last of the old, old guard. The ones who remembered a time when the Manix thrived and we had wars with Lycanthropes over some bullshit. When we were stronger than we were now. He'd had both a female and male Omega. Legend had it that Lorso's Omega female had been the last one in existence.

When his Omegas died of old age, Lorso had withdrawn from society to die right along with them, and the Legion Generals had let him, happily. His power was too great, and he had no desire to be Alpha General. But if he had, he could have taken it easily.

No one had seen him in decades, and honestly, I'd thought he was just an urban legend by this stage, pulled out by old-timers at Pack gatherings so they could lament how far our species had fallen with the introduction of human blood into our gene pool, blah blah.

I stared at Beckett. "Tell her to take us home, in Latin. Otherwise we're gonna have to take her back to Maxton."

He winced, and I got it. She was a half-blood, and a female. The Legion didn't give a shit what happened to half-bloods, and the Alpha General strongly believed in survival of the fittest. If she couldn't hold her own in the Legion group homes for half-bloods, she'd be fucked. We'd recently seen the older kids kick the shit out of one of the new half-bloods, who'd been unfortunate enough to appear in town in his teen years. Beckett and I had been about to go kick some ass when Gatlin and Finlo stepped in. Gatlin was the Alpha General's kid, but if anyone hated the Alpha General more than me and Beckett, it was Gatlin and Finlo.

Nah, we couldn't take her back to Maxton.

Beckett said something in Latin, and the girl cocked her head to the side. "Don't think she understands, Beck."

"I said I knew Latin, not that I could speak it, Corvin," Beckett said in his pissy voice.

Eventually, either he got the pronunciation right or

she finally understood, because she froze and looked at us warily. Or more specifically, me.

I raised my hands. "I mean you no harm," I told her softly, and then I thrummed deep in my chest. Her eyes went wide, her pupils blowing out. Aw, yeah. I'd been working on my thrum.

Either she'd decided she liked us or she just didn't know any better, because she stood and pointed back into the trees. She gave me another wide-eyed look, and started to jog out of the clearing along an animal trail.

We followed along behind her. After about twenty minutes, we were nearing the edge of Pack grounds, and I was beginning to wonder if we were jogging into a trap. But just as I was about to grab Beckett and head back, we found ourselves in front of a tiny shack. It was little more than a rough-hewn shelter, though now we were this close, I could see a small amount of smoke from a chimney.

The girl pushed through the door and basically chirped something to whoever was inside. There was no doubt that this was her home. We stepped cautiously in behind her, and there was a deep growl from the darkness that made every hair on my body stand on end. The smell of Manix and Alpha permeated every inch of this cabin.

"Lorso? Um, we mean no harm? We come in peace."

"Seriously, Corvin? He's not a fucking alien," Beckett hissed, while the girl bustled around the one tiny room.

"In," came the grunted command, and Alpha or not, I obeyed. Beckett and I stood in the middle of the room, and that's when we saw Lorso.

He was so fucking old, his body withered and gnarled, as he lay on a pallet on the ground. He looked like an ancient, petrified tree, but his eyes glowed brightly even in the darkness. "Who are you?" His voice sounded rough, like he didn't speak much.

"Uh, I'm Corvin Fletcher, and this is my Packmate, Beckett Reid. We, uh, stumbled across the girl in the forest."

The girl said something incomprehensible, and the old man grunted back. "She says you caught her in a trap."

"We were after rabbits, I swear, Sir. We couldn't have known..." That an ancient fucking Manix lived in the forest with a kid.

"No, I suppose you couldn't." He let out a deep sigh. "I'm glad. The Ancestors have been calling me home for a while now, but I couldn't leave her out here defenseless. Couldn't send her there. You'll take care of her now."

His breath rattled, like he was moments from death, making my heart thunder a million miles a minute. "What? No, wait. You can't die!"

He grunted a laugh. "No one's dying this minute, boy. Sit down and ask your questions."

Oh man, did I have a thousand goddamn questions.

Six years later

It was hard to believe the girl in front of us was the same creature we'd caught in a net over half a decade ago. Her dark brown hair was shiny and full, her body slightly plumper now she didn't have to hunt for all her food.

She sifted through the box of essentials we'd brought with us, cooing at the things she liked as she packed away the food. Beckett watched her, his eyes shining with affection.

She hadn't had a name when we met her, but now we called her Kitten. Lorso had just called her Girl.

Fate was funny. Lorso had died days after we first met him and Kitten, like he'd been waiting for someone to shoulder the burden he'd been carrying. Turns out, Kitten was actually a teen when we met her, not a child like we'd thought. She was just tiny for her age, a little due to malnutrition, and a little because of genetics. Lorso said he'd found her abandoned on the northern perimeter of the Packlands, close to death by exposure, only a few weeks old.

He'd intended to take her to town, but he'd run

into Legion soldiers bragging about beating the shit out of a half-blood for fun, and heard how the Alpha General had just laughed when the half-breed complained. Lorso had decided that a life as a hermit was better than a life of torment.

So, he'd raised the baby, and taken care of her long after his spirit became restless and ready to move on. But he'd held onto life, because in his own way, he'd loved her.

After his death, we'd started bringing her food and clothes—she'd been wearing rough dresses fashioned from Lorso's scraps when we met her. We'd taught her to speak English, which was its own hurdle. She was fiery, our Kitten. And easily frustrated. But then we'd introduced her to books, and it was like she was a sunflower in full bloom. You couldn't help but stare at her brilliance. She still couldn't write, but at least she could read.

Every week we'd visit, until it became the best part of our week. "Oh, I've been waiting for this author to release the sequel. Thank you, Beckett." She hugged my Packmate, and he held her tightly.

"I found you something else," Beckett told her, pulling out a laminated card from his back pocket. "Four-leaf clover. People say they're good luck. Thought you could use it as a bookmark."

She took the card, and read it slowly. Beckett had inscribed something on the back, though wouldn't show me what it was. Kitten looked up and gave him a smile so joyous, it made my heart want to burst.

"Thank you, Beck. I'll keep it forever." She walked over to her bed and pulled out a small metal box, no bigger than a loaf of bread. An old munitions box was my guess. We'd both seen the box before—it held the keepsakes of a girl who had no need for material possessions. It wasn't jewels she kept in there, but the wing of a butterfly she found, and the stick and string doll Lorso had made for her when she was a child. Dried flowers and shiny rocks. A small hunk of gold she found in the creek bed sat right next to a piece of river-polished quartz. She didn't see that one was worth more than the other.

She went outside to collect some of the wood I'd just chopped, and we followed behind her. It was hard to tell when we'd stopped being kids raising another kid, and started acting like a Pack, but at some point it had just occurred naturally. Not officially, though, because Lorso had instilled a fear so deep into Kitten that it was part of her core nature.

That fear? Maxton and the other Manix.

We hadn't tried to dissuade her—partly because we liked not having to share her. She was our Kitten, and we were inherently selfish.

But everything changes eventually.

"Kitten?"

"Yes, Corvin?" she mocked, mimicking my deep voice.

"Do you want to be part of our Pack?"

She froze, then turned slowly toward me. "Would you move out here?"

I chewed my lip. We couldn't. I had an apprenticeship as a Legion mechanic, and Beckett taught at the high school. Plus there was—

"We can't. You'd have to move to Maxton," Beckett said softly.

She frowned. "No. You move here."

Beckett shook his head. "We met an Omega, Kitten. He's agreed to be part of our Pack. We want you to be a part of that Pack too."

She gasped like we'd slapped her. "You found someone else?" She paused. "Do they know about me?"

There was real fear in her voice now, under the note of pain. But we'd sworn, first to Lorso, and then later to Kitten herself, that we wouldn't tell a soul about her. We wouldn't break our word, but it burned to keep secrets from Darius and Cooper.

"No one knows. But they'd love you, Kitten, if you just gave them a chance." I watched as she shut down, and began building the walls inside her to block us out.

Beckett made a low noise of pain in his throat. "Please, just think about it. *We* love you."

She looked between us, but was already shaking her head. "I love you too. Both of you. But I won't go. I won't be part of a Pack." She stepped back into the cabin, which we'd been steadily improving over the years until it was actually comfortable, with a solid front door.

"Kitten..."

She shook her head furiously. "Leave. Don't come back. It's better for all of us." Then she slammed the door in our faces. Beckett knocked, thudding against the oak wood repeatedly, until I grabbed his fist.

"Leave it, man. Let her think about it. We'll talk to her again next week."

I'd been so fucking wrong about that though. Next week, she hadn't been home when we arrived. Or the week after. It was like she knew when we were coming, even when we mixed it up. Week after week, she wasn't there, and if it wasn't for the lack of supply boxes, or the subtle signs that the cabin was inhabited, I'd suspect that she'd left.

For a whole year, we went back every week. Then, we'd go back every month with supplies. We mated Darius, and cemented the Wiley-Fletcher-Reid Pack. We were happy, and our monthly trips became bi-monthly, until we eventually stopped going altogether.

But Kitten was a ghost that had left behind a wound which refused to heal.

1

BECKETT

Four years after that

There was a strange feeling in the air, a pulsing wildness that made the air in my lungs burn, and my Beast stir from the depths of my body. Darius, Corvin and Coop were at the Sanctum, and I felt the urge to go over there, just to make sure they were safe.

I chewed my bottom lip, and then nodded to myself. Better to be safe than sorry, and besides, shit around here had been weird lately. A new Alpha General had enacted all sorts of crazy change, and even though I liked Courtland, it was going to stir things up. Then Bonnie, who worked with Darius at the Sanctum, had collapsed into a coma from some mystery illness. Honestly, it was all too unsettled for my liking.

Just as I grabbed my keys, I heard Corvin's ATV pull into the driveway. He was home early. Coop was staying at the Sanctum with Darius tonight, but normally we'd all hang around over there until after the kids had all gone to bed.

I looked out the living room window, and stiffened as I watched him run toward the house. I'd known Corvin my entire life; I knew when something was wrong. He looked more disheveled than normal, his strawberry blond hair mussed and wild.

I raced to meet him at the front door. When I wrenched it open, Corvin—the Alpha of our Alphas, I guess—was staring at me with wild blue eyes.

"Corvin, what's wrong? Is it Darius? Coop?"

I didn't realize I'd reached out and grabbed him until he flexed beneath my hands, like he'd been electrocuted.

"Bonnie turned into an Omega. And so have the other unmated Betas."

My heart stopped beating. "What?" That didn't make sense, not even one little bit. You didn't just change your designation. Bonnie was one hundred percent Beta. She was the best of them, really.

"I don't fucking know, Beck. I ran into Radic taking an unconscious Bonnie into their Packhouse, and my nose doesn't lie, man. She was Omega. Radic said that they were all turning Omega, and that the new Alpha General was predicting a frenzy." He paused, staring me dead in the eye. "Because all the unmated Betas are turning into Omegas in heat. *All of them.*" He said the last bit slowly, and it finally dawned on me.

"Kitten," I breathed, horror constricting my throat. I started peeling off my clothes, preparing to shift. She'd be alone out there, and the other Alphas would be in rut.

But when I got to my jeans, I slowed. We'd be in rut. What if we hurt her?

"Is it safe?"

Corvin looked more serious than usual. "I was around Bonnie and didn't turn into a slavering animal, so I think so?"

We both knew there was a difference between Bonnie, our friend, and Kitten, the girl our Beasts had claimed as Pack all those years ago. But I'd rather take the risk than leave her out there defenseless.

I finished shedding my clothes and shifted. "Let's go."

I was out of the door and heading for the woods behind our house, not letting any thoughts but getting Kitten to safety enter my brain. I knew the path instinctually, having walked it so many times I could do it with my eyes closed—or in this case, close to full-blown panic.

Corvin had his nose to the wind, scenting for

threats, listening for other predators in the woods. There were very few creatures that could take down a Manix in full Beast form, and the large predators of this ecosystem stood no chance.

I could tell the moment that Corvin caught her scent though, because his whole body went rigid. I turned, raising my face to the breeze. Omega, in heat.

I went instantly hard.

Fuck.

Fuck, fuckity, fuck, fuck fuck.

My feet stilled, and I heaved in lungfuls of air as I got ahold of myself. Then I changed back to the man. It was too hard to keep ahold of my Beast in my other form, and right now, Kitten needed the man, not the Beast.

Corvin had a backpack clutched in his claws, and right then I loved the hell out of him, because even in a crisis, he'd remembered to bring clothes and supplies. He dropped the bag in front of me, his chest still vibrating with a rumbling growl. I grabbed out my discarded jeans, forgoing a shirt. If she was okay, she'd freak out if we rocked up naked and fully beasted out. But we would all be more vulnerable in our human forms.

"I'll stay shifted," Corvin said, in his deep, rumbling voice that would have made a human shiver with fear. "Just in case."

I looked up at him, letting my pure appreciation shine through. "Thank you."

He waved a clawed hand, and I knew he just wanted to hurry. There were no other scents around Kitten's house, and I had a feeling that Lorso had his own wards put on the place all those decades ago to keep people away. It was why he'd always been considered more of an urban legend than a real figure in Manix society—there was just a general sense of unease once you got past a certain point in the woods. You felt like you were reaching the edge of Pack territory and then a strange foreboding started to sink in.

In reality, there was another mile between Kitten's house and the border of the Packlands. When the first female Omega we'd had in centuries arrived in Maxton, forcing the former Alpha General to strengthen the wards, I'd breathed a sigh of relief, though I didn't say anything to Corvin. No one could sneak over the back side of the Packlands and hurt Kitten now.

As we moved around to the front of the cabin, I noticed there was no light burning in the window, and my heart pounded in my ears. What if she'd passed out while bathing in the stream and drowned? What if she'd fallen into her fire? The Manix could survive a lot of things, but drowning and burning to death weren't included in that list.

I pounded on the rough wooden door that had

weathered with a run of hard winters. "Kitten! Kitten, are you in there?"

Silence. I couldn't breathe.

Corvin walked up beside me and kicked in the door. It banged open, and I knew something was wrong. It was too still, too silent. "Kitten?"

We moved into the house in unison, checking everywhere for the girl who'd stolen our heart. There was food on the table, uneaten—as if she'd just stepped out—but the ashes in the fireplace were cold. Wherever she was, she'd been gone for a while.

A roar from the bedroom had me racing to the only other room in the cabin. Corvin was hovering over an unconscious Kitten. She looked paler than normal, her body limp, like a lifeless doll. I was on my knees beside her before I even consciously thought to move. I checked her pulse, but it was strong, and her skin was warm and dry. It was like she was just asleep.

I checked her over for any cuts and bruises, anything broken, but she was perfect. Corvin's rumbling growls in the background were a distraction, but I didn't chastise him. He was as scared as I was.

"She feels fine. Strong and healthy." I shook her a little. "Kitten? Kitten, can you hear me? It's Beckett."

"*Wake up, Omega,*" Corvin roared, the Alpha power in his voice making my skin prickle, but Kitten remained still.

"Obviously, Corvin is here too." I looked up at my

best friend. "She's completely unconscious. We need to take her back to the Packhouse."

I didn't think about the fact that Darius was going to lose his shit that we'd kept this from him for years, or the fact that she was now a female Omega—something I knew he'd prayed to the Goddess for after the Huxley-Grey Omega had appeared from nowhere like a gift.

I wasn't even sure I believed in the Goddess, but it was hard to deny now though. Changing designations, your actual biology? That was fucking insane.

Corvin bent down, scooping her up into his arms with a gentleness that belied his scales and huge claws. We were monsters, but not with Kitten. Kitten was everything.

"Let's go."

2

DARIUS

The whole fucking town had gone insane. It had started about an hour ago, the scent of female Omegas in heat permeating Maxton like the most delicious scent you'd ever inhaled.

The ache in my gut had started around then too, and I could hear my pulse as it whooshed through my ears. Most of the kids at the Sanctum were too little to be affected by the pheromones, but the teenagers weren't. While they weren't in frenzy, their emotions were heightened and aggressive. Cooper had to use his Alpha voice to send them to their rooms, because otherwise there'd be fights all night.

"Where the hell are Corvin and Beck?" Cooper grumbled. "We could use some fucking help down here before I hogtie some of these little shits and throw them in their closets."

"What did Merrick say?" Merrick and his Packmate Murphy were Legion Force, and if there was shit going down, they'd know.

"He said that all the female Betas had spontaneously turned into Omegas, and all went into heat at once. He said it happened to Bonnie first." He shook his head. "Goddess save them all if we go into a frenzy. I messaged the Alpha General and told him we'd take care of the Sanctum so he could take care of the town, and Bonnie."

Anyone with eyes could see that the Alpha General wanted Bonnie more than he wanted his next breath, and I was glad for my friend. She deserved it. She deserved to be worshiped, because she'd spent her whole life being as selfless as a goddamn saint.

"Well, that would be easier if Corvin and Beckett would answer their phones and come by." I hesitated. "You don't think they're frenzied, do you?"

Cooper stepped toward me, pulling me tight into his arms. "No, Omega. They love you, and they are in control of their Beasts. They are probably out cracking skulls and keeping everyone in line. Corvin has definitely been waiting for an appropriate time to punch some people."

He was right, but the scent of the Omegas was getting to me too. I was going to go through the yearning, which was like the male Omega version of a heat, and that was always crap. Almost like, I don't know, when you're working yourself up to a giant sneeze, and then can't.

But as much as I loved Cooper's reassurances, we couldn't know how we'd react until faced with an Omega in heat, begging for someone to give her relief. It was our biological imperative to make her feel better.

I heard low voices outside, and the rumbling growl of an Alpha. My Alpha. Cooper stiffened, and I strained to hear what was happening in the front yard. The scent of Omega increased outside the Sanctum, and I wondered if that meant that Bonnie was awake.

I walked to the door, and pulled it open. Standing in the doorway, naked, was Corvin. Behind him was Beckett, his face closed down into something unreadable, the falling night casting even more shadow over his broodingly dark features.

In Corvin's arms was an unconscious woman. No, scratch that, an unconscious Omega female.

"What the hell has happened?" I hissed, searching the woman's face. But she wasn't familiar at all. I knew everyone in Maxton, but not this woman. This Omega.

"What have you done?" Cooper's sharp bark echoed my thoughts.

"Nothing," Corvin growled, the sound more Beast than man. "And I don't like what you're insinuating."

I growled back. "Coop isn't the one who's just turned up naked with an unconscious Omega, Corvin Fletcher." I looked out into the darkness behind him. I could hear the shouting, and sense the insanity in the air. "Get in the house. Goddammit. Why would you bring an Omega to a house filled with kids?"

"She's stirring, and we're still too far away from the Packhouse," Beckett answered. "Plus, it didn't feel right without you two."

"What doesn't feel right?" Cooper demanded, and I hushed him.

"Take her up to the top bedroom. She's in heat, and she'll want something smaller and cozier." I always did. The top floor was unused at the moment, and mostly we kept it for emergencies. My body buzzed just being in her presence, and I gritted my teeth. We were not mindless animals. "Then you can tell me who this is and what the fuck is going on. And be quiet; the little ones are finally all asleep."

Corvin bowed his head softly, and as he walked past me, he leaned forward and kissed my temple. I watched his naked ass climb the stairs. It was a great ass. Fuck it.

I looked at Beckett, and he had the good grace to look a little ashamed. "It's not what you're thinking. Let us explain."

Cooper grumbled and strode off after Corvin, but I watched Beckett's face, cataloging the earnestness of his expression and the shadow of guilt around his eyes.

"Lock up. I want this place more secure than Fort Knox."

I turned and headed up the stairs, stopping at the linen closet and grabbing all the extra blankets and pillows I could find. She'd need somewhere soft, as her skin would begin to feel too tight and her whole body would soon feel like it was on fire.

I walked into the still dark bedroom, noticing that Cooper had found Corvin some pants. The girl who was lying in the middle of the bed like Sleeping Beauty was gorgeous. Wild brown hair, full pink lips, and a face that was wholly unfamiliar. Her skin was almost inhumanly pale, like a ghost.

"Who is she?"

Corvin looked over his shoulder, dragging his eyes away from her. I didn't blame him though; with her hair fanned out like that, she looked enchanting. "Her name is Kitten. Well, at least that was the name we gave her."

They gave her? I didn't understand.

Cooper cleared his throat. "We should let her sleep."

Corvin hesitated. "I'd rather she didn't wake up alone, somewhere unfamiliar."

My heart stuttered in my chest. Was he choosing her over me? Was that what was happening right now?

My face must have displayed the pain in my chest, because Corvin was across the room immediately, pulling me into his chest, and thrumming hard only seconds later. "No, Darius. Whatever you're thinking is wrong, I swear it. I love you with everything I am." He paused. "I'll explain everything when Beckett gets here, but I promise, you're my very soul, Darius. There's no choice for me but you."

I nodded, because I could feel through our connection that he was telling the truth. There was no doubt in my mind that he loved me.

But he obviously knew this woman. And he'd kept her a secret.

Beckett came in, leaving the door open just a crack so we could hear the rest of the house. Cooper frowned in the corner, but I saw how often his eyes slid back to the woman, this Kitten, in the bed.

"One of you better start talking," I muttered, keeping my voice lowered.

Corvin sucked in a deep breath. "We met Kitten years before you looked our way. We actually trapped her in the forest hunting for rabbits one day. She was a tiny, hissing, wild child, an unknown Beta Manix. I would have been less surprised if we'd caught a damn dragon. She was dirty and skinny, and it sounded like she just babbled incomprehensibly, but Beckett worked out she was speaking Latin. We convinced her to take us to where she lived. We met her guardian, Lorso. She looked like a small child back then, but she was thirteen."

I frowned. Lorso? Like the ancient fucking Manix who everyone thought was dead?

"How long ago was this?"

"Eleven years."

"Hold up... *Lorso?* Of the Raku-Lorso-Niles Pack?" Cooper asked incredulously. "Isn't he a myth? Or long dead, anyway?"

Beckett snorted. "Well, dead now. Back then, I'd never seen someone so ancient who wasn't an immortal. He died a couple of days after we met them both, like he'd been waiting for us."

I shook my head. Okay, mystery girl and an urban legend who was, in fact, real.

Corvin picked back up. "We started going out there, making sure she was okay. It was obvious that she and Lorso had been living in the old ways, catching and killing their food, hunting from the woods. But you know what it's like—after a long winter, there's never quite enough. So we supplemented her food, bought her clothes, taught her to read and speak something that wasn't a bastardized form of Old Man Latin and wild beast."

He hesitated, looking over at me. "We loved her. But she was terrified of Maxton, of the Manix. Of civilization in general. I don't know what she learned about us at Lorso's knee growing up, but whatever it was, it warped her forever. She wouldn't move here with us, so we planned to move to her, one day. Once we had good jobs, and saved up enough money to do the upgrades to her cabin. Always something else and something else, but we were never ready." He smiled sadly at me. "Turns out you were the something else we'd been waiting for. You and Coop. You completed our Pack, and for the first time, we had something in our life that rivaled what we felt for Kitten." He trailed off, his eyes still filled with an old pain. I recognized the expression on his face, that wistful longing, but I'd never registered that maybe he was longing for something he'd lost.

Beckett sighed. "We begged her to come with us, to let us introduce her to you guys, but she said no. She was adamant. She shut us out and never let us back in again. We chose you. And we've never regretted that choice," he said quickly.

"But a part of you still longed for her," I said softly.

He nodded. "Don't get me wrong, Omega. I have been happy every single day since the moment you walked into our life."

But he would have been happier if she'd been here too?

Yes. I wasn't a jealous man, despite my earlier worries. I sat in silence for a moment, digesting everything I'd just learned. The guys finally showed good sense and didn't interrupt as I rethought every moment in our relationship under this new lense. Could the happiest moments have been better with her here? The hardships have been weathered better with a Beta beside me, helping me soothe the wild Alpha emotions?

A Beta may have helped me care for these three stubborn, bullheaded Alphas over the years, and I would have been glad for it. But right now, she was just a shining neon sign, pointing to a betrayal by two of the men I loved more than any other beings that walked the earth.

I wasn't sure if it was the silence, or the scent of the Omega that got too much for Cooper, but he left, mumbling something about checking on the Sanctum kids.

I stepped forward, brushing the hair from the forehead of the woman on the bed. She was going to be so scared when she woke up. I traced my finger along a scar that curved around her forehead. What kind of life must she have lived, up there all alone?

I pulled back my hand, but with lightning-fast reflexes, there were fingers around my wrist, gripping me tightly and scaring the living shit out of me.

"Ah!"

"Help me," came the whimpered words as I looked down at her wide brown eyes. "Please. I hurt. Everything... hurts." She writhed on the bed in pain, like she couldn't escape the sensations under her skin. I knew that feeling, knew it intimately, the blissful torture of it.

Something inside me snapped, like a rubber band pulled too tight, and the ends wrapped around this ethereal creature clutching my arm. The Omega inside me recognized the fear and pain, tempered with lust, staring up at me from the depths of her soul.

"It's okay, Kitten. I'll make all the pain go away." I clamped my lips shut. That hadn't been me, the man, making that promise. Oh, shit. The Beast was out to play, and I had a feeling that he wasn't going to let me hold the wheel again anytime soon.

3

KITTEN

My body felt like I had lead rather than blood coursing through my veins. I tried to swim out of the darkness, but it was hard. I felt... wrong. That permeated my brain before I was even fully conscious.

As I waded back to consciousness, and my senses finally came back online, I knew there was something very, very wrong. I wasn't in my bed; this one was too soft, but even that couldn't cushion my itching, burning skin. The scents in the room were both familiar and foreign. The ache in my gut was only exacerbated by the fear that was beginning to flood my body. There were fingertips brushing my head that seemed to chase away the pain for a moment, making me almost purr. Then those soothing fingers began to pull away, and the pulsing pain began to crowd back in.

I grabbed the first body part I could, which was a wrist. As if having my eyes shut was the only thing holding back the residual ache, it all flooded in when they snapped open. I writhed on the bed, and it felt like my body was betraying itself, the pain growing and growing until it was unbearable.

"Help me," I gasped. "Please. I hurt. Everything... hurts." Even my eyelashes hurt, and instinctively I knew that this dark-haired man, this stranger, could make it all go away. I curved toward him, trying to drag him down onto the bed. But he was tall and strong, and I could sense his Beast close to the surface.

Manix.

Where the fuck was I?

"It's okay, Kitten. I'll make all the pain go away."

His words were like a balm, and while I would normally be afraid of him, all I wanted was for him to get down into the bed with me and roll my body across his. I just *knew* he was an Omega.

Scents overwhelmed me, but there were two I knew. "Corvin? Beck?" Their familiar scents calmed me, and when Beckett's soft face appeared, I cried. He looked exactly the same as he had all those years ago, when I'd loved the boy he'd been. "What's happening to me?"

"Kitten, listen closely." He was using his Alpha voice on me, and I had no choice but to listen. "An illness swept through Maxton, affecting only Beta females, changing your biology. It's made you an Omega." He swallowed hard, and I was transfixed by the bobbing of his Adam's apple. "And you're in heat. That's why you feel this way."

None of that made sense, and it was like I was that kid again, trying to understand the boy in front of me as he spoke a foreign language. It just made me cry harder. "Make it go away," I sobbed as another stabbing pain hit me. "It hurts so much."

There was a low, savage growl in the room, and for some reason, it soothed me rather than scaring me. I knew the timber of the growl, knew the Alpha pheromones that were coating my skin. Corvin. He was here too, and another knot of tension eased in my chest.

The pretty guy with the soft eyes was there again, pieces of his auburn hair falling across his forehead. "I know it hurts. I've been there. Unfortunately, you just have to wait it out." His face looked torn.

"You're theirs? The Omega?" His face crumbled, but he nodded. Part of me hated the sadness in his eyes, though I wasn't sure why he was sad. "I understand now. Now that I see you." I tried to give him a reassuring smile, and he cupped my cheek.

"I didn't know about you."

My eyes flicked to Beck, who had his head in his

hands. I felt bad, because that was my fault. I'd made them swear. "Good men. Kept their word." Fuck, this Omega male's hands felt so nice, cooling my skin where he touched, and chasing away the pain. I needed more. "Lay with me?" It was a whine. "You make it hurt less."

He hesitated, looking at the Alphas in front of me. Finally, he nodded, taking off his shirt and climbing onto the bed with me. "Skin contact will help. I, uh, I'm only going off my own experience. I don't know what happens with female Omegas."

I sighed as his chest met the skin of my back. I wanted to press myself against him until I was inside him. It soothed, but didn't chase away the pain altogether. I needed more, but I didn't know what that more was. Honestly, I would have given my left nut for it. I didn't actually have nuts, but it was one of those English sayings the guys had taught me, and it stuck.

"Name?" Pain was killing my language, slurring my words until I was reverting back to that wild language of my past.

"Darius. My name is Darius." I froze as I felt the hard length that could only be one thing pressed against my ass. He grunted as he felt my body stiffening, and he bent his body away. "Ignore that."

Oh sure, I was going to ignore the giant dick pressed against my back. The Beast inside me—the one in heat—arched back against him, chasing the feeling again, and the human part of me was horrified.

"I'm sorry." But I couldn't drag myself away.

He grunted again, his hand on my hip stilling my grinding. "Don't be. Our biology is urging us to do the very thing we were created for. Male and female Omegas were made to fit together like this, made to ease the pain of the other. We are two sides of the same coin." He cleared his throat. "My body wants to soothe the ache of yours in the only way it knows how, and your Beast is fully on board. But we aren't just Beasts; we're people too, and logic is what's needed right now."

His hand stroked up and down my hip soothingly. I realized I was still in the yoga pants and sweatshirt I'd been wearing... however long ago. They were nearly threadbare, and if I stood in the sun, they were basically transparent, but they were the last items of clothing that Beckett and Corvin had gifted to me before we'd cut ties. I mean, before *I'd* cut ties. Lorso had taught me a few things when I was a kid, and one of them was how to know if another Manix was approaching. I'd avoided them for months, until they'd finally just stopped coming altogether.

The pain dulled at Darius's touch, but it was still there, like a burning in my abdomen. "How would you stop the pain?"

He stilled, and I could sense him looking at the Alphas again. His Alphas.

"Kitten..." Corvin's voice was filled with longing and pain.

"I want to know."

"Tell her. She has a right to know. Doesn't mean we'll act on it," Beckett said softly, always the cool voice of reason. God, I'd missed their bickering. Not that I'd tell them that.

I felt Darius stiffen behind me, but he didn't stop the movements of his hand. Skin to skin, that's what he said. But my sweatshirt was still in the way. I tugged it up, tucking it up under my chin, baring my back to his front. The moment our skin met, I shuddered. This was better.

The relief from pain made me lightheaded, but the pain haze that had been fogging my thoughts was starting to lift. This was like the worst period pain ever —it felt like PMS cramps, if your eggs were ninja stars. "Speak."

Darius's heavy sigh puffed against the back of my neck, cooling it softly, which told me that I was sweating. "The heat, and the yearning for male Omegas, is nature's way of ensuring that we, uh... procreate. The only way to naturally ease your discomfort is to do what nature intended and have sex." He trailed off, leaving me with a suspicion that wasn't the whole truth.

"And?"

Darius let out a whine, making something in me

keen with him, and I wiggled my ass back against him subconsciously. Like I was trying to ease his pain too.

"You would still hurt, but it would be less. It could take around a week for the heat to subside this way, and basically, it would be five to seven days of constant sex to make sure your body was too flooded with endorphins to realize we weren't *quite* doing what Mother Nature intended."

He was talking in circles, and I growled low in my throat, making the energy of the room shift. I could almost feel them all stretching toward me.

It was Corvin who answered my unspoken question. "We were made to breed during this time, Kitten. Traditionally, to ease the heat, Darius would fuck you, drawing your eggs into his body for us to fertilize. You would have to impregnate our male Omega."

"Oh." That did seem drastic.

Beckett snorted. "Fuck, I missed you, Kitten." Then he pressed his lips closed, like he'd said something bad. His dark brown eyes were shining in the dim light and his normally light brown hair seemed almost black from the shadows.

I realized, too late probably, that I was rubbing up against his Omega like I had any right. I twisted, looking over my shoulder at Darius. He looked like he was in pain. "Sorry."

He shook his head, giving me a tight smile. "Not

your fault." He gave the guys the stink eye. No prizes for guessing whose fault he thought it was.

"Third option?"

"Cooper said they're putting the new Omegas in the bottom cells of the Legion building to keep them safe, then sedating them as best they can with human drugs."

Oh hell no. That wasn't an option for me. I wasn't going anywhere near the Legion Building.

"I can't go home and..." I cut off as my body curled in on itself, a cramp doing its best to set my insides on fire. Seven days of this torture sounded just as impossible. There was only one solution that my brain, or maybe it was my Beast, would even remotely consider. "Can we do option one?"

Everyone in the room stilled. Even the air stilled. The silence was like a heavy blanket across us all, suffocating and comforting all at once.

It was Corvin who broke the silence. "Excuse me, what?"

4

COOPER

I'd left the guys and the sleeping girl alone about an hour ago, but judging by the soft hum of voices, she'd woken up. This secret Beta-turned-Omega that the guys had hidden from us for nearly half a decade. My Packmates. The men I loved more than any other people in the world, and they'd been lying to Darius and I like it was nothing. But you only had to see the way they looked at this woman, this Kitten, to know that they'd loved her at some point. Maybe they still loved her.

Now, everyone's feelings were all mixed up in the heat pheromones, and it was hard to know what was legit and what was just horny Alpha desire. I paced up and down the hall, but all was quiet here.

"Coop?" someone called softly, and I looked

around the corner at Beckett, who looked guilty as fuck.

"What?"

"We need you here. Pack decision."

I raised both eyebrows. "Oh, now it's a Pack decision? You and Corvin don't want to unilaterally make decisions for all of us?"

His jaw tensed. "Come on, man. It wasn't like that. Please, just come and meet her. Speak to her. We need to have a Pack discussion."

"Is she Pack now?"

He hesitated, and I knew she could probably hear. I was being a dick, but one of us had to keep their goddamn head.

"Please, Cooper."

I sighed and pushed off the wall. As I got closer to the room, the scent of Omega became dizzying. I gritted my teeth. What the fuck were we going to do about the fact that we had a house full of kids?

I huffed as I walked past Beckett, ignoring the comforting hand he placed on my shoulder. The pheromones in the bedroom were like being hit in the face with a baseball bat, and my eyes went straight to the bed, to my Omega wrapped around this girl.

I couldn't deny the way my Beast reacted to the sight though, his purr of approval bursting past my lips before I could clamp them shut. I looked over at

Corvin; he hadn't dragged his eyes away from what was happening on the bed.

"What's the decision?" I already knew, of course. I wasn't an idiot. But you bet your ass I was going to make them spell it out for me in the most painful, awkward way possible.

"Kitten, this is my Alpha, Cooper. He's been my best friend since we were four and my mate since we were eighteen, and part of the Wiley-Fletcher-Reid Pack for six years. He's a good man." Darius's voice was soft as he whispered in the woman's ear.

She turned her head and smiled at me. It was a pained smile, and I knew she was probably feeling like every single hair on her body was being plucked out. At least, that's what Darius said the yearning felt like. It was why we'd pursued Naja, the first female Omega, when she first appeared. Though I understood why she turned down our request that she donate her eggs.

All this flitted through my brain as my eyes locked with this Omega, this Kitten, and stayed there. Ensnared. She moaned as her body scrunched in on itself. I resisted the urge to go to her, to fuck her with my mouth to ease the pain. To make her come over and over until she was too blissed out to feel anything.

"I'm sorry. I didn't mean to..." It was like she lost the words, muttering something that sounded like a different language.

"Intrude, Kitten. But you aren't intruding, is she

Cooper? It isn't her fault at all. None of this is," Beckett said softly.

I looked over at Beck. "What language is she speaking?"

Corvin huffed. "Kittenish. It's her own language. A little Latin, a little grumpy Old Manix grunting, a little animal. Beckett learned so we could teach her English. Guess you didn't keep up with it, Kitten?"

She gave Corvin a narrow-eyed look, and there was something in the stubbornness of her chin that intrigued me. "Not much point," she said peevishly, before groaning. "It hurts... Please," she gasped, and I took a step toward her before I even realized.

"She wants us to help her through the heat. It might go for the normal full week, or hours, or days. Radic couldn't tell me when I messaged him. Doc doesn't know. There's no manual on spontaneous acts of the Goddess," Corvin muttered.

My Beast roared his approval, but the Beast and the man sometimes had different views of what the Pack needed. Helping an Omega through her heat? That kind of thing created a bond, whether we wanted it to or not.

I looked between my Pack members. Who was I kidding? They already had a bond with her; they just hadn't mated her.

Though Corvin didn't seem convinced. "Maybe we

can get something to knock you back out? This shouldn't be how your first time goes."

The female Omega made a choking noise, which I quickly realized was laughter. "First time? I haven't been sitting around my cabin waiting for you, Corvin. I went to town and had sex a long time ago."

The wash of Alpha vibes that poured off Beckett and Corvin could have choked a dragon. The sudden tsunami of possessiveness was almost tangible. I had no doubt that if things had even gone slightly differently, the woman in front of us would be Pack.

Every writhe of pain, every whimper, grated against my very nature until I said, "Fine. Help her." I turned to leave, but Corvin was there, his arm blocking the door.

"It's going to take all of us, Coop."

My whole body thrummed, but I kept my face impassive. "Corvin, I do not know this woman. It's been, what, five or six years? You don't know her anymore either. I'm not about to take advantage of a situation where her consent is already a bit sketchy. Now move. I have to call my family and see if they'll take over caring for the Sanctum while both Darius and Bonnie are otherwise indisposed."

I stomped out of the room and down the hall, not taking a deep breath until I was around the corner in the living room. My dick felt so hard that I was convinced it was about to snap off.

I'd meant what I said to Corvin though; despite what the Pack—and my dick—wanted, I didn't think that Kitten was in any head space to be agreeing to have sex with an Alpha she didn't know. I could understand maybe Corvin and Beckett—she knew them, and had obviously loved them at one time in her life. I could even understand Darius, because her new nature would've meant she had an instant, undeniable attraction to my Omega.

Me, on the other hand? I was a stranger. An Alpha during not only her first heat, but during a frenzy. I had control of myself, and I was going to keep all these insane fucking feelings locked down tight.

I grabbed my cell phone from where I'd dumped it on the hall table. I pulled up my parents' number, and they answered on the second ring.

"Cooper? Are you okay?" My mom sounded panicked.

"I'm fine, Mom. The whole Pack is fine. How about you guys?"

Mom snorted. "Your father had to bonk Freddie on the head because he was snarling and shifting and generally acting crazy, but everyone else is fine."

Freddie was my youngest brother, who was nineteen. He was already filled with hormones and crap without the insanity of simultaneous Omega heats doing a number on him.

"That's good. Do you think you could do me a

favor, Mom? I hate to ask you, but it's kind of important."

"Of course, Cooper. Anything."

I sucked in a deep breath because I hated lying to my parents. "The whole crazy biological event is hitting Darius hard, and we thought it would be best to get him back to the Packhouse." Technically not an untruth. "Could you come and take care of the Sanctum for us? It'd be a day or two at max," I cajoled. I knew she wouldn't say no. My parents were soft, especially when it came to Darius.

"Yes, Cooper! All you have to do is ask." I could hear her cover the phone as she yelled, "Leo! Pack a bag! They need help over at the Sanctum. No, you won't need your damn sword, you silly old fool!"

I held back the chuckle that wanted to burst from my chest. I loved my parents. I couldn't hear what my father said back, but I can imagine it was just as sassy. I had six fathers, which was why I had so many damn brothers, and two sisters—both happily mated, thank fuck. Pretty sure for two decades my mother had been permanently pregnant. But they loved every single one of us, and I couldn't have asked for a better childhood.

"Okay, sweetheart. We'll be there in twenty minutes."

Not for the first time, I was overwhelmed with gratitude for the woman who'd raised me. "Love you, Mom."

"I know, son. I love you too." When she hung up, I dropped my phone back into my jacket pocket. Time to go tell everyone we were having a change of location.

In the back of my mind, I knew that Kitten being in our house was forever going to change our Pack. What I didn't know was if it was going to be for the better, or for the far, far worse.

5

CORVIN

K itten was curled into a ball of pain by the time we'd bundled her up in soft blankets and transferred her to the ATV before Cooper's parents turned up. I liked Coop's folks, but we didn't need the questions right now.

Now she was in the back, pressed tightly between Darius and Beckett, as I drove possibly a little too fast back toward our Packhouse. I hated hearing her soft mewls of pain, and the scent of her need was driving me crazy.

Thank god Cooper was keeping his head, because I wasn't sure that I'd possess any reason once I got a taste of Kitten. I could already feel my Beast beating down the door, desperate to please, and fuck, and mate the Omega whose scent was begging for all those things. But Cooper was right; although she seemed clear-headed enough to tell us what she wanted, now wasn't the time to be making big decisions, especially when we were all high as kites on pheromones.

Radic was going to kick my ass. I'd sworn that we wouldn't touch her, even if she begged, but dammit, I wasn't as strong as I thought I was. I couldn't sit back and watch her suffer for a week.

As if she could sense my thoughts, she moaned and pushed against Darius, seeking some kind of relief. He stroked a hand along her overheated skin, thrumming deep in his chest while Beckett whispered small reassurances.

Yeah, we needed to be at the Packhouse already. Like, right now. I watched the road with laser focus as I willed us there faster, and when the house finally came into sight, I could have cried with relief. I didn't, of course, but it was a close thing. I skidded to a stop near the front door, gravel spraying up and thudding against the cladding. I was glad that we'd chosen a Packhouse so far away, despite the fact that I'd just been cursing that very point right up until we arrived. It meant the houses were less crowded together, and our neighbors were a fair distance away. If we got her into the house fast, hopefully no one would know she was here at all, and I wouldn't have to patrol the perimeter.

Even just the thought of someone lurking out there had my Beast rattled. "Get her inside. I'll secure the house."

I slid from the car before I followed them like a lovesick hound, moving toward the back of the house instead. I tested every window and door, ensuring they were all locked. When we'd built this place, we'd done so to impress our Omega, which meant that if we wanted it to be, it was practically a fortress.

Once I was satisfied the rear of the house was locked up tight, I went through the front door and locked it. I followed my nose to Darius's nest, which made sense, even if I was a little surprised. A nest was an intensely personal place for an Omega, and it said something that he'd decided to take her there instead of the guest room.

Along the way, I gathered pillows from everyone's beds—even Cooper's—as well as extra throws from the blanket box at the end of my bed. When I was so laden down I couldn't carry any more, I decided that was enough. Taking a deep breath, I walked into the nest.

Most of the floor was covered in a soft cushion, which had a cover on it made of wine-red faux mink. It was incredibly soft, and zipped into ten different pieces so it wasn't a nightmare to clean if we got extra dirty. Darius always said it felt soothing against his skin when he was in yearning, and given the fact that Kitten was rolling in it like a bed of catnip, I guess it felt good for her too. She had a death grip on Darius's arm though, holding him close.

I looked at the strain on his face, and guilt washed

over me. Did he actually want this? I mean, I knew he
wanted a female Omega, but it wasn't just about biology, especially not this moment. You still had to like a
person to have sex with them. At least, you did if you
weren't a monster.

"Are you okay, Omega? We can take care of this, if
you would rather..." I didn't know what the right
word was here. Wait? Tap out? Not take part in something that was intensely intimate with a near
stranger?

He looked over Kitten's dark brown hair at me. "I'm
okay, Alpha. I want this." We used the formal terms,
referring to each other by our designations. Sometimes
we did it affectionately, the way humans called their
spouses Husband or Wife instead of their name. But
today, there was a lot more gravity to the word, as the
heat reduced us to Alpha and Omega.

I shed my shirt, but left my jeans on. I dragged my
shirt over one of the pillows, knowing the scent of it
would soothe her, then crawled onto the bed beside
them, watching Beckett out of the corner of my eye. He
was still dressed, and though he was trying to keep his
face impassive, he was eyeing the entwined Omegas
with so much hunger, I could almost hear his balls
rumbling from over here.

"Omegas," I growled, catching both of their atten-
tions. "Kitten," I said in a softer tone. "Are you sure this
is what you want?"

Kitten let out a frustrated noise. "Yes, Corvin. I'm sure. Are you going to ask me every step of the way?"

It was Beckett who answered. "Yes."

She huffed, which was a sound I remembered all too well, and then she reached for me. Grabbing my arms, she pulled me along her body and let out a shuddering sigh, burrowing her face in my neck.

"I remember your scent. Sometimes, I think I still smell it in my cabin." It was a soft murmur that managed to break my heart in two. I pulled back and gave into the one desire that I'd had for years, ever since she'd stopped being an annoying little kid to me and Beckett, and started being more.

I kissed her. Her lips were softer than I could have imagined, and coupled with the Omega pheromones, I felt like they were dragging me down to an abyss that I knew I'd never claw my way out of.

She moved into the kiss, but still refused to let go of Darius, who didn't seem to mind that he was being used as a security blanket. She wrapped one leg around mine, twining us together as she curled against me. I was thrumming low in my chest, my whole body vibrating as I purred. Thrumming was a weird Manix trait. It was as universal as a hug. It could be comforting, friendly, or wildly sexual, depending on the situation.

We all knew which situation this was though.

Kitten was grinding up against my aching cock,

trying to find relief. "Easy, Omega. I've got you. Let's get you some relief in the form of several mind-blowing orgasms," I said soothingly. I pulled back, and Darius took over kissing her while I started undressing her slowly, starting with her threadbare yoga pants.

Her legs were long and muscular, but they were marred by both old scars and new scabs. I traced a scar that ran down the length of her thigh from a hunting accident. She'd gotten banged up bad tripping down a ravine. It had taken Beckett and me a whole day to find her, and I still remembered that fear like it was yesterday. If she'd hit the wrong spot, bled out, she'd be dead.

Suddenly, the need to taste her was overwhelming, and I tore off her underwear, not giving her time to feel shy as I dived between her thighs.

I groaned against her clit as her taste burst on my tongue. Goddamn. I was gonna blow in my pants like a brand new fucking Manix teen. The heat had ratcheted her natural pheromones up to eleven, and she was like eating your favorite meal, if it was cooked to perfection by a Michelin-starred chef.

She tasted like everything that had been missing from our lives.

I pushed that thought down as I flicked out my tongue and twirled it around her clit, a pleased rumble bursting from me at her gasping moan.

"Oh god, Corvin."

Mmm, that's it... Scream my name, Kitten.

Well, that's what I would have said to her if my tongue wasn't already busy. The taste of her slick was making me dizzy, but I sucked, licked and tongue-fucked her until it was coating my face and my girl was screaming. Her hand was wrapped painfully in my hair, and I relished every single strand she ripped out. My Kitten was feral, in more ways than one.

"Oh, oh, oh," she chanted in a voice that was so high-pitched it might be heard only by bats and dogs, and then she was coming all over my face. I lapped up her slick, refusing to let even a little bit be wasted.

She uncurled her hands from my hair as she panted, trying to regain her breath. I licked and nibbled her thighs, my Beast roaring for me to bite hard, to mark her as mine, to mate her. Instead, I let my tongue trace down to her knee, appreciating the way her legs still shook.

She grabbed at my shoulders, her fingers curled into little claws. I looked up, along the lean lines of her body, at her face. Her eyes, and Darius's, looked back at me. Her cheeks were flushed but her eyes were even more wild.

"Fuck me, Corvin. I want you to fuck me. Please..." She trailed off, and looked at Darius. "Or you." Then she met Beckett's gaze. "Or you. Why does this still hurt so bad?" It was a whimper of pleasure and pain, and it tore at my chest. She needed more.

Darius brushed his fingers across my cheek. "Let me, Alpha."

My Omega, the man who had nearly all of my heart, was far more Beast than man, but I still couldn't deny him anything.

6

DARIUS

It was a fever dream. The small amount of control I was clutching turned to dust in my palms. I kissed Kitten like she was an illicit drug, drinking her down. I needed more though; the more relief she got, the more I began to ache with a need to be inside her.

I can control myself, I repeated inside my head, all the while kissing her—this stranger I'd known for mere hours—like she was my salvation. I devoured her lips, her tongue, and replaced them with mine. I dragged her on top of my body, giving her an element of control when it probably felt as if her own body had a mind of its own. I knew that feeling, that helplessness as biology took over and it felt like free choice went out the window. At the time, it didn't matter. You needed. You craved. Reason was something that came later, after your needs had been met and that burning in your gut was gone.

I felt that madness on the edges of my own consciousness now, waiting for me to give myself fully over to instinct and take what was finally within reach —that one act I'd ached for since my first time in yearning. But we weren't going to do that this time. This was all about appeasing the heat, easing her pain, and then we could figure everything else out later.

I could control myself.

She ground down on my dick, and I wanted to tear my own underwear off so I could be inside her already. Dangerous feeling, but we both needed this. I let her move rhythmically up and down my dick, finding some relief, though her whines and the heat of her core told me she needed so much more.

"One more orgasm, Kitten," I said with as much authority as I could muster, gripping her hips and dragging her up my body, coating myself in her slick. I purred at the thought of combining our scents, of her soaking my skin with sweat and her juices.

I pulled her up until she was sitting on my face, and she submitted to the urge to ride it straight away. I speared my tongue inside her, and I was pretty sure I was drowning in the best way possible. Give me a snorkel and I wouldn't come up for days. She arched forwards so she could rest her hands on the wall behind me, her whole body undulating. I bet she looked beautiful; if I didn't have the best seat in the house—or was I the best seat?—I'd be jealous of the show the Alphas were getting right now. I held onto her hips, and her clit bumped on my nose as my tongue went wild. When I felt her coming on my cheeks, I thrummed with happiness against her clit.

"Oh my god," she gasped, her pussy fluttering against my mouth. "Do that again, Darius." Reason left me at the sound of my own name moaned like that. I pulled her clit between my lips and thrummed hard. She curled forwards, like the stacked orgasm was pulling her muscles tight. Her slick was running down my cheeks now, and she was panting through the pleasure.

With a growl, I flipped her onto her back, moving up over her in a single, lithe movement. I pushed down my boxers with rough hands until I could take my aching, dripping cock and slide it inside her with a grunt.

"Yes," she hissed, not hesitating to thrust up so I was balls deep.

Out of control.

Things had spiraled out of control as I pumped inside her, my body pressed along hers, her teeth on my chest, not breaking the skin but the promise making me roar. I could mate her right now, make her mine, make her ours. *We could be a Pack, a proper one,* the voice of my Beast at the back of my mind begged.

But then there was a hand between us, and then a face. Beckett's eyes were wild, but his face was pulled into serious lines. "Woah, woah, Omegas. No biting," he murmured in a rough voice. He said it, but he was eyeing those cute little crescent marks on my shoulder with so much longing that it didn't take a genius to know where his head was at.

While my mind acknowledged the command, I shook it off quickly as I fucked her harder and harder. I wanted to tattoo my cock inside her body; I wanted to be one with her. I wanted everything. She came again, her scream echoing around the room.

Something shifted inside me, and I knew. I knew my body was trying to take her eggs, trying to draw them into my body. Trying to make cubs with my evolutionary counterpart.

I dropped her torso—I hadn't realized I'd been clutching her close to my chest as I fucked her—and pulled out, with a mammoth display of willpower I hadn't been sure I even possessed until that moment. My Beast keened, the sound leaving my chest so heart-breakingly mournful.

So damn close, the Omega inside me whined, but the man was adamant that now wasn't the time.

Maybe one day, but not like this.

"Finish her," I growled at my Alphas, writhing as my body clenched at nothing, like a fucking phantom sneeze. The urge was an ache, but there was no completion. No nothing.

Both Alphas jumped into action, Corvin launching toward me. His hands were all over my body, trying to ease the yearning that was riding me worse than I'd ever felt it. It was like my body was both hot and cold, aching and languid. The yearning was such a contradiction, a painful one at that. His hand went down to my dick, dragging his rough palm across my cock still coated in Kitten's slick, making the slide smoother. I closed my eyes, leaning back against my Alpha.

"You did so fucking good, Omega. So good. I'm proud of you." His hands dropped to my balls and he squeezed softly. "Now let me make you feel good too."

His hand moved back to my cock, and he stroked me just how I liked it. I was lucky; my Alphas cared more about my pleasure than their own, but not all Alphas were like that. I could feel the hard press of his length against my spine. He pushed me forward until I was on my hands and knees, pouring lube over my ass and sliding it up and down his own cock. He pushed inside me slowly, since he hadn't prepped my ass at all, curling his body over mine. "Watch, Omega."

Beckett gathered a gasping Kitten up until she too was on her hands and knees.

Kitten looked over her shoulder. "Change."

We all froze. "What?" Beckett said, his voice a whole octave higher than normal.

"I want you to fuck me in your Manix form."

Holy shit. I thought that's what she'd said. We didn't fuck often in full Manix form. Sometimes in the half-shift, where we kept our same proportions but were coated head to toe in soft fur. It was an interesting experience. But in full shifted form, we grew substantially. Every part of us did. Beckett's cock would split this girl in goddamn half.

"Kitten..." he started.

She grabbed his hand, pulling him close. "Please, Beckett. I've dreamed about it for years. I want it. I can take it."

The whine in her voice made my dick pulse with need, and Corvin began to slide in and out of me in slow, measured thrusts. I knew they'd give her what she'd asked for; turning down a needy Omega wasn't in their biology. We just had to hope to the Goddess she could take it.

I t took every single ounce of willpower to hold myself back and talk about her request.

"Kitten..."

She lurched up toward me, grabbing my face and dragging me back down to the bed with her. Suddenly, I was pressed along overheated flesh, and her soaked little pussy was tight against my cock. It was hard to be logical in the face of that.

"Shift, Alpha," she purred, and there was no doubt in my mind that it was mostly her new Omega speaking. But when I looked into her eyes, it wasn't just the insanity of the heat staring back at me. No, the earnestness of the girl I had known burned in there too, and I crumbled.

I pulled back, still kneeling between her thighs. My Beast burst free, and my body elongated, twisting and growing until I was at least a foot taller and the rest of me was... bigger. My huge thighs, now scaled, brushed the insides of her thighs, and she clamped her legs around me, trapping me close. My now footlong—and then some—cock sat like a baton between us. My Beast thrummed as her tiny fingers traced over my chest plates, flicking my nipple.

The heat momentarily put on the back burner, she cataloged me again. The scales, the fangs, the fluffy ears. I was a monster, but she was looking at me like I was the most spectacular specimen she'd ever laid those soft hands on.

Finally, her hands traveled down to my length, and she strained to fit her hand around me. Fuck, it looked tiny wrapped around my cock, and my Beast paused, despite the urgent need to claim, and claim *now*. We didn't want to hurt her.

Never hurt Kitten.

"So big," she gasped, sliding her hand up and down my length a few times, making me grit my teeth.

"Too big," I groaned, and she huffed.

"That's for me to decide."

"You and physics," Corvin grumbled. He wasn't wrong.

But the grin Kitten gave me was pure sexual goddess. Corvin had thrown down the gauntlet. She was going to rise to the challenge.

She kissed me, and she didn't need to sink her

teeth into my flesh for me to feel claimed. I grabbed her up into my hands, her body seeming tiny and delicate. She kissed me softly though, unperturbed by the fangs that pressed tight into her bottom lip, or the soft down of my facial hair.

I tried really hard to enjoy this moment I'd dreamed about too—well, not quite like this, but close. It was hard when all I could feel was her tight core against my dick, just begging me to impale her on it.

I moved my hand between her thighs, and she held her breath as my sharpened nails brushed against her tender flesh. I would never hurt her like that though; I was in better control of my body in this form than in my other form.

I pressed the heel of my palm against her clit, and her hips jerked up hard, increasing the pressure. Kitten didn't have a Manix form; she was soft and stuck in her human form all the time.

I leaned forward and brushed my lips over the softness of her collarbone. She tasted of salty sweat and the sweet undertone of pheromones. Her little gasps of pleasure fanned over my cheeks as she rode my hand, and I gritted my teeth to hold myself back.

When she finally soaked my hand with her slick, I decided she was probably as wet as she was going to get without me dipping my dick in an entire bucket of lube. I wrapped one large arm around her back, pulling her tightly to me so I could roll onto my back and she could be on top.

There was a moan from my left, and I realized that Corvin was slowly making love to our Omega. Darius and Corvin together was always a beautiful sight, like two serpents entwined around each other. But even though they were fucking, their eyes were on me and Kitten, who was now looking down at me with a purely primal grin.

"Go slow, Kitten." There might have been a little bit of an Alpha command in that, but fuck it, I was worried.

"Women stretch to push out babies, Beckett. You're big, but you're not the size of a tiny human."

Darius grunted—whatever Corvin was doing was obviously good—and both Kitten and I watched them for a moment. Then I reached up, grabbing her chin. My voice was low and guttural in this form. "Sometimes they still need stitches, Omega. Slow. I mean it." There was just a touch of growl to the command this time, and I watched as her pupils blew out.

"Yes, Alpha." Then she was moving down my body, reaching beneath herself to grab my cock in her hand and line it up against her entrance.

I clenched my jaw with bone-shattering force to hold myself still, even though my dick knew it was so fucking close to home. After a little working, where I held her hips and she rubbed herself down, the head of my cock popped past her entrance.

The clench of her around me was like a vice, and my eyes rolled back in my head. "Sweet fucking Goddess."

I thrust up just a little, going a bit deeper, as the noise she made was more animal than Kitten. Her nails clawed into my chest, and the sting told me they'd broken skin, but I loved it.

"More?"

"Yes!"

She met my eyes with her own wild ones, her lips parted, looking like a feral cat in a fight. Not liking my slow response time, she slid down further.

"Oh god, I feel you everywhere," she moaned, and then like a fucking lunatic, thrust down in one movement, taking as much of me as would fit inside. She panted, and I watched, mesmerized as a drop of sweat slid down her neck and between her breasts.

"That's it, Kitten. Take all of me. Such a good Omega." I thrummed hard, turning my dick into a monster vibrator.

"Beckett!"

The sound of my name in that gasping scream set something loose in me. Fuck, I was an idiot for agreeing to this. That was my last thought before I flipped her onto her back, caging her with my arms.

She was so tiny. Completely in my control. Completely... "Mine."

"Yes," she purred back, rolling up to meet my shallow thrusts. Even though I was wild, I didn't want to hurt her. I just wanted to consume her completely, so she'd never think of leaving me. Leaving us. I wanted her addicted to my cock, then to me, and then to the Pack I could provide for her.

Her tiny human legs barely fit around my hips as her body responded to the pheromones, getting wetter and wetter until our bodies slapped together loudly, almost drowning out the sounds of moans.

"Yes. Beckett. Please. Fuck, more. Please." Her eyes were huge and imploring, and I went harder. Filled her so completely that there was no doubt that I would be tattooed inside her body in the morning.

I was going to fill her with my seed, with my cubs. I was going to see her heavy with child and in the arms of our male Omega. I was going to fuck her until I was dripping from her pretty little cunt. Then I was going to fuck my other Omega, until he had a whole litter weighing him down.

Yes. But first, I would fuck her harder, deeper...

"Beckett!" Corvin roared loudly, snapping me out of it in time for me to pull out and come all over Kitten. My seed painted her stomach as her legs shook with the force of her orgasm. Her hands smeared my cum all over her torso, and I grunted in satisfaction. That was fucking close, but I couldn't deny that she looked heavenly coated in my seed like that. I wanted Darius to come over and lick it all off, but not today.

Kitten's lips curled into either a grimace or a smile, and the raging heat of her skin cooled with the sweat that coated her. Her eyelids fluttered a couple of times and then she drifted off to sleep, her fingers still curled in the sticky mess I'd spread all over her torso. I tried to convince my Beast to recede, but there was no chance. I gave up and lay down behind her, pulling her tight into my body until I could curve myself around her completely.

Pressing my fangs into the back of her shoulder, I scraped them gently over the place I knew I'd one day mark her. Where I would make her my Mate.

The sound of Darius reaching his release too made me lift my head—watching my co-Alpha pleasure our Omega was too perfect to miss. I met Darius's eyes, and I saw the knowing in them. He knew what I wanted.

The sadness that pulled at the edges of his eyes broke my heart, but I couldn't make myself release Kitten. No, I would take the consequences of this, but I refused to give her up.

The bedroom door opened, and I growled low in my throat, but it was just Cooper. His eyes widened as he saw me, in my Beast form, wrapped around a very naked, unconscious Kitten.

"What the *fuck* have you guys done?"

8

COOPER

It had been hard, but I'd managed to convince Beckett to shift back into human form and go and take a shower. Corvin was dozing quietly against the wall. Darius was passed out beside Kitten, his hand wrapped in hers reassuringly, even though they were both asleep. Well, for now. She was so coated in Beckett's cum, she was about to harden like a Christmas cookie.

After I'd gotten Beckett unwrapped from her, I'd grabbed a clean washcloth and some warm soapy water. She needed a shower, but this might do for now.

I touched her shoulder gently. "Kitten? Wake up— you need to wash this off before you turn crusty."

One eye barely slitted open. "You do." Then it closed again.

Um, no. I could not bathe a woman I didn't know. I shook her arm, and she batted at my hand.

"Come on, woman. You've known me for three seconds. You definitely don't want me rubbing on your naked body."

This time, two deep brown eyes opened and looked at me. "Mate." She yawned as my heart thumped hard in my chest at that single word. "You're their mate," she clarified, and I let out the breath I hadn't even realized I was holding. She gave me another soft smile, her eyes drifting closed again. "So tired. You do it. I trust you."

Well, if that didn't make me feel like a gooey mess. I wasn't done being mad at the guys yet, but man, this chick was getting under my skin already. She was snoring gently by the time I shook myself out of my stunned stupor, lifting the cloth from the warm water and squeezing it out.

I slid it across her stomach first, wiping away the bulk of the stickiness. She seemed to have smeared it all over her torso, because there wasn't an inch of her that didn't have the light sheen of Beckett's seed making her glisten gently in the moonlight. I tried to remain impersonal and not pervy as I ran the washcloth over her breasts, rinsing and warming it again in the hot water. Making sure to get up beneath her chin—and dammit, did he even get it in her hair?—I made sure she was as clean as I could make her without being wildly inappropriate. She was going to have to decrust her own pubes when all this was over.

I realized she was making a soft hum of content-ment, and that warm feeling that had been growing in the bottom of my gut suddenly burst to life.

Dropping the washcloth back in the bowl, I smoothed back her wild hair with my hand, taking in her features properly. Her skin was like captured moonlight, paler than any of ours. We were a product of Maxton through and through. It automatically set her apart as an outsider, but I couldn't help but admire how creamy it looked beside Darius's light tan, and the way her full lip jutted out a tad when she slept, like she was pouting. I wanted to rub my thumb over its pillowy softness, but that would probably be too far.

Actually, what I really wanted was to see those lips wrapped around my dick, but that was way, *way* too far.

"She seems precious somehow, doesn't she?"

I turned slightly until I could see Corvin in my peripheral vision. I gave a sharp nod, because I wasn't mad at the woman in front of me. No, I was mad as hell at them.

"It's a bit of a disguise, really. She's tougher than nails. She doesn't need me or you; she's been living just fine without anyone for most of her life. I saw her chase down a fucking deer once. On foot, in her human form. She knows that forest better than any man, woman or child in this goddamn town." He moved closer until he was staring down at her. "I want her to want us, Coop."

"Us? You don't get to make those decisions for us all, Corvin. You or Beckett."

The Omegas on the cushions stirred, and I threw Corvin an aggravated look. Standing up, I thrust the bowl of now lukewarm water at him. Then I grabbed a light, fluffy blanket and pulled it up over both of them. With one last longing look, I uncurled from the kneeling position and moved softly to the nest door. Corvin, smartly, followed behind me. We made it downstairs and back into the kitchen before my anger boiled over.

As soon as he put down the bowl, I turned around and punched him in the jaw. "You fucker! How could you keep this from us for so damn long?" I hissed. I didn't want to wake Darius or Kitten. "Did you see the hurt on Darius's face? Did you even give a damn about anyone but yourself?"

He bared his teeth. "What did you want me to do? Leave her out there to suffer? Be preyed on by other Manix in frenzy? You know what they would have done. How can you look at her and think that was the right alternative?"

I growled low. "I would never even suggest that, and you know it. I would have been the first one to go and rescue her if Darius and I *had known she even existed.*"

His cheek wasn't bruised from my hit, but I still felt guilty. I swiped at it with my hand, and he didn't even flinch.

"Shouldn't have hit you."

He shrugged. "You probably deserved a free shot." He wrapped his arms around me and hugged me tight, thumping me on the back. "She made us swear, Coop. Otherwise I wouldn't have been able to keep my mouth shut, especially at the beginning. We loved her, Coop, but we loved you and Darius just as much."

"He won't forgive you as easily. He won't take a swing—he probably even likes Kitten—but he's still hurt."

Corvin dropped his arms with a sigh. "I know. How about we get past this insanity, and then we reorientate ourselves, okay? She mightn't even want to stay. Might be just as angry with us as you are right now."

I sucked in a deep breath. The scent of Omega now permeated every inch of our house. Both Kitten and Darius's scents had combined to make something mouthwateringly exquisite, and I wasn't sure I would ever forget it, even if she did decide to leave.

Something inside me ached at that thought, but I pushed it away. An Omega in heat made you feel insane things, and I wasn't going to give into the sensations quite yet. "You guys need to wrap your shit up before Kitten has her own damn litter."

"Unless you have Saran wrap and a roll of duct tape, no condom was going to fit on Beckett's shifted dick," Corvin joked, though he probably wasn't exaggerating. To even imagine that tiny woman riding that...

"How does that even work?"

A throat cleared behind us, and I knew the sound like I knew my own laugh. "Well, Coop, when two people feel mutually attracted to each other, sometimes they fornicate. This involves—"

I flipped Beckett the bird. "I know what it involves, asshole. I just spent fifteen minutes cleaning up all your damn 'involvement.'" I looked at him hard, taking in his relaxed shoulders but the wild flash of his eyes, showing the Alpha was still riding him. "I just hope you guys know what you're doing." I slapped a hand lightly down on the countertop. "Go and cuddle the Omegas. I'll make some food and bring it up."

Corvin quirked an eyebrow. "Stepping into the role of Beta, are you Coop?"

I opened the fridge door, looking at the meager offerings we had in there. It was difficult to think about food when your dick was sitting hard against your stomach. Gritting my teeth, I tried to block out the smell of Omega.

"Someone has to stop you fuckers from going feral

and wasting away into nothing. Now get the hell out of here before I decide to abandon the lot of you to your own devices."

Corvin swaggered off, the light in his eyes telling me he was excited about what was happening here right now. Beckett had always been the more sensitive of us, which kind of made his betrayal worse. Corvin was big and fearless. His word meant everything to him. But Beckett, while still being big and fearless, also had an empathy, which was what had attracted Darius and endeared him to me in the first place.

He paused, his jaw tense like he wanted to say something to fill the silence between us. "You shouldn't hide yourself away down here. When she's a little less needy, you should meet her properly. I think you'd like her."

I chewed my lip as I stared into the fridge. "That's the problem though, isn't it? I know I'll like her, because you and Corvin love her, and you are the best males I know. But she doesn't have to love us at all."

Beckett reached out and gripped my chin, pulling me close so he could rub his cheek against mine. Sometimes we played as a group, because I mean, there was only one Darius and some days just called for an orgy. So we all played, but it was a casual thing, more when you needed an extra hand, or mouth, or both. What we had, more than that, was affection. A bone-deep love for each other, and that love was physical as well as emotional, not just always sexual.

It was hard to explain. But the cheek rubbing, the hugs—they were as integral to our Pack as mate marks and sex.

They were expressions of love.

"If you trust our judgment about her, just trust me about this too. I can't promise it won't end bad, but I just feel it deep down in my gut, you know? This is going to be something good."

With that, he patted my back once more and turned on his heel, heading back up the stairs after Corvin. I trusted Beckett with my life and with Darius. I guess I could trust him with my heart too.

9

KITTEN

When the heat broke, it was like a rubber band snapping. Days of sleeping and fucking and eating and fucking and sleeping on repeat, and suddenly all that was left was a overwhelming tiredness. I sat up, looking over the naked bodies strewn around me. Most of the past few days were hazy, but I vividly remembered the begging, the expression on Corvin's face while he made love to me, the softness of Darius's lips. Beckett's monster coc—

"Your heat's broken?"

I looked over at the other Alpha in Darius's Pack. Cooper, that was his name. He looked like a Cooper. His hair was a messy blond, his eyes a pretty blue, and he looked like he'd be more at home on a surfboard than in the wilderness. But he had slight lines between his brows that told me he took the world seriously, in the same way that the small creases at the corners of his eyes told me he laughed often. A perfect balance.

I stretched, ignoring my nakedness. Too late for modesty now. Pretty sure the guy in front of me had wiped more bodily fluids off me than my own mother had. "Yes." I held his eyes so he knew I wasn't ashamed of what had happened.

That didn't mean I wasn't angry. Or scared. I just didn't know who to be angry at just yet, and there was no need to be scared because my two white knights had appeared just when I needed them. Again.

I was pissed about that too.

"Do you need help to the shower? I could run you a bath, maybe?" He was speaking in a soft voice so he didn't wake up his Packmates, and when I looked at him, I could see the slight edges of the same anger that burned low in me. He was mad, but not at me.

I tilted my head at him, trying to figure out what his deal was. Shrugging, I said, "A bath would be nice."

He gave me a soft smile. "Come on, I'll help you up." He stepped carefully between the exhausted bodies, covered in scratches from my nails. Following my gaze, his smile turned wry. "Living up to the name there, Kitten." He pulled me gently to my feet, and my knees shook. Man, I felt like I'd run a marathon. My thighs were jello.

I took a couple of steps and nearly tripped on the

soft, cushioned flooring. Two strong arms scooped me up gently. "Woah there, let me carry you. You'll get your land legs back soon enough."

I breathed in the scent of him, and while it no longer drove me crazy as it had when I was in heat, he still smelled really good.

When I was in heat.

I was an Omega.

"Flying fuckballs."

Cooper tripped, catching himself at the last minute. "Did you just say... Jesus, I forgot the guys said they taught you English. It didn't occur to me that it would be a seventeen-year-old boy version of English." He didn't put me down as he kept moving down the hall. "You don't talk much."

I shrugged, trying not to let my blush show. "No need. English got rusty."

He snorted. "Except flying fuckballs." He gently nudged open the door of the bathroom with his hip, before placing me down gently on the toilet lid and then turning on the taps of a deep clawfoot bath. It was decadent, with a pretty white porcelain interior, deep blue exterior and gilded feet. It looked like the kind of tub a princess would bathe in.

He picked up a small amber bottle but then hesitated. "Do you want bath oils? Does your sense of smell feel too heightened?"

I was unexpectedly touched by his thoughtfulness.

He could have dumped it in, and it still would have been done with good intentions, but this? It showed he actually cared about people.

I thought for a moment. "Let me sniff it?"

He leaned over, wafting the small uncapped bottle beneath my nose. It smelled faintly of Darius, and I found that scent unusually soothing. I closed my eyes, huffing out a long sigh. "Yes. Please."

Cooper was watching my face closely; I could feel his eyes on me. But when I opened my eyes again, he was back across the bathroom, pouring the tiniest drop of the oil in the bath. The steam dispersed it around the room, and I instantly felt more centered. Damn, that Omega had a hold on me already.

Cooper pulled a fluffy towel out from a cupboard in the corner of the room, and sat it on top of the vanity. "I'll leave you to it. Yell out if you need help, okay? I'll be just downstairs making dinner. I can be here in a flash."

I nodded, giving him a soft smile. I needed space to think over the insanity of my life at this moment. He left, shutting the door quietly behind him, and I took a moment to relieve myself. Then I stood in front of the bathroom mirror and stared at myself. I looked the same. At least, the same skin suit stared back at me, but emotionally, I felt like an alien had possessed my body. It felt like all my emotions had been amplified times a thousand, that the Beast who shared my skin was suddenly so much more than she was when I was a Beta. I couldn't shift, but I didn't really know what I was missing. I was still free enough that the Manix who shared my soul didn't chafe too badly.

At least she hadn't until now.

I ran the tips of my fingers over small bruises left from sucking kisses on my chest and shoulders. Darius. He enjoyed the feel of my skin between his teeth, and I enjoyed it too. My lips seemed swollen, like they'd been kissed one too many times.

And my vagina felt like I'd been fucking a fire hydrant. The vivid flash of Beckett above me, his Manix form staring down at me, fangs glinting in the moonlight like he wanted to taste my flesh as well as my body.

I spun back toward the tub a little too fast, and had to steady myself on the side. Reaching out, I turned off the taps and stepped in. I lowered myself gently, hissing at the stretch of sore muscles, until I was fully submerged in water that was just the perfect temperature.

I let out a relieved sigh and rested my head on the back of the tub. Right. Lorso hadn't raised me to run from the trap placed in front of me. He'd taught me to think my way out of my problems, though I doubted he could have thought himself out of this either.

A dull ache flooded my chest at the thought of my surrogate father. He'd been a stern man, but he'd loved me. He'd taught me everything I knew about life, about Manix, about predators and prey.

Omegas had always been considered prey amongst the Manix, and mixed-heritage Manix even more so. I'd trusted Lorso when he said I would suffer in Maxton, and I trusted his wisdom on Omegas just as much.

Omegas like me. There hadn't been a female Omega in a century or more—Lorso's mate had been the last—though I'd heard whispers on the wind that one had appeared from down the mountain and been snaffled up by a Pack like she was the last piece of candy.

Was that going to happen to me? Would they fight over me like a favorite chew toy?

No. I'd get over this heat bullshit, and then go back to my life. I wasn't a prize for anyone, not even the men who'd once been the boys I'd loved enough to let go.

Water splashed down my face, and I realized I was crying. Damn, I hadn't cried in years. But once the tears started, I couldn't make them stop. They flowed freely down my cheeks, splashing silently into the cooling bath water.

The bathroom door slid open, and Cooper was there. I swiped at my tears like I could hide them with wet hands, but one look at his face told me that I wasn't fooling him. His eyes saw too much, his look of understanding threatening to open the floodgates further. He moved further into the bathroom, taking off his clothes until he was just in his tight boxer shorts. I didn't say anything—not encouragement, not to tell him to stop.

"I can scent your pain, Omega. Your distress sours on my tongue." He stepped into the bath, pushing me forward a little so he could settle down behind me. He wrapped his huge body around me, and I held myself stiff. He ran a hand up and down my arm reassuringly. "Rest, Kitten. It will all be okay. I'll make sure of it."

I let myself ease back into his chest, the hair tickling the damp skin between my shoulder blades. He tucked my head beneath his chin and wrapped his huge arms around my waist, until I was wholly anchored to this man who was a stranger, but a stranger who spoke to my soul.

"Rest," he whispered once more, and I felt myself beginning to succumb to the Alpha command. When his chest began to vibrate with a silent thrum, my whole body went limp.

Relax. Yes.

10

DARIUS

When I woke, I was alone in my nest. A nest that smelled like sex and sweat, but mostly of a certain Omega. I stretched, ignoring the way my Beast searched the air for her scent. As I pulled on a pair of sweats, I told myself I needed to pee, not that I was chasing the Omega in the bathroom. She probably wasn't even in there anymore.

But when I slowly slid open the door, my lips parted. Cooper was in the tub with her. As I moved further into the bathroom, I realized that both Cooper and Kitten were sound asleep. I waited for the stab of jealousy, and while it was there, it was muted. It was hard to be jealous when you'd just spent three days balls deep in the woman in his arms. That would be hypocritical. But the heart was rarely rational or logical.

I was just glad that me and that bloodied organ were on the same page.

Cooper had his arm banded around her ribs, holding her tightly into his chest even as his head tipped back against the tiled walls, his eyes closed. She looked tiny against his chest, black smudges beneath her eyes the only sign of her exhaustion. I dipped my finger into the water, and it was cool. I touched Cooper's cheek, and his eyes snapped open, his arm tightening around Kitten instinctively.

"It's okay," I whispered softly. "The water's cold though."

I noted that while Kitten was still gloriously naked, Coop had his boxer shorts on. The small part of me that still felt betrayed by Corvin and Beckett was oddly satisfied that Cooper hadn't just jumped on the heat train. As selfish as it sounded, I had been the center of Cooper's world since we were kids. That was when he'd decided I would be his Omega, and no amount of dissuading would convince him otherwise.

As much as part of me preened at the idea that he was holding out for me, I hoped he'd form some kind of kinship with Kitten, because I had a feeling she was going to be around for a while.

Cooper rubbed Kitten's arm gently, and I hid my smile. Okay, maybe I didn't have to worry about them bonding. "Time to wake up," he said gruffly, his voice always grizzled when he first woke.

Kitten blinked and yawned, and when her eyes met mine, she gave me a smile that made my chest feel shaky. It was a dangerous smile.

"Darius." She breathed my name, and I admitted to myself what I'd been fighting for three days. I had feelings for her. Feelings born from a crazy situation and way too many pheromones, but feelings all the same. We'd just have to see if they'd stick around. Or if she felt the same pull.

"Hey, Kitten," I replied, giving into the urge to touch her. "I see you stole my favorite bath pillow." I raised an eyebrow at Cooper.

A small crease appeared between her brows. "Sorry. I didn't..."

Fuck. Now I'd made her feel guilty. "It's okay, sweetheart. I didn't mean it like that. Come on, out you get, before you turn into a raisin. Or Cooper's balls turn into Rocky Mountain Oysters."

Cooper gave me a droll look, but hefted Kitten up onto her feet, standing up behind her. I grabbed the fluffy towel from the vanity and held it out. She stepped out of the bath on feet that were still delicate, despite being weathered. You could tell she spent a lot of time barefoot in the woods. I wrapped the towel around her tightly as Cooper climbed out and grabbed his own towel from where it hung behind the door. He gave us both a smile, then hotfooted it out of the room.

We stood in silence for a little while, and for the

first time since Corvin had carried her unconscious into the Sanctum, it was awkward. I gave her a tight smile. "I'll go and grab you something to wear. I'll leave it outside the door so you can have a moment." Then I ran away like Cooper. Apparently, we were all allergic to these kinds of situations.

At the door though, I paused. "I'm not mad you're here, Kitten. I'm mad that I didn't know you existed, but that's not in any way your problem. What I'm trying to say is, well, if you want to stay, it's okay with me. More than okay, even. But I'm going to give Corvin and Beckett seven shades of hell about this whole thing, so don't think any of that is coming your way."

She gnawed on her lip, and I resisted the urge to replace her teeth with my own. "Okay."

That was enough for me. I shut the door to the bathroom softly behind me, heading down the stairs to the open plan kitchen and dining room. As I walked in, my wayward Alphas tensed.

Yep, they knew they'd fucked up. Corvin's chin was raised slightly, so I knew he wasn't remorseful, and Beckett just looked like a damn kicked puppy with those big, dark eyes.

Instead of chewing them out about it, I headed to the kitchen. "I'm starved."

Beckett, predictably, launched himself at the refrigerator. "Let me cook you something to eat. Waffles, smothered in fruit and chocolate sauce?"

Oh, my favorite breakfast. He definitely knew he'd done bad. "That would be wonderful. You might want to make enough for all of us, and any other love interests from the past that you might have secretly squirreled away in some rustic hideaway lovenest."

"Darius, it wasn't—"

I waved a hand at Corvin. "It doesn't matter anymore, Alpha. The damage is done."

Beckett reached out, grabbing me and pulling me against his bare chest. Dammit, I was a sucker for this man's chest. "There are no other secrets between us, Omega. I swear on my life. On our bond. I'm so sorry this hurt you."

The sincerity in his voice was so earnest, it was hard not to believe him. "You both hurt me. Not Kitten, she's..." I trailed off because she was so many things, but I wasn't sure I could find the right words to describe her.

Corvin crowded behind me. "Yeah, she is."

I glared at him over my shoulder. "Her good nature doesn't erase the fact you both lied to me. For our entire relationship, you never told me that you loved someone else, someone who you *still* love, if the way you raced to her rescue is to be believed. That's something you share with Pack. Something you share with your lover."

"I'm truly sorry, D." Dammit, even Corvin was

sounding remorseful. "If it makes you feel better, Cooper punched me in the face for the insult."

I frowned. "Surprisingly, acts of physical violence between my Packmates doesn't make me feel better." I sighed, because I hated ill feelings in the Pack. They festered like old wounds. "No more secrets?"

"None, Omega. I swear it," Corvin murmured against my ear, and I leaned back against his chest as Beckett kissed me softly.

"We swear it."

I huffed. "Fine. You're forgiven. You're lucky she's so damn sweet."

Beckett snorted. "Yeah, she's sweet but a little spicy, that one. Don't think she's going to let us off quite so easily, though she seemed to like you. Maybe she'll just forgive and forget too."

"I wouldn't bet on it," came the sweet, yet furious, dulcet tones behind us.

I peeked around Beckett's arm. "Kitten. Do you like waffles?"

She frowned. "Never had them."

I audibly gasped. "Beckett. The poor thing has never had waffles. What the hell were you guys feeding her out there? You can cook while she yells at you." I smiled in her direction, my dick instantly hard again at the scent of her. Fuck, I'd thought the heat was over. "I think I'd definitely enjoy that more than doing it myself."

Cooper strolled into the kitchen then, a frown on his face. "It'll have to wait. Radic just turned up, and he's got that officious look on his face."

Ah, fuck. I was kind of hoping he'd give it a little more time, but Radic was as straight-laced as they came. The only person he'd bend for was Bonnie, and that was because he was so in love with her, it was both painful and awe-inspiring to watch. I'd once watched the Beta square up to Corvin when he thought we were trying to steal her away from him. Like we ever could —Bonnie loved Radic just as wildly.

Once he'd realized that we were all just friends, he chilled the hell out, but still I thought maybe he was waiting for us to make our move. Like it was inevitable that we'd want the beautiful Beta in our Pack.

I'd never tell Rad this, but I'd thought about it once or twice. I loved Bonnie—she was one of my best friends. She was beautiful and caring, but she was also ferocious when it came to her charges. It just never felt like quite the right time, and I got it now. She wasn't meant for us. She was meant for that crazy Pack she was creating over in the old Sanctum dorms.

I looked over at Kitten. It felt perfectly right with her. The realization wasn't a surprise exactly, more of a problem.

When Kitten's scent reached me though, I frowned. It smelled sour. Like fear. I stepped toward her and realized she was trembling.

"Kitten, what's wrong?"

Everyone turned, but it was too late. Radic stepped into the house, looking pleasant as always. He stopped in front of Kitten. "Hello, my name is Radic. It's nice to finally meet you."

That's when Kitten hissed, like a legitimate cat, and all hell broke loose.

11

CORVIN

I t all happened at once, really.

Cooper telling us Radic was here to check on Kitten's wellbeing, just like he said he would.

The smell of Kitten's distress.

Radic appearing.

Kitten hissing.

Me shifting to Manix and launching myself at the unsuspecting Beta male.

"The actual *fuck,* Corvin?" Radic growled, jumping backwards out of my reach. He might be a Beta, but he was a strong one. "Get a fucking grip before the Alpha General gets here and tears you a fucking new asshole," he hissed, dodging my swiping hands.

I had to protect Kitten. She was scared and vulnerable here.

"Corvin!" Darius's voice cut through the din of yelling. "Stop!"

We liked to pretend that Alphas were the top of the food chain, and in a way, we were. We were stronger, faster, more deadly. But a mated Omega could turn an Alpha into a lap dog if he was so inclined.

I pulled up, still growling low in my chest. Beckett and Cooper were there, still in human form, and they stepped between me and Radic.

"Fucking hell... Did you guys mate the new Omega? Because someone should've let me know—I wouldn't have come within a hundred yards of here."

"You mean you wouldn't have come without backup. We both know that Bonnie would have made you come check on Kitten anyway," Darius teased, trying to lighten the mood.

Radic got a blissful look on his face. "You aren't wrong." Yeah, he was in love with his new Omega too. He looked back at Kitten, his face turning somber. "I'm sorry if I scared you." His voice was soft, the voice he used with the kids at the Sanctum. Non-threatening and reassuring. "I just came to make sure you were happy here with the Wiley-Fletcher-Reid Pack. If you feel uncomfortable in any way, or wish to return home, I can help. You aren't obligated to be here unless you want to be."

The growl in my chest hadn't stopped, and only got louder at the insinuation he would take Kitten from us.

Or that she wasn't happy here. But Radic was used to dealing with the strongest of us on a daily basis, and just stood taller, meeting my eyes.

"I'll bring back the Alpha General to enforce it himself, if I have to," he said, not dropping my gaze. Ballsy move.

"No!" Kitten yelled, setting my Beast off all over again at the sound of her distress. Then I remembered her past, and the fact she didn't know we'd recently had a change of leadership. Beckett, who'd already worked this shit out because he was way more intuitive than I was, stepped closer to Kitten, putting a hand gently on her arm, and when she leaned into the touch, pulled her into the safety of his hold.

"It's not the old Alpha General, Kitten. We've just gotten a new one, and he's a good guy, I think. He doesn't hold the same old-fashioned beliefs. He won't care that you aren't pure-blooded Manix."

Radic snorted. "He'll probably like you more because you aren't. He hasn't exactly got a lot of respect for the 'Old Guard,'" he said, doing air quotes. He eyed Kitten again. "He's not from Maxton either."

Kitten remained quiet, and I could see Radic using that sharp intelligence to try and work out what the hell was going on.

"Do you want to stay here?" he asked softly once more.

I held my breath, but didn't look at her. I didn't

want her to feel pressured, and I knew I wouldn't be able to keep the longing out of my eyes if she looked.

"For now," was all she said, but it was more than I'd hoped for.

Radic seemed happy enough with that answer too. "Fine. I'll leave you guys to it." He stepped toward Kitten once more, making us all tense, even Darius. He pulled out a business card from his pocket and gave it to her. "If you change your mind, you can call us any time of the day or night. I'll bring Bonnie. She's better at these things than I am." He moved away quickly, because like I said, he was a smart guy. "I'm sure the guys will bring you around for dinner sooner rather than later to meet everyone."

I stared him down, but Darius made an affirmative sound. "I'll be back at the Sanctum today or tomorrow. Cooper's parents have been watching the place while we... dealt with a few things."

Radic shrugged. "I doubt Bonnie will be far behind you. She's dying to get back to work. She misses the kids, even though she was just in a coma for what felt like an eternity."

Darius and Cooper walked him out, and I shifted back to my human form. Beckett sent me a disgruntled look. "Seriously, dumbass? Jesus, we'll be lucky if he doesn't go home and tell the Alpha General you almost ate him just because you're a jealous douche."

He went back to the waffle maker, pulling out a

pastry that was more a cookie than waffle now. He tossed it on a plate and started again, acting completely normal. Like we didn't just witness Kitten having a freak-out.

And maybe me too, just a little.

When Cooper came back, I knew I was in the shit with him too. "We need to talk. All of us." He looked at Kitten. "Are you staying or going?"

I frowned. "It's a bit more complicated than that, Coop, and you know it."

He shook his head, sitting down at the table and stretching out his long legs. He met my eyes, and I knew then and there he wasn't going to budge. "It really isn't. Now she isn't all hopped up on hormones, and she's met Darius and me, she can decide if she wants to go back to her life or stay here in Maxton." He gave Kitten a soft smile. "Either with us, or by yourself. We'll help you get settled in your own house here, if you want to be closer to civilization."

"Manix civilization. Been going to town for years among humans."

My Beast growled at the reminder she'd been going to town to have sex with humans. With other men who'd touched and tasted what was mine. I didn't notice I was growling again until Darius cleared his throat. I threw him a sheepish look, tamping it down.

Kitten was silent, but that was her way. Lorso had taught her to think like a strategist, to analyze every move before acting. It was what made her a good hunter.

Finally, she sighed. "I like my cabin. I like the woods and the silence. I like the trees and the animals. I know who I am there."

My heart constricted in my chest. She wanted to go home. I understood—it was where she felt the most comfortable, where she thrived. It wasn't her fault that it broke my heart. I wasn't sure I could survive giving her up a second time though.

After a small pause, she looked around at us all. "But I like you guys too. I don't want to go *away*, but I want to go home."

Poor Kitten. Torn. It was a feeling I knew well. The scent of her sadness had me bundling her up and placing her on my lap before my forebrain even caught up to what I was doing. "We'll follow your lead, Omega. Prop you up while you find your feet. Then the decision is up to you." She buried her nose in my chest and breathed me in, appeasing us both a little.

Beckett placed a plate of waffles in front of Darius, kissing him softly on the top of the head with the casual affection of a couple who had been lovers for years. I wanted that casual affection with Kitten too, not this awkwardness. We'd had that once upon a time.

Beckett placed the second plate in front of Kitten. "There's some more for you guys over there," he said to me, tilting his head toward the kitchen counter. Then he cut a piece of waffle, making sure to get the perfect amount of melted chocolate and strawberry chunks on the fork. "Open, Kitten."

I wasn't sure how much Lorso had schooled Kitten on Manix ways, or if we'd even mentioned Manix courting habits to her back when we were teenagers. But feeding an Omega was a significant act, and Beckett was declaring something silently, to us, if not to Kitten herself.

As she took the bite into her mouth, moaning as the sweetness of the breakfast food hit her tongue, I had a feeling that she didn't know the real statement behind the gesture.

We'd tell her eventually, but not now. At this moment, I was happy to just watch her experience this first, hopefully one of many that we'd get to see firsthand.

She looked at Darius with wide eyes. "Oh my Goddess." She babbled something in her weird bastardized version of Latin, and it made Beckett grin. I was rusty. Once upon a time, when we were teaching her English, she was teaching us Kittenese. Beckett obviously had a better brain for languages than me.

Cooper grabbed a plate of waffles for himself. "How are you feeling now, Kitten? Apart from over-dosing on sugar from Beckett's pastries."

She froze, and I gave Cooper a stern look. I held

her tighter, and eventually she relaxed. "I'm an Omega."

I was glad she was looking at Cooper and not me, because I couldn't keep the pleased look off my face, and quite frankly that was an asshole thing to do.

Cooper's dirty look in my direction when she wasn't looking confirmed it. He softened his expression when he nodded at her though. "Yep. Did anyone explain what happened?"

She frowned. "Maybe? During the..." She let the words trail off.

"Sexfest?" Darius provided helpfully.

A snort. "Yes."

Cooper nodded, giving Beckett the stink eye again too. Yeah, he wasn't going to stop being pissed anytime soon. Unlike Darius, we couldn't just feed him, hug him, and send him all the good Alpha pheromones to make him feel better.

Cooper pointed to the plate of waffles. "Have some more and I'll explain what I know. When the guys first arrived with you, I called down to Doc and he answered some questions. Apparently, the doctor who came to take care of Bonnie called it a mass survival event. Our species was slowly dying out, so evolution or mother nature or the Goddess—whoever you want to attribute it to—decided to kick it up a notch. When the Huxley-Grey Pack came across a female Omega, it was the first female Maxton had had inside its borders in nearly a century. When she went into heat a second time, it triggered something in the female Betas that forced you to evolve."

"Like a Pokémon?"

I barked out a laugh, and Kitten threw me a furious stare.

Darius too. "You taught her about Pokémon but not the courting habits of the Manix? Figures," he grumbled. "But she isn't wrong. They kind of leveled up like Pokémon."

I was looking at Cooper, who I expected to be furious but he just seemed a little more smitten. The man did love his classic anime. Anime, *not* cartoons—don't even get him started.

He cleared his throat. "Uh, yeah. But that makes it sound like Betas aren't as important to the Manix as Alphas and Omegas, and if Radic proves anything, it's that Betas can wield just as much power, with considerably more tact. Don't tell him I said that though. He'll get a big head."

Now it was my turn to snort. Radic knew who he was, knew the exact amount of sway he had. He didn't need to be reminded.

Cooper reached out and squeezed Kitten's fingers. "Do you have any questions?"

12

KITTEN

Did I have any questions? I had a million.

"The heat will happen again?"

"Yes. But you can prepare for it so it isn't such a big deal like it was this time around. You won't be taken by surprise again."

"Can I talk to the doctor?"

Darius flushed. "Of course you can. We should have offered before now. We can go today, if you'd like?"

I nodded. I hadn't had a checkup in... ever. I couldn't go to human doctors and there was no way I could've come into Maxton. It would be nice to know that everything was where it was supposed to be. "Thank you." I felt the flush start at my toes over the next question, but I had to know. "Can we still have sex even though I'm not in my heat?"

Everyone fell silent. Then as one, they looked at Cooper. He was the only one who hadn't eased the ache during the heat, though he'd appeared regularly with food and water, and cleaned me up when I could barely move my body. As far as I was concerned, that was as intimate as sticking your dick in someone.

"You can't pick and choose between the Pack. No matter what you feel for Corvin and Beckett, or what they feel for you, splitting the Pack like that would hurt us all."

I frowned. "What do you mean, pick? You don't want to... Oh. I'm sorry." I wiggled off Corvin's lap. I'd just assumed that Cooper would want to have sex with me too, like I was some irresistable bombshell, rather than a half-wild mixed-blood who lived in a hovel in the hills. What an idiot.

I looked at Cooper, who was easily one of the most gorgeous males I'd ever seen, with his shoulder-length blond hair and blue eyes. Every part of his body was big and broad, the perfect golden Alpha. He didn't have the same childhood attachment to me as Corvin and Beckett.

"That's not what I meant—"

"No, it's fine. I'll get dressed and see the doctor now. Then I think I'd like to go home." Back to where my life, and my body, made sense to me.

"Cooper!" Darius hissed, and then suddenly, the big blond Alpha was in front of me.

He grabbed my arms gently in his huge hands, holding me still. "Kitten, I'm going to kiss you now." His voice was soft, and his grip loosened slightly so I wasn't restrained. "If you don't want this, you just have to say." He was giving me the chance to get away if I wanted. I stared up into his sparkling blue eyes, my lips parted as I held my breath. I didn't want to go anywhere though.

When he leaned forward, the brush of his lips against mine was the gentlest kiss I'd ever received. It was tentative, and I had a feeling it would stay that way until I made a move. So I slid my tongue along his bottom lip and melted into his arms a little more, pressing my body along his.

He groaned softly, pulling his lips from mine. "I didn't mean I wasn't interested, Kit. I meant that I didn't want you to feel pressured to take us all."

I froze up. "I'm not *taking* anyone. Sex doesn't mean I want to mate into your Pack."

Not yet, at least. I wasn't ready to give up my life just yet. But I wasn't opposed to being in a Pack. Lorso had spent most of my childhood telling me stories of his Pack, and his Omegas. They were dashing tales of battles and romance, and they'd created this dream Pack in my mind that I wasn't sure any real-life Manix could live up to.

The Wiley-Fletcher-Reid Pack would come close though.

Cooper kissed me again, a quick, hard kiss this time. "Sex means something. It doesn't have to mean commitment, but you can't go into this thinking we aren't going to get attached." He leaned closer, until his lips were beside my ear. "We are already attached, Kitten. You hold all the power in those beautiful hands. Be careful how you wield it." Then he nipped my earlobe, making me gasp. Pulling back, he straightened to his full height and gave me a lopsided grin. "Go and get dressed. We'll take you to see Doc and maybe pick you up some more stuff. Then, if you want to go home, I'll take you."

A low rumbling noise came from behind him, but we both ignored it. He was giving me choices, and I desperately needed them.

My life as a carefree Beta in the woods was over. I didn't want to admit it yet, but I knew deep down that I could never go back again.

PEOPLE WERE STARING. After visiting the doctor and being given a clean bill of health, as well as an awkward procedure involving a contraceptive that would be immediately effective—because we all knew that things were going to get wild and *soon*—and a crash course in Omega biology that apparently I'd missed out on by not going to school, we went to a store that sold clothes. Darius called it the commissary.

Corvin hovered and refused to let anyone closer than six feet, which I didn't care about, but he couldn't stop their whispers. Most of them seemed to think Corvin had been keeping me in his basement or something. There were a lot of sneers about my parentage as well, along with some outright lustful looks since I was an Omega. I hated it. I felt like a bug under a microscope, just waiting for someone to come and squish me.

Darius and Beckett were at the Sanctum, which was the home for unwanted baby Manix apparently. It was also the place where Darius worked with the infamous Bonnie. My lip curled silently at the thought of him being close friends with another Omega, a completely visceral response that horrified me. I wasn't a jealous animal; I'd let the two men I'd loved go all those years ago so they could be with their chosen Omega. It was like the heat hormones had flicked a switch in my brain, making me a territorial shrew.

Cooper picked out some things from the extremely limited range in my size. At first, he wanted me to choose, but it was all too much. I could feel people watching me as I searched the rack, so I just gave up and let Cooper pick. He was no nonsense about it, and I knew he wanted to be in and out of here just as fast as I did.

The guy behind the counter was a hundred years old if he was a day, and while his eyes had a small light of interest, he didn't stare. "There's a package for Darius as well. I think it's that new weighted blanket he ordered."

Cooper thanked the man with a smile, paid, and then hurried us out of the store.

Doc had said that there was no going back to being a Beta. He'd also told me that the heat was usually once a year, and that the pheromones I gave off would attract unmated Manix from all around, sometimes even other shifters. He'd insinuated that it would be best if I found a Pack to stay with during my heat, or come into town and be protected, either at his clinic or in the Legion building.

The Beast, he said, could sometimes not be controlled by the whims of the man, unless the Manix was very strong. I thought about Cooper, and how I was in his house, fucking his Packmates at the height of my heat, and he'd still resisted. That must have meant he was strong, right?

I was so lost in my thoughts, I nearly ran into a huge Manix Alpha. He caught my arm immediately, and I looked up into a hard, smirking face.

"Careful, little Omega." His words sent shivers down my spine.

Corvin grabbed my hand and pulled me back behind him. "Fuck off, Wilkie."

"What's wrong, kid? Scared I'll take your Omega?" He looked me up and down. "Don't need it now. Got my own. Pureblood at that. You can keep your mutt."

His words were like tiny knives in my heart, confirming everything I'd ever thought about the Manix and Maxton. I clung embarrassingly to Corvin's back, and I felt his muscles bunch like he wanted to hit the older Alpha, but he wouldn't leave me defenseless.

Cooper, apparently, had no such qualms. His fist came out of nowhere, and then he pummeled the Alpha. Blood sprayed, but the other Alpha was no weakling either. He soon rolled on top of Cooper, landing his own blows, the crunch of bone telling me that they weren't pulling their punches.

A huge Manix waded into the fight, grabbing Wilkie by his too long hair and dragging him off Cooper. Another Alpha, with hair as blond as Cooper's, grabbed him up and put him on his feet, keeping one restraining hand around his bicep.

"What the fuck is going on?" the big Alpha holding Wilkie growled, and I could feel his power against my skin. He was strong, and scary as hell.

"None of your fucking business, Huxley," Wilkie snarled. "Let me go before I tear you to shreds."

The big Alpha just laughed. "In your dreams, dickhead." He let him go with a shove, making Wilkie stumble. "Get the fuck out of here before I lose my control and give you the ass-kicking you so desperately need."

Wilkie spat at the guy's feet and strode off. He didn't seem to have any Pack with him, and I wondered if he was a bachelor Manix. Though he'd said something about an Omega, so he must have a Pack.

I stepped out from behind Corvin's broad back, running to Cooper. "Are you okay?"

I rubbed at his bloodied cheeks. It was smearing the crimson liquid but I wanted to see if he had anything that required stitches. He hissed when I ran my fingers over his nose, which was now sitting at the wrong angle.

"Your nose is broken. We should realign it." I placed my fingers at the very top of his nose, right between the eyes, then molded my palms down the sides, holding it snugly between my hands. "You're going to want to take a deep breath. This will hurt, but it will hurt more trying to do it once it swells." I ran my hands as straight as I could down his nose toward his chin, and he hissed in pain as it crunched back into place. I stepped away, looking at my work. It was straight, but already starting to swell so I wouldn't know if it was crooked until it went back down again. By then, it would be too late, but hey, I tried.

A woman with a toddler bustled over, waving tissues at me. Oh, actually they were wet wipes.

"Man, what I would have given to accidentally put the boot into Wilkie's ribs," she sighed. She passed the child to the big blond Alpha, who snuggled her close to his chest. The woman looked between Corvin and Cooper. "You guys okay?" They nodded. "Well then, there's no excuse not to introduce me to your friend."

Cooper's sigh was a higher pitch than normal. "Kitten, this is my cousin Finlo, and his Packmates Gatlin and Naja. Also, Naja's little sister, Luisa. They are part of the Huxley-Grey Pack."

I looked around the group, at the smiling face of Finlo and the equally welcoming expression of Naja. Gatlin frowned. "You're one of the new Omegas?"

I nodded, and Naja flushed a deep red. "My bad."

Doc had told me that it had been Naja's heat that set off the chain reaction. I gave her a tight smile. "Not your fault."

Corvin gathered me back into his arms protectively, and Finlo raised an eyebrow. "Friend of yours, Corvin?"

"Yes," he said through gritted teeth.

"And where did you come from, little Omega? Down south?" He used the same endearment as Wilkie, but this time, it didn't give me the creeps. There was something to be said about tone and body language, and while this guy was huge and scary, he wasn't threatening. Gatlin was still frowning, but he wasn't leering like Wilkie. He seemed worried and perplexed, but not in a weird way. He looked at me like I was a puzzle.

So I answered, but I thought it through first,

ensuring I had the right English words, and didn't embarrass Corvin and Cooper. "I was raised by Lorso in the woods on the north-western border."

Gatlin tilted his head. "You have an accent."

Well, so much for that. "Didn't learn English until I was thirteen," I told him that in the bastardized Latin Lorso had taught me, making the blond one laugh.

"She's speaking Latin. Holy fucking shit. Lorso was real. That's insane."

Naja threw him an exasperated look. "Don't swear in front of Luisa, Fin." She leaned closer to Gatlin. "Who the fuck is Lorso?" she whispered, and a giggle passed my lips.

"An urban legend." He looked between us. "Come for dinner one day soon. Bring Darius and Beckett too. I'd like to know more."

With that, he bundled them away, even though Naja rolled her eyes. "See you soon. Call me if you need anything. I'm sure you have questions."

Questions about being an Omega. Doc had been reassuring but he didn't really know much; it was all theoretical. The closest I had was Darius, since he was also an Omega, but it still wasn't the same.

I gave Naja—the reason I was in this situation in the first place—a relieved look. "Thank you. I'd like that."

Corvin pushed me toward the ATV. "Home now."

Yeah, he'd reached the end of his patience, and honestly, I'd had my fill too. That was enough people for one day.

13

COOPER

My nose throbbed as I stood between Kitten's thighs while she held a cold pack to my face, her butt on the bathroom vanity. "Where'd you learn to set a nose?"

She cleaned up the blood on my face, and treated a small cut on my cheek that I didn't even realize I had— the sensation had been dulled under the throbbing of my nose. By tomorrow I'd be fine, but I let her fuss.

"When I was eight, I fell out of a tree trying to untangle one of my traps. Hit every branch on the way down with my face. Broke my nose, and Lorso made me fix it myself. Said it was a *doctrina experientia.*"

"A what?"

"Uh..." She paused, screwing up her nose adorably. I traced my finger down the bridge, feeling a slight bump. "A learning experience?"

I huffed a laugh. "Apparently, he was right."

She smiled, and I noticed her front tooth was slightly crooked. Not noticeable from a distance, but this close, I could tell one sat just in front of the other. Probably from that same fall that broke her nose.

"What was it like, growing up wild?"

She shrugged. "Like growing up." She shrugged, her hair bouncing, and I inhaled the scent of her. It was like sunshine and the forest. "Lorso loved me, like I was an unruly cub and he was a near ancient old man."

"So not full of warm gestures then, I guess?" I touched her lips. "Your English is getting better every day."

"The more I am forced to use it, the more words come back to me. What is that saying? Like riding a bike."

I laughed as she taped my nose. Wouldn't want it to rapidly heal wrong. She was sitting up on the bench so we were similar heights, and I soaked in her features as she worked.

"There must be more to it."

Her lips pinched slightly. "I didn't know there was any other way until I met Beckett and Corvin. Or they caught me, at least. They were like devils to me. Lorso had made sure that I feared the Manix enough that if I ever spotted one, I'd run in the other direction as fast as I could. Then he died." I could see the old pain in her eyes, but I didn't poke at the wound.

Instead, I leaned forward until I could feel her breath on my lips. "Can I kiss you, Kit?"

She froze in my arms, but then her heels hooked behind my thighs, dragging me closer. "I like that you call me Kit."

She leaned forward and captured my lips. She tasted as sweet as she smelled, and I felt like I was drowning in her. I let her explore, answered her tentative nibbles with soft ones of my own, the flick of her tongue past my teeth with a stroke of mine against hers. Her fingers buried in my hair, holding me close, but I wasn't going anywhere. I couldn't think of a better place to be at this moment than right here.

She pulled back, resting her face in the crook of my neck. "Is it greedy to want you too?" she whispered, and my heart almost stopped.

"Not greedy. Are you sure?" My Beast growled at me. He was already pissed that we'd missed out on her heat, but he was way too attached considering we'd only known Kitten for less than a week.

"Yes." There was no doubt in her voice, not a pause or a quaver. She wanted this.

And I was more than happy to give it to her. I cupped her jaw with my hand, stroking my thumb along her high cheekbone. She was so beautiful. Not like a delicate flower, though she was certainly delicate in stature. No, she might be slight, but there was a fierceness to her, a strength that said she didn't need us. It made the fact that she wanted me so much sweeter.

I stroked my hands down her ribs until they settled on her hips—still too skinny but beautiful all the same. Once she was well fed, these curves would be soft beneath my fingers. I slid my hands beneath the waistband of her borrowed shorts, tracing the line of her underwear, asking for permission.

"More," she growled, and it was cute as fuck. I wondered if she could shift. The guys seemed to think she couldn't, but who knew?

That was a question for another time though, because right now, I wanted to taste. I wanted my mouth on every single inch of her as quickly as possible. I pulled at the shorts, and she lifted her ass so I could wiggle them off her legs. Grabbing her knees, I spread them wide and groaned.

"Aw, Kit. You're so wet for me already. God, how could you be so perfect for us?" I bit the inside of her thigh gently, a claiming kind of bite. My Beast was screaming things I refused to hear, but they may have started with M and rhymed with the word Fate.

Dragging my teeth away from her creamy flesh, I stroked my tongue toward the apex of her thighs. Sliding between her folds, I lapped at her juices with a groan. Oh, yes. As I flicked my tongue over her clit, she curled against my mouth, showing me what she liked. A little soft, a little rough. My girl liked a variety. I could do that. I alternated plunging my tongue inside her with sucking gently on her clit until she was holding my hair and panting out her release.

I wanted this so bad that I was going to come right now. I thought about baseball, that one time I fell on a roofing job and broke my arm, anything at all that was completely unarousing so I could hold on.

But when she moaned my name? I was fucking done for.

I stood, grabbing her thighs. "You're sure that you're sure?"

"Cooper, please," she whined, and that was it. Pushing my sweats down to my thighs, I lined up my dick and thrust into her with more enthusiasm than finesse, filling her balls deep as she clung to my back.

"Yes," I whispered, pulling her hips even closer and propping one arm against the wall so I could slide in at a slow, deep pace that was making her squirm.

Sweet fucking Goddess, she was tight around me. I'd never had a woman before. It had always been Darius for me. This was entirely different—not better or worse, just different. And I was going to blow.

"Touch your clit, Omega. Help me get you off."

Then I thought about football scores. And that one time Jeremy at work slipped with a nail gun and attached his balls to a roof. Yeah, that one did it. The urge to blow ran away and hid after that visual memory. So I upped my stroke, going deeper and harder, until she was whimpering around me.

"Knot me," she moaned. Oh fuck. I wanted nothing more in this moment than to fill her completely. I sent up a small prayer of thanks to her IUD, and succumbed to her moaned request.

I kissed her hard, drinking her down between large gulps of air. "Come for me," I said, my voice all Alpha now. The Beast had risen at the idea of knotting this pretty Omega and he wasn't going away. Like the good girl she was, she came around my cock, clawing me to her body and hanging on for dear life.

I heard the open and close of the front door, scented Beckett and Darius arriving home from the Sanctum. They'd smell what was happening in here too, but I didn't know if they'd leave us to it or come in and join us. It didn't really matter though; I would continue whether I had an extra set of hands to plea-sure Kit with or not.

I pushed my swelling knot against her entrance, begging to be invited in. Nudging gently past the resis-tance of the outer ring of muscle, we were suddenly locked together, two halves of a whole, and she came again, shaking around me as I pumped softly, rubbing all those happy places inside her with my swollen dick.

Finally, with one more sloppy kiss, I filled her with my seed. It was everything and more. I looked down into her pretty brown eyes as she clung to me, her softness wrapped around my hard edges, one being just for a small moment.

I was so screwed.

The door burst open, and Darius stood there, his face pale. He looked between us—Kit wrapped naked around my body, me buried knot-deep inside her.

"I'm sorry to interrupt, but Cooper, there's been a coup. The Alpha General is fighting for his seat. They say it's to the death." His breaths came in heavy pants. "I tried calling the Sanctum, but there's no answer."

Fuck.

14

BECKETT

I tried to make Darius stay at the Packhouse with Kitten, but he refused. Fucking stubborn Omega. But at least Kitten agreed. She didn't want to be involved in Maxton bullshit or Manix politics, and for that, I was glad. Cooper stayed behind to protect her, but I knew he burned to be with us.

We drove the ATV at breakneck speed toward the Sanctum. We pulled up out the front, and already I knew something was wrong. I shifted forms, and the scent on the wind made me freeze.

"Blood," I whispered, and Darius let out a pained cry, racing toward the front door of the Sanctum.

"Darius, wait!" Corvin yelled, but he was already halfway to the door. I sprinted to catch up, and grabbed him just as he reached for the handle.

"Me first, Omega," I hissed. I pushed him behind

me as the door swung open, and I sucked in a breath. A pool of blood stained the entry hall.

It smelled like Bonnie.

"No," Darius breathed, pushing into my back to get in. I held him back—or maybe it was Corvin—as I let my senses search the house. No one else was here. I let him pass, and he rushed in. He squatted down, dipping his fingers in the now tacky blood. "Bonnie."

Tears poured down his cheeks. Mine too. The loss of this much blood would be tough to survive—it meant extreme violence. Possibly death. But there was no body to be seen.

"Where are the children?" Corvin whispered.

Darius was up on his feet instantly, running further into the house like his own senses were wrong. "Kids? Taylor?" he shouted, running from room to room.

Corvin came up beside me, his body tense. "This is bad. I'm going to check next door." Then he was gone.

He wasn't wrong. This was worse than bad. This wasn't an Alpha Challenge, this was a targeted attack on an Omega female. On *Bonnie*.

Darius reappeared. "They're gone," he whispered.

I grabbed him and pulled him close, rubbing a reassuring hand on his back. "No one would hurt the children, Darius. I'm sure they're somewhere safe. The only blood here is Bonnie's."

I tried to reassure myself that the words were true. The Manix were many things, but we didn't kill children. They'd kicked them around a bit in the old days, but we were past that. I was sure we were past that.

When Corvin reappeared, he shook his head. "No one was there either, but there was the blood of the Alpha General's Omega out the back. Pryce."

This wasn't right. I didn't care how many times the other Alphas fought for power, there were too few Omega—too few Manix, even—to endanger them this way. What the hell was going on?

"Call Radic. Or Murphy. Call someone and find out what the hell is going on," Darius said, his voice wavering. Corvin nodded, pulling his phone from his pocket and stepping back outside.

I pulled Darius back into my arms. "It will be okay, Omega. It will all be okay." He was staring at the pool of blood on the floor. Judging by the coolness of the blood, it was an hour or more old.

"Thanks, man. I owe you one," Corvin muttered into the phone as he walked back into the room. His face was grim, and I knew I wasn't going to like this. "The Alpha fight is happening now at the Arena. We need to get down there. Someone is saying that they've hobbled the Alpha General to stack the odds."

Fear washed through me. Fear of the unknown, fear for my friends and family. Fear that we would be shunted back to the old days, where the Sanctum kids were seen as less, and your worth was based on your bloodlines and designation.

Everything I thought I knew about the Manix was turning out to be wrong. And that scared me most of all.

I'D ATTENDED the last Alpha battle, when Courtland De Léon had taken down Alpha General Huxley. The old Alpha had reigned for all of my life, and I'd disliked the man and everything he stood for. Racial purity. Money. Power.

However, the vibe was far different at this Alpha fight. The crowd was dead silent as Legion soldiers dropped the mangled body of the Alpha General in the center of the ring. Even from here, I could see that his knees were well and truly fucked.

We kept Darius between Corvin and I, to protect him if things went crazy. As I looked around at the faces of the people of Maxton, all I saw was worry. Worry and fear. Eldridge, a Legion General and close friend of the former Alpha General, stood in the center of the ring, giving a speech about his greatness.

"We can't let this happen," Corvin said softly, but I hushed him. Maxton had been divided. I couldn't tell who of these people—people I'd known for my whole life—were loyal to Eldridge, and who had put their faith in the new Alpha General.

I shook my head. "We can't stop it," I whispered back, though it hurt me to say it. We could dive in there to protect the Alpha General, but the result would still be the same. He'd still lose his position. And there was a chance we'd lose our lives on top of it. Call me selfish, but I wasn't nearly as strong as the Alpha General, or even just a Legion General.

And then they were fighting. The true strength of Courtland De Léon was on display, because he kept Eldridge on the back foot even without the use of his legs. He had to be in incredible pain.

"This is wrong!" someone yelled, and I looked over to see Doc arguing with one of Wilkie's Betas. Fuck.

"Stay with Darius," I told Corvin, moving toward them. Doc wasn't going to just lie down and bare his belly to the Legion soldiers; he'd never had that much respect for the institution. However, now was not the time to invoke that fight. Not while everyone's blood was up. Not while violence and bloodlust hung in the air like a bad perfume.

I pushed through the crowd, shoving shocked bystanders out of the way as I heard Doc continuing to shout. "Get the hell out of my way, or so help me Goddess, I'll make you piss blood for a month."

The Beta just laughed. "I have to warn you, stepping foot into that ring would be a bad idea." It wasn't a warning. He was goading him.

And Doc was going to dive headlong into the trap.

Doc spun on his heel, stepping into the ring, pulling a gun from who knows where and firing.

"Doc, no!" I yelled, but I was too late. The Legion soldier swung a sword, slicing off Doc's head with shocking ease.

I gasped as it rolled across the ground, shocked. The shock turned to confusion as I watched a vampire appear from nowhere, and stick his fist into the Beta's chest, removing his heart.

Gatlin appeared beside me, panting, his eyes wide. "Fuck. No," he breathed, and I looked at the horror show in front of me. The vampire moved quickly so he was beside Courtland's prone body. Dominic, the Alpha General's wolf Beta, was there next to him.

It was carnage. Eldridge's head was in pieces, Doc's beside him. Vampires appeared from nowhere, and the entire arena was locked down tight, making every person inside of it anxious. You didn't fuck with the vampires. It was a life lesson taught right around the same age as 'don't eat the yellow snow.'

The vampire with the scary face—still coated in the blood of the Beta—disappeared out of the arena with our wounded Alpha General in his arms.

This was a nightmare. I pushed back toward Corvin and Darius, barging past people who were gaping at the blood-soaked sand in shock. I could see Corvin standing, Darius pressed between his back and the wall of the arena. Corvin's eyes were wild, and he looked seconds from shifting. But he didn't, not with so many vampires around. They were our friends, or at least that's what they'd told us. But still, friendships ended, sometimes in the bloodiest ways possible.

"We need to get out of here," I said, stepping behind him and grabbing Darius by the arm.

We didn't get far, as Raine—Convocation Member, vampire, and if rumor had it correct, bakery owner— appeared in the center of the arena.

"Well, we've rightly fucked this up, haven't we? Honestly, I expected better from you." She managed to give us the look a disappointed mother would give an unruly child, which was a true feat if you considered the fact that she looked like a preppy eighteen year old. "Go home. I'll catch up with those who made a poor choice today." She gave us all a smile that sent shivers down my spine, and I hadn't even done anything wrong. "Trust me when I say, we'll know. We always know."

15

DARIUS

It rained the day we buried Doc. My heart ached for the man who had been a stalwart of Maxton for decades. He'd delivered Corvin, Beckett and me. He'd set Cooper's leg when we'd fallen off the school roof trying to skip weapons training class.

He'd been an integral part of our society for so long, revered just below the Alpha General, and now he was dead. Senselessly dead.

The kids from the Sanctum were gone, squirreled away in Canada in an academy for supernatural children until we were sure Maxton was safe. Safe for the young. The world had been turned on its head, and I wasn't sure we'd survive as the people we once were.

Kitten had come, dressed in red and standing between us all. She'd wanted to pay her respects to a man she'd only met briefly, and that made me like her even more. We ignored the curious looks, instead focusing on the words of Joshua, who was leading the funeral in the place of the Alpha General, who was still recuperating in hospital.

Joshua's speech was solemn, filled with the many accomplishments of a man who'd lived almost a century, who'd worked hard to fill the dark depths of our society with light, who'd taken in an orphaned Beta and raised her like a daughter. Who'd stood toe to toe with the old Alpha General to ensure that half-bloods were treated better, who'd raised his daughter to harbor them, nurture them.

"Doc was the best of us," Joshua ended, and it was a truth that spread through the crowd and landed heavily on our hearts.

We dispersed slowly, moving away from the grave strewn with carnations. A hand gripped mine, small and rough, and I looked down to see Kitten's fingers entwined with mine. I squeezed it back, soaking in the comfort she was giving me so freely.

We had to walk back to the Packhouse, as the Manix didn't bring vehicles to funerals. In the old days, we came in our Beast forms, and we'd burn our dead on a pyre. But they were traditions that were long dead, as the older generation died out and the younger generation—a generation without Omega females, a generation that got smaller and smaller each decade— became the ones who made decisions.

We walked slowly, the death walk a solemn trudge of respect. "Are you alright?" Kitten whispered beside me, and I nodded.

"I'm okay. Lost, I think. And sad."

She stepped closer so our footsteps synced and our shoulders rubbed together. "When Lorso died, I dug his grave myself. I knew he'd probably like to be burned on a warrior's pyre, but he made me promise to bury him. He didn't want the Legion to see the smoke and come to see what it was. Protecting me even in death." She gave a sad little smile that I wanted to kiss from her lips. "I was thirteen. It took me two days to dig a hole deep enough that the animals wouldn't uncover him for food. Though he probably would have liked to be devoured by wolves too. He was a great believer in *ordo naturalis.*" She paused. "The natural order of things. But I was young, and the idea of the only person who'd ever wanted me being torn apart by wild animals seemed wrong."

I squeezed her hand, and my Alphas stayed quiet. Kitten hadn't spoken much, which I think was a combination of not knowing the words and not knowing what to say.

"So I dug a hole under his favorite tree, dragged his body from his bed, and dropped him in it. No bindings. No rites. I still think about it."

Beckett stroked his hand down her spine. "Lorso would be proud of the woman you've become."

She snorted. "Lorso would kick my ass for doing the one thing he made me swear not to do." She looked at us all. "I want to stay in town. I want to stay with you."

My breath seized in my lungs as I tried to think of the right thing to say. I didn't want to blow this. "Are you sure? I know you didn't want all this..." I waved at the rows of housing, at the crowds still around us, even if they were no longer in hearing distance.

"I was raised in the woods, and they'll always be home." She chewed her lip. "But sometimes people can be home too, you know?" She cleared her throat. "We deserve to see where this goes. I deserve to know if there is more to life than hiding in the shadows."

I stopped, pulling her to a stop with me. "We'll take it slow. Go at your pace. This?" I waved at the three Alphas who stood silently around us. "This feels right, like it was meant to be." I tugged gently on her hand and we continued our trek home. "I'm not going to lie —I was pretty pissed when the guys turned up with a mystery woman." I stepped closer, so my lips were against her ear. "But I'm kind of glad they did. Don't tell them I said that though."

She smiled up at me, and it lit up an otherwise gray day. "Your secret is safe with me."

Cooper put a heavy hand on her shoulder. "But first, maybe you should take us home."

. . .

RUSTIC WOULD BE a generous way to describe the place where Kitten had grown up. It was made from stone and small logs, roughly piled together. The area around it was clear, but only for about ten feet in either direction. After that, the clearing was subsumed by the woods, the towering trees hiding the cabin from view. The most innovative thing about the place was the chimney, which seemed to disperse the smoke so that it didn't create any real beacon, rather just a haze that would be difficult to pinpoint from far away.

She'd lit the fire as soon as we got there, so she could make us coffee. There was no electricity out here, so everything was run through that fire. Cooking, heating water, and keeping warm in the winter. She started the fire with practiced ease.

"You should get solar panels for this place," Corvin suggested. "We can get you some of those, now that you aren't hiding."

She made a non-committal noise, and slid a cup of coffee in front of him. "Sorry, I only have three cups. I've never needed more." She looked around at how the four of us filled the room. "Actually, I don't think I've ever had this many people in my home."

I laughed softly. "Let's go outside. It's a nice day, a bit of a break from the oppressive heat this year."

She handed the Alphas the rest of the coffee and we all followed her outside. The woods weren't silent, of course, but it was peaceful out here. I hadn't realized how suburban Maxton had actually become.

"It really is beautiful out here. Peaceful."

She gave me a bright smile, such a genuine expression of happiness for the first time. "Thank you."

It was in that moment that I knew we couldn't move her to our Packhouse. She'd be happy; we'd make sure of it. Maybe deliriously happy, if I had my way. But she'd be happier out here.

I watched her face as she explained about extinguishing the wild boar problem out here, about cultivating a herd of deer, and only picking off one a year to feed herself. About salting and drying the meat and storing it to eat over the year. She pointed out small areas where she'd planted patches of vegetables in convenient locations without having to clear a bunch of land. The only things she bought from town were bags of flour and curing salt.

"It's a bit different this year. The season has been historically dry after last year's rains. The undergrowth is too long, which makes it dangerous."

Beckett was murmuring something about talking to the Alpha General once he healed up, or even Radic, but I stopped listening. The way the sun touched her head, the warmth of that golden hour before the sunset made her look angelic.

I wonder if I could love a person this quick. I knew I was definitely in awe of her, but I'd been an Omega my whole life. We were drawn to Pack life—we didn't thrive by ourselves. Now that I'd been here, seen her home, where she lived, I was beginning to understand what she'd really lost when she became an Omega. She was free once.

Now, no matter how we tried, she'd always be caged.

She led us over to a log that sat under a large tree. A small stone cairn sat below it. "I come out here sometimes and still talk to Lorso. I know that he isn't here anymore, not even in spirit. But it gets lonely."

I grabbed her and pulled her into my arms. "Not anymore, Kitten. Never again. Whether you stay with us or not, you'll never be alone again. Unless you want to be. No pressure."

Corvin snorted. "You're so fucking cute, Darius."

I gave him the finger, and kissed her sweetly. "Just want you to be happy."

I looked down at the grave in front of us, and silently thanked Lorso for raising her. For keeping her safe. Corvin and Beckett hadn't been wrong all those years ago; Betas were treated as second class, and half-blooded Betas were basically chew toys for orphaned Alphas. Or full-blooded Alphas. For anyone really. No, they may have been dumb kids, but they'd made the right choice.

We sat out there for hours, listening to the animals in the woods, long after the sun went to bed. Corvin lit a small fire, and we sat around and bonded, the way a Pack should. My Beast rumbled happily from where I rested back against Corvin, his fingers stroking through my hair. Kitten was snuggled between Cooper and Beckett as they rested against the log.

This was right, perfect, and all I had to do was convince Kitten the same thing.

16

KITTEN

"**F**uck, Corvin, please!"

Cooper laughed against my back as he stroked his thumbs over my nipples, then pinched them with a firmness that was just on the pleasurable side of pain. He seemed to know that line intimately, and he was teaching me my limits, one teasing bite at a time.

But it wasn't those teasing fingers on my breasts that had me panting right now. No, it was the man between my thighs, whose tongue was doing truly wicked things which were driving me insane.

Trapped between them a position I often found myself in now, and I wasn't even a little bit mad about it. It wasn't always Corvin and Cooper. Sometimes it was Darius and Beckett, or Beckett and Corvin, or all four of them.

Those times were my favorite. We were just a mass of bodies, writhing in pleasure, and it didn't matter where one of us ended and the other began. It was more frenzied, more animalistic. That was when the Beasts really came out to play.

I hadn't managed to get any of them to fuck me in their full Manix form since the heat, but honestly, without all those pheromones giving me huge lady balls, I wasn't sure I could take it.

Corvin nipped at my clit, dragging me from inside my head with a scream. "Goddess, fuck!" Then I was coming all over his face, while he continued fucking me with his long and surprisingly dexterous tongue.

I flopped back against Cooper's chest with a heaving pant. "Uh-uh, Kit. You aren't done yet." He slid me up his body a little, before impaling me on his cock. "Oh fuck, sweetheart," he groaned against my ear. He slid me back up, taking control. My body was sweaty, helping me glide along his chest with ease, and I looked up at Corvin kneeling at the end of my bed, stroking his cock.

"One day, Kitten, we'll both fuck you like this. My cock and Coop's, sliding in and out of your delicious little sheath. We know you can take it. You took the Beast." He flicked my engorged clit, just once, making both me and Cooper moan as I clenched around him.

"Fucking hell, Corvin. Stop or I'll blow, and I'm not ready to be done yet." As if to punctuate his words,

Cooper slid me up and down his dick at a faster pace, before grunting and banding an arm around my waist, pushing forward until I was on my stomach and he was behind me, fucking me into the mattress. He kissed between my shoulder blades as he went deeper, hitting new places, places I didn't even know I had.

"You're so perfect for us," he whispered against my skin. Or at least I thought he did—it was hard to hear over the slapping of our skin. "Omega," he growled in an inhuman voice, and his teeth scraped my shoulder. The Beast was out to play too.

I arched toward his mouth. I wanted him to bite me, but I also didn't. My heart said yes, but my head was arguing. She was still a scaredy bitch.

Stuffing his hands under my hips, he tilted my pelvis a little, and hit a spot that made me scream so loudly, I wondered if the Legion would come.

I was definitely coming. I buried my screams of pleasure into the mattress, and Corvin splattered his seed over my body. Yes. I wanted to bathe in his cum. I wanted him to own me, scent me. I wanted all of them to mark me as theirs.

Fucking Omega hormones.

Cooper pounded into me through my orgasm, dragging it out until I was a whimpering mess, before he collapsed against my back, groaning his own release.

"I thought after a month I'd stop coming like I'm a

teenage boy with no self-control, but you undo me, Kit," he murmured, licking the sweat from my spine, and maybe a little of Corvin's cum.

It had been a hell of a month. The heat, the coup, moving into the Packhouse with the guys. It had been wild, but I was happy. I thought I'd long for home, and I did sometimes. But I'd miss them if I left—I was honest enough with myself to admit that.

"You know, when you said you were coming up here to change for the party, I didn't realize you were getting naked and sweaty, or I would have joined you." Darius stood in the doorway, one eyebrow raised. He looked stern, but his eyes were laughing.

I grinned at him, attempting to blow hair out of my face. It just fell right back over my face limply. "There's still time?"

He laughed, moving into my bedroom. They'd given me my own room, and I'd brought some stuff from my cabin to make it feel more like mine. I had to admit, I liked it. My Omega liked it.

Darius stopped in front of me, brushing the hair off my forehead for me. "I wish, baby, but there really isn't any time. Not if you want to shower off Corvin's cum first."

The Alpha in question grunted. "I say leave it. I want everyone to know that I please my Omega."

Cooper pushed up off my back, no doubt sticky with Corvin's seed too. Mmm, I liked that. "It's your cum, not hers. The only proof it provides is that you blow your load at the drop of a hat."

Corvin growled, diving at the other Alpha, and they wrestled around on the floor naked, play fighting. Well, I'm sure it would look like real fighting to humans, but it wouldn't even leave a bruise on a Manix. It was something these Alphas did all the time, over any little thing. The last scoop of ice cream? Wrestle until someone tapped out. Wanted to have Darius on his lap during the movie? Wrestle for it. Wanted to make me breakfast? Or eat me for breakfast? You got it. Winner gets dibs.

It was so ridiculously endearing.

Darius rolled his eyes, then bent down and kissed me. "You have ten minutes, and then we're meant to be at the Alpha General's house. Shake that pretty ass." As if to punctuate his point, he slid a hand down my back, and squeezed my butt with a groan. "On second thoughts, who cares? No one is going to know we're missing, and I haven't tasted you in like twelve whole hours," he said with another squeeze, before reaching up for his tie.

Beckett saved the day, letting out a loud whistle and stopping the two Alphas fighting on the floor. Coop had Corvin in a leg bar around his neck, which was a bit courageous considering how close Corvin's teeth were to his balls.

Beckett gave them an incredulous look. "Omega,

leave your clothes on. You two, get dressed already. Goddess, you're basically children." He looked at me, his eyes softening. "Later, Kitten. Right now, we need to go."

"Yes, Alpha."

Beckett's lips parted, his eyes hooding with lust. He was halfway across the room with a low growl before he stopped in his tracks. He waved a finger at me. "I think I liked you better when you were hissing and spitting, Kitten Wiley-Fletcher-Reid. You know you have way too much power over us poor schmucks now."

My heart stuttered at the fact he gave me his Pack name. I'd never had a surname. Lorso had called me Girl. The guys had always called me Kitten, which had stuck as a first name. But that was it. A singular name.

I swallowed hard and tried to keep the emotions from my face. "I'll get dressed now, Alpha," I said softly, and the room was unnaturally quiet. They'd all heard Beckett's slip. Or maybe he did it on purpose? But no one said anything at all for a moment, waiting for my reaction. When I ignored it, they all went about their business.

Beckett's smile was sweet, and it made my heart thump harder in my chest. Not a slip then. "Ten minutes, you guys, or I'm leaving without you all."

Darius huffed, kissed the top of my head, and left with Beckett. The two remaining Alphas, still naked and entwined on the floor, looked up at me. Cooper cleared his throat and released Corvin's head from between his huge thighs.

"We better change. I'll start you a shower." He shifted to his feet, and I don't care what the ancient Romans thought, naked wrestling wasn't all that glamorous unless you were in the middle of it. He came over, pushed me onto my back and kissed me. "Just so you know, I like the way it sounds too." Then he hauled me into his arms like a rag doll and carried me to the bathroom.

We were definitely late.

17

CORVIN

Kitten may have washed my seed from her body, but there was no doubt who she was with. We'd all scent marked her at some point, and she smelled like Pack now, even if she wasn't officially mated to us.

We stood around at Bonnie's mating party to the De Léon Pack, and I smiled at how deliriously happy she looked. As if she felt my gaze, she turned to look at us. She was holding a baby in her arms, and Hamish, one of the Sanctum kids, was clinging to her leg.

That was Bonnie in a nutshell. A nurturer. She deserved to be an Omega, not that she couldn't be the best goddamn person there was as a Beta. But that maternal drive she had, the softness, her mission in life, would only be aided by her Omega biology.

Shuffling over the best she could, she smiled at us blissfully. "If it isn't the Wiley-Fletcher-Reid Pack. I haven't seen you all together in so, so long. I've missed you."

Hamish scaled Cooper's body like a spider monkey, settling in his arms. If Bonnie was like a mother to the Sanctum kids, I guess we were like fathers. Though I wondered if we'd be as important now that she had her own Pack, and her own Omega Male to help?

She raised an eyebrow at me, which seemed faintly chastising, and then turned to Kitten. "I'm Bonnie. I've heard so much about you—I'm so happy to finally meet you."

Kitten blinked at Bonnie, and I got it. Bonnie was like a warm hug after a life of grayness. It was her super power, I think. Look who she'd managed to snag as a Pack.

"It's nice to meet you too. Darius says only nice things about you."

Bonnie grinned, handing her a baby. Kitten took it —this tiny, fragile being—like she was holding a bomb, and I stifled a laugh.

"Darius says only wonderful things about you too. You have a fan." Bonnie looked at me sternly. "He was a little less impressed with his Alphas for a hot minute though."

I shrugged. "Had to be done, Bon."

She harrumphed, reaching out to fix Kitten's hold on the baby absentmindedly. "They aren't as breakable as you think. Hold him here and here." She placed Kitten's hands in the proper position. "There you go—you're both happy now." She turned back to me. "I trust that you're taking care of her? Giving her choices and not being all caveman now that she's an Omega? Showing her she has options other than your Pack?"

I flushed. "Of course," I said in a strangled voice. Bonnie and Radic had always been a good team, and were a great couple. They believed in what was right, and stood their ground to get it. "I'm glad you and Radic finally made it official. I know the Alpha General is in charge, but he looks like a man who listens to his Pack. You two will be good for this town."

She gave me a narrow-eyed look that told me she knew I'd changed the subject on purpose. "Courtland is what's best for the Manix and for Maxton. I know it deep in my soul. Doc did too."

I watched her eyes shine, and pulled her into a hug. Well, at least I did until Courtland, the Alpha General, appeared.

"Corvin," he said curtly, dragging Bonnie back to his side and dropping a proprietary arm around her shoulders. It made me grin. He bowed low at Kitten. "Omega. It is good to meet you."

Kitten blinked big brown eyes up at the Alpha

General, and she looked skittish. Swallowing hard, she nodded her head back. "Alpha General."

I understood though—Courtland De Léon radiated power. It made my own Alpha wanna lie down on the floor and bare his belly. Luckily for us, subjugating us didn't seem big on Courtland's agenda.

"You seem to be holding my cub, Omega. Do you have a name?"

"Uh, my name is Kitten. Sorry. Here," she mumbled, thrusting the baby in his direction like she was offloading drugs during a drop. And if rumor was true, it wouldn't be the first time Courtland had been at the receiving end of a drug drop.

He smirked, taking the baby easily. "Kitten. Interesting. Maybe I should introduce you to my Beta, Dominic, one day."

I frowned at the amusement in his eyes, which was reflected in Bonnie's. An inside joke then, but hopefully not one at Kitten's expense.

The Alpha General cleared his throat. "Actually, while you are both here, I would like you to meet Tanner." Courtland pulled Bonnie closer to his side, like he was shoring her up for something, and his next words confirmed it. "Tanner is here to act as temporary town doctor until another one can be trained up. Tanner?" He said the words softly, but suddenly there was a vampire in our small circle, right in front of my

Omega. A low growl bubbled in my throat but I pushed it down. Now was not the time.

The vampire was big and blond, with a goofy, yet perfectly white and straight smile. Except for, you know, the fangs. "You rang?"

Courtland nodded. "This is Kitten. Kitten, this is Tanner. I've tasked him with chasing down the lineage of all the new Omegas and their Packs, just to ensure when the next generation is grown and ready to start Packs of their own, no one is accidentally mating their cousin."

I narrowed my eyes. "Not to ensure the purity of the Manix bloodlines?" It was a short, sharp fall from protecting the health of the Pack to using lineage to control who should get a Pack and an Omega.

"Corvin, I couldn't give a flying fuck about lineage. I just don't want the Manix to perish because in three generations' time cubs are being born with an extra head."

Kitten coughed, or maybe it was a snort. "I'm not sure what I could tell him, Alpha General. I was found in the woods. I have less knowledge of my lineage than a feral kitten born in a barn."

Bonnie frowned. "Sometimes, who your parents are isn't as important as who your family will be." She shifted her eyes to me. "You've chosen well, if this is who you've chosen."

Bonnie had a pretty shitty childhood. She was a little older than us, only by a couple of years, but when you're a kid, that may as well be a century. I knew enough to know she'd been bullied for being rejected by her Manix parents. Defective. Pushed from the nest.

Such was the deep-rooted prejudices of the Manix people. Yes, Courtland was definitely needed as the Alpha General.

Tanner smiled. "Honestly, a DNA test will sort it out. This is the Manix; there's only like six degrees of Kevin Bacon."

I blinked. "What?"

Bonnie rolled her eyes. "He means that there aren't very many of us, so bloodlines aren't hard to trace. Maybe you'll come out of this experience with some answers."

Yeah, but sometimes answers weren't a good thing. I'd leave it up to Kitten, not pushing her in one way or the other. She was silent for a moment, and then nodded. "I think that would be fine?"

Tanner grinned. "Excellent. I've done most of the other Omegas, but Radic said to give you guys extra time because you might be busy. Don't know what you guys do that you can't give me ten minutes to draw some blood, but hey, Radic knows best, am I right?"

I held my mirth on the inside. "Radic knows best."

Bonnie patted the huge vampire on the back. He was like a fucking golden retriever with fangs. "Tanner is actually an excellent doctor. He has senses even better than a Manix."

Tanner grinned broadly. "Hell yeah I do. I can tell you who the rest of your Pack members are just by scent, and I can tell how many weeks along your Omega is by the strength of the fetuses' heart rates. Well, it isn't really a heartbeat at this stage, more like a whoosh. But you know, it makes it easier to date that way."

The world froze. It was like a record scratch, or when someone hit the brakes and your stomach suddenly felt like it was in your throat.

"Excuse me?" Kitten squeaked loudly, drawing the attention of those around us.

Tanner laughed. "Oh, not this Omega. The other one. Pretty fucking amazing reproductive system you guys have got there, if you ask me." He pointed to Darius who was talking to one of the Legion Generals across the room.

Blood rushed in my ears. It was like a wave of white noise that got louder and louder until it threatened to consume me.

Darius was pregnant. Darius was pregnant.

Bonnie dropped her voice. "Darius is pregnant?" she echoed my thoughts in a whisper.

My Beast surged up in me along with an uncontrolled growl.

"I don't think he knew. I suggest you take your Pack home, Alpha," Courtland said softly.

It wasn't a suggestion, it was a command, and I was already bundling Kitten up in my arms and moving her through the crowd toward the other side of the room. Beckett frowned, making his way over from where someone was mixing drinks.

"Home," I growled, all Beast right now, and Beckett had the wisdom not to argue. I caught up to Cooper and Darius, who both took one look at my face and started making their excuses to leave. Beckett grabbed Kitten from my hands and led her outside. The other Alphas in my Pack were on alert for a threat, but there was no threat.

There was only a fucking miracle.

"Corvin, what's wrong? Kitten? Are you okay?"

Kitten swallowed hard. "We need to discuss this at home."

I loaded them all into the ATV, driving home as fast as I dared. Which meant ten miles under the speed limit. At this rate, it would have been faster to crawl home, but I wasn't taking any chances. Not Darius, not with Kitten and not with the babies.

The babies. Our cubs.

I let out a shuddering breath and when we reached the Packhouse, Darius climbed out, folding his arms over his chest. "Corvin, not one more step until you tell me what the hell is going on. You're freaking me out right now."

I looked at the man that I loved with my whole heart. For nearly a decade, he'd been my whole world. And now...

"Darius, you're pregnant."

18

DARIUS

I laughed at Corvin. Right there, in his face. "No I'm not." I looked at Kitten's stricken expression, and my humor faded away. "I'd know if I were pregnant. You guys would know. You'd be able to smell the changes in my scent."

"Not for a while. Apparently, our senses aren't quite as good as a vampire from Australia who sounds like he wrestles crocodiles for fun," Corvin grumbled.

I slumped down on the grass. Shit. My brain couldn't comprehend what Corvin was telling me. Not really.

"Do we believe him?" Cooper's voice was a rough whisper. "Do we trust that he knows what the hell he's talking about? I mean, up until a few weeks ago, he'd never met a Manix, let alone a pregnant male Omega."

Corvin shrugged. "He seemed pretty sure. Didn't even realize that we had no clue."

"How?" Beckett asked, and I noticed he was holding onto a still gray-looking Kitten. "We were safe."

Well, mostly. I mean, we weren't the gold standard of safe sex, because things got a little wild during the heat. But we'd been careful. Careful of Kitten—the last thing we wanted to do was trap her into anything when she was still learning she was an Omega.

"Well, when five people are overcome with hormones, and love each other dearly, they sometimes have sex. Sometimes sex makes—"

"Shut up, Corvin. We were safe."

"We were careful with Kitten. Obviously, Darius's dick had other ideas, and was a little overeager in its new-found abilities. And we weren't exactly Safe Sex Extraordinaire with Darius."

The whooshing noise in my head got louder and louder.

"The how doesn't matter. What do we do now?" Corvin asked slowly, like he was scared of the answer.

I pushed up off the ground. I walked to Kitten and picked her up in my arms, striding into the house. "I just need a minute."

After a squeak of surprise, Kitten snuggled into my chest. A cold sweat coated her body, and I knew she was freaking out too. I took the stairs up to my nest two at a time. I wanted to be in there with her, snuggled away from the world, just for a little while. Kicking the door shut behind me, I laid her down on the pillows. I tore at my tie, ripping open my button down shirt so the buttons flew everywhere. Then I climbed onto the nest behind her, pulled all the blankets up around us and nuzzled my face into the back of her neck.

For a moment, we just breathed. I let the warmth of her body soak into mine, and felt her heartbeat beneath my hand. We'd created something together, all of us, but it wouldn't have been possible without Kitten. I was hoping we hadn't destroyed something equally as precious in the process.

"Are you okay?" I whispered against her neck.

She sighed, rolling onto her back so she could look at me. "I don't know." She wiggled back toward me. "Are you okay? You're the one who's pregnant."

I turned onto my back as well, and together we stared at the ceiling. I placed my hand over my abs. "I don't know either. I'm freaking the hell out, if I'm honest."

Six months ago, this had been the only thing I wanted, but it was a fairytale wish back then. Now it was a stark reality, and I wasn't sure I was ready.

She slipped her hand on top of mine, lacing our fingers together. "Explain this to me. Are they part mine?"

I nodded. "Yes. Fuck, I thought we'd have more time to explain this. So during the heat, my dick, I don't know, pulls an Uno Reverse and sucks instead of spits? Dammit, Beckett is the teacher. He'd be better at explaining this."

She tightened her fingers around mine. "I want to hear it from you."

I sighed. Birds and the Bees talk it was then. "So I have an extractor, which is like a secondary urethra. Like, I don't know, a second hole? And during the heat, you ovulate, but your eggs drop lower into your secondary cervix and my extractor kind of sucks your eggs into my womb. From there, they're inseminated by the Alphas when they knot me. Theoretically, anyway. We didn't do any of that perfectly, and yet, here we are?"

"So it's an accident?"

I snorted. "I prefer a miracle, but yeah. Basically."

"So, they are half me, half one of the Alphas? But not you?" She was frowning. I guess it was kind of a weird evolutionary hiccup. No part of my DNA would be passed onto the cub, or cubs. I was like an impressive incubator.

"Yep. If I want my own biological offspring, it would occur in a more traditional manner. You—uh, I mean the female, not *you* you—would carry it to term. And it wouldn't result in a litter the way it does with me." I flushed bright red. "That's Manix reproduction

101. Don't ask me any questions because I'm really not sure I know the answers."

"A litter?" she squeaked, and I laughed. She huffed out a breath, laying her head on my chest. I stroked my fingers through her hair as we lay there silently, coming to terms with the fact that everything we'd known, everything we'd planned, was now irrevocably altered. No matter how much I wanted to tell her that this didn't change anything, that she wasn't tied to us forever just because we'd accidentally made cubs, it would be a lie.

"You think we can call one Lorso?"

I want to shout yes, wanted to take that small commitment and hold it close. Instead, I squeezed her a little tighter. "I think we can definitely make that happen, Kitten."

I'D BEEN BLESSED with attentive Alphas. Even from the first moment we met, I knew that they were the ones for me. That they would love me and cherish me, protect me if I needed it, even from myself.

But I swore on the Goddess herself, that if they tried to feed me one more time, I was going to stuff this hot bread roll somewhere unpleasant.

"Get that roasted Swiss mushroom ravioli away from me unless you want to lose an eye, Cooper."

"D, you are eating for—"

"No! Don't say it. Oh my Goddess, I will explode—and not with cubs—if you try to feed me one more thing. Fuck, I've eaten eight meals today. Eight. Yesterday, I didn't even know I was pregnant. I'm not about to keel over if you haven't fed me my body weight in food."

"We just want you and the"—Corvin cleared his throat, and I could hear the emotion he was trying to suppress—"the cubs to be happy and healthy."

I softened, because it was all coming from the right place. "I know, Alpha. I want that too. But that won't happen if I'm stuffed like a Christmas turkey."

"I think being stuffed like a turkey is the reason you got yourself knocked up in the first place," Beckett joked. Kitten snorted a laugh, making me chuckle along with her. Soon we were all laughing, and Cooper fed the ravioli to Kitten piece by piece with his fingers instead. Not that Kitten had escaped much of the overindulgence either; they were just less inclined to make a fuss about it.

I looked over at the unexpectedly solemn face of Corvin just as he spoke. "What will you do now, Kitten? Will you stay?"

She stilled, like a prey animal caught in the trap of a bigger predator, and I hated that. "Leave it, Corvin. Let her have time to think," I said softly.

"She isn't going to get less attached to the idea as time goes on, Darius." He turned back to Kitten, squatting down in front of her so she had to look down on him. An Alpha supplicating himself to his Omega. "We aren't going to get any less attached. I love you, Kitten. I loved you years ago and that love never went away—it just dimmed to a dull ache in my chest. But if you stay, if you watch those cubs grow inside Darius, *our* cubs, and then choose to leave..."

He trailed off, but he didn't have to finish. He would be heartbroken. He would be angry. He wouldn't be able to understand how she could walk away from this gift that we'd been given, even if it had been an accident. But he'd let her go, if she wanted to, if she went now. While the cubs were more of an idea than a reality.

She swallowed hard. "They're ours."

Cooper stroked a hand down her back. "Yes, Kit. Ours." He leaned closer, kissing her cheek. "You can be ours too. We could be a Pack. A family."

She let out a choked breath. "I want to stay. I don't want to do to them what my parents did to me. Don't want to throw them away like they are nothing. Left for the wolves."

With a growl, Cooper pulled her onto his lap, his chest vibrating with a thrum so loud, I could almost feel it across the room.

Beckett reached out and held her hand too. "I swear, Kitten, that no matter what your choice is, your children will grow up happy and loved. Cherished."

Tears sprung in her eyes, falling gently down her cheeks faster than Cooper could kiss them away. She cried, a sorrowful sound that tore at my heart. She turned her face into Cooper's chest, and my strong Alpha held her close, even though the scent of her sadness made us all want to cry with her.

"I want to stay. I want to have a family. I want to be loved."

We all surged toward her, and I got my arms around her, pressing her between my chest and Cooper's. We huddled together like that for a long time, the beginning of a Pack that would last forever.

19

COOPER

Maxton had never been as shaky as it was in the aftermath of the coup. People were side-eying their neighbors, rumors flew about who'd supported Eldrige, and the trial of the Legion officer who'd shot Bonnie only exacerbated that. As he'd been operating under the orders of Eldridge—who was Legion General at the time—the other Legion Generals urged Courtland for clemency. He wasn't inclined to give it, but I was pretty sure Radic's careful urging about what a tinderbox the social environment currently was in Maxton pushed him to grant it.

However, he still exiled the Legion soldier from the town, sending him to fucking Mexico. I didn't know what the hell he was going to do down there—maybe they'd just bury him in the harsh Mexican sun instead —but out of sight, out of mind.

The flip side of that was everyone had to go back to work, and dragging myself away from Darius and Kitten was... difficult. I was in construction with my cousin, Finlo, who owned the business. I didn't mind. I liked building things, but hated paperwork.

"Just go, Cooper. You're going to be late," Darius urged, pushing me toward the door. "The job site is literally half a mile away from the Sanctum. You'll be able to stick your nose out the window and catch my scent, I'm that damn close. And Kitten's coming with me. Bonnie said Dominic will be there too, on babysitting duty."

Surprisingly, the crazy wolf being there didn't exactly make me feel better. It wasn't a reflection of the man himself, since Dom had been perfectly nice every single time I met him, but him being there just made me antsy. Though I guess it was better than another Alpha.

"Okay, fine. But I'm coming down to see you guys for lunch on my break."

He lifted up on his toes so we were nose to nose, lips to lips. "Love you, Alpha." He kissed me softly. "Now go to work."

"Love you too, D. I'm going, I'm going. Just have one more stop to go first."

He smiled and shook his head. "She's in the

kitchen having breakfast with Beckett before he goes to school."

I kissed him once more, before hurrying downstairs. I paused in the doorway to the kitchen just to watch Beckett and Kitten. She was laughing at something he was saying, her dark hair wild over her shoulders. She was wearing one of Darius's T-shirts and some soft sleep shorts she'd grabbed when we were back at her cabin.

Beckett was spoon-feeding her yogurt and berries, his eyes intense as he watched each mouthful pass her lips. I mean, I got it. Her lips were fascinating. I was fairly sure Beckett would feed her every single meal by hand if she'd allow it.

We were waiting for her to be ready to take things to the next level. To be comfortable with the idea of living in a Pack. She didn't say it, but sometimes I could see her struggling, especially when it was loud or busy. We tried to curb it a little, but we'd lived together so long that we didn't even think twice about wrestling on the ground, or chasing each other around, hollering about who ate the last chocolate bar.

Darius insisted she'd adjust. We had set her up her own nest and bedroom so she could have space alone if she needed it, and we made sure to respect that space.

She finally scented me and turned, giving me a smile that made my heart happy. Her expression was full of joy, like she couldn't imagine anyone she'd rather see more in that moment.

"I have to go to work."

Beckett snorted. "Quit pouting. We all have to go to work."

I flipped him the bird. "I'm not pouting. Well, only for a kiss." I made a smoochy face at Kitten, and she kissed me hard until our teeth clacked together, making me laugh. "Brutal, Kitten. Are you looking forward to heading to the Sanctum today? Darius loves that place, and I think he's pretty excited to introduce you to all the kids. When we were sure we'd never have cubs, he threw all his paternal instincts at them. Which means we basically now have sixteen adopted kids that we co-parent with another Pack. Christmas dinners are intense."

She gave me a tight smile. "I'm not sure how I'll be with kids. I've never met any, except the baby I held at the Alpha General's party the other day." Her face fell. "What if they don't like me?" She dropped her voice. "Or I don't like them?"

She looked so fucking worried, and it tugged at my heart. "You aren't running the Sanctum, sweetheart. No one expects you to love them." I paused, tilting her face up. "And if you mean our cubs, it's okay to feel nervous. It's okay to be scared." I stroked her cheek. "You didn't ask for this, and if you feel that way after they are born, we'll figure it out then. But it isn't a you or them situation, Kitten. You're stuck with us as long as you'll have us. Or if Beckett and Corvin are any indication, we'll probably stalk your ass even after you kick us to the curb."

"Hey!" Beckett protested, holding a travel mug. "I made you coffee to go but now I don't think you deserve it."

"Noooo!" I made grabby hands. "I'm totally thankful that you guys are stalky bastards with no boundaries." He went to pour the coffee down the sink, and I vaulted the kitchen counter, making a grab for it. "Beckett!"

"Say 'You were right, Beck. And you're the most attractive Alpha.'"

I snorted. "Fuck off. Second most attractive, at best."

He laughed, handing me the travel mug. "Asshole. Lucky I love you."

I punched him in the arm teasingly, before walking back around to stand in front of a giggling Kitten. "Have a good day today, babe. Don't overthink it, okay? Maybe tonight we can go for a run." I leaned closer. "I'll even shift to my full form."

She flushed bright red, and Beckett cleared his throat. I bet he was vividly remembering the last time he was in full Manix form, as was Kitten. Good.

I leaned down so my lips were beside her ear. She smelled sinfully good. "Mmm, Kitten. You feel that ache between your thighs? That promise of pleasure? Everytime you rub your thighs together today to ease that feeling, I want you to think of me." I straightened and grinned at Beckett. "Have a nice day, kids."

I grabbed an apple and my coffee and left, Beckett's soft curse following me out the door. As I reached my ATV, I bumped into Corvin coming back from his run.

"Fucking work," he grumbled. He looked as annoyed as I did about having to restart our lives today. "If I quit, could you bankroll me? I'll take care of our Omegas all day."

"Your job pays better. How about I become a stay-at-home Alpha instead?"

He grinned, and it was an expression of pure happiness. If you'd asked me before the frenzy whether Corvin was happy, I would have said absolutely. But now, he looked carefree, and I realized the weight of leaving Kitten had sat across his shoulders for so long, it had become a loss he'd learned to live with. Always there, but he'd managed to be happy despite it.

Now he was like a whole new guy. Still an asshole, but a happy asshole.

"I'll fight you for it?" he joked, rubbing the sweat from his brow onto his forearm. Corvin was a mechanic for the Legion, which was a pretty relaxed job but the bureaucratic red tape could be killer. It was better now though, under the new Alpha General. And

Radic, who'd basically kept the town running under the old Alpha General, was no longer hampered by that old fucker anymore, so real changes were happening.

I slapped him on the shoulder. "Maybe we'll have to suck it up and both go to work so we can provide the best for our Pack. And our cubs."

Our cubs. I was still in fucking shock.

Corvin's face softened. "Yes. You're right. Cubs are expensive."

Darius's scent had changed this week, confirming what we'd all come to accept as the truth anyway. We were pregnant. We'd go and get an ultrasound with Tanner sometime this week, and see how many cubs we were having. I didn't think any of them would be mine biologically, because I hadn't been with Darius during that crucial fertilization period, but I didn't care. They were going to be mine just as much as anyone else's, because we were a Pack.

I said goodbye to Corvin and drove down to the job site. Darius was right; it was pretty close to the Sanctum. We'd demolished a dilapidated old building and were in the process of replacing it with a modern home for a young Pack. With the influx of brand new Omega females, most of the Packs were upping their game in the hope they could woo one to bond with them. I didn't have to worry about that, since I was the luckiest guy in the world. But hey, it was good for business.

Finlo looked tired when I pulled up. "Hey man, you look like shit."

"Fuck off, Cooper. Stop being so goddamn happy this early in the morning." He rubbed a hand over his face. "Sorry, man. The cubs are teething, and I don't think I've had a full night's sleep in a week. I'll be glad when they all have a full set of chompers." He smiled, raising an eyebrow. "Lucky they're cute. But I hear you'll know about all that soon enough."

That damn Maxton grapevine. You couldn't keep a secret here. "Yeah, it was an accident, or maybe a miracle." I let the goofy grin that had been threatening to crack through all morning finally spread itself across my cheeks. "I can't wait to be a surly, sleep-deprived bastard, just like you."

Finlo laughed, pulling me into a hug. We were cousins, but we were a tight-knit extended family. "I'm so happy for you, kid. You guys deserve the miracle."

20

BECKETT

T he work day dragged on, mainly because the kids were feeling restless too. I mean, teenagers in general were a handful, but Manix teenagers coming into their designations, plus the newly returned shifter kids who had arrived with the Alpha General combined to make it worse. Add to that the shifter kids having somehow formed a posse with the Sanctum kids—with Rosa appointing herself avenging angel for them all—and it made for interesting detention breaks.

Mostly though, I let it go. Rosa was fierce, and it was time for a little bit of a shake up in the social hierarchy of the high school. The full-blooded Manix kids had kicked around the half-breeds for long enough, so sure of their superiority. They could learn a valuable lesson or two at the hands of this righteous tiger shifter.

So I didn't interfere unless I thought it would cause injury, but I made a note to let Bonnie know that Rosa was fighting on school grounds for dominance every lunchtime. Seeing a tiger in the playground had scared the shit out of me the first time, and I didn't think all the teachers would be so lenient.

Letting myself into the Sanctum quietly, I ran into Bonnie first. "Beckett," she said with a wide smile. Beautiful, that's what Bonnie had always been, but she was even more so now that she was content.

"Hey, Bon. Happy to be back?"

She grinned, grabbing up a toddler who was clinging to her leg and handing him to me. "Denis, look who it is! Becky!" Baby Denis wrapped his arms around my neck, blowing a wet kiss on my cheek. He was a cutie. "It's wonderful to be back, but I'd forgotten how exhausting it can be. It's been helpful having Darius and Kitten here today though." She waggled her eyebrows at me. "She's very pretty, Beckett. And obviously smitten with Darius."

The subtext was there; she was wondering if we were going to bond Kitten, which was hilarious considering the fact Bonnie had avoided the same fate like the plague up until this year.

"Geez, Bonnie. Is Pack life treating you so good that

you're trying to convince everyone else to do the same?"

She waved a hand at me. "Beckett, we both know you want to. No point hiding it from me." She patted me on the cheek. "Darius is upstairs helping Theodore with his algebra homework. Kitten is out the back with Alexi."

"How did she go?" I whispered.

She gave me that maternal smile again. Yeah, Bonnie should have always been an Omega. "She was a bit put off during the morning insanity, but I think she's relaxed into it. She definitely has a niche age though—old enough not to be breakable, young enough not to have an outrageous attitude."

"Ah, the golden age," I said with a laugh, trying to hand Denis back to her, but she waved me away.

"Nope, your limpet now." Bonnie kissed the boy on the cheek, all but skipping away. I decided to leave Darius to his mathematics and searched out Kitten.

Stepping through the back door, I saw my Omega and a small boy both looking at the setting sun by the edge of the forest. Making a conspiratorial shushing noise at Denis, I watched her talking to the small boy. Alexi was a pretty quiet kid. He'd been dropped off when he was four, but I had a feeling he'd been neglected before that. He didn't speak much, and had been pretty behind developmentally when he'd arrived. He'd caught up now, thanks to a lot of hard work from Bonnie and Darius, as well as Radic and my Pack. We all took turns spending one-on-one time with him, helping him become more confident. He was such a great kid.

Kitten squatted down, so she could touch the grass. "It's not so hard to find if you know what you're looking for. It becomes a bit like reading a book."

"I can't read words," Alexi told her, his voice a little wobbly.

"There's no words out here? Can you see any?" Alexi shook his head. "It's more like a picture book, where you look and see what's going on in each drawing, and after a while you get the whole story. Like this, you see this?"

Alexi squatted beside her. "It's poop."

She laughed softly. "It is. But it's small and round, so we know it's probably a rabbit. It's also a little shiny, so you know that the rabbit has been here recently. That's one picture." She duck-walked over a few feet. "Now see this? This grass has been nibbled down, and if you look around, you can see that most of the grass around it has been too. That means there's a lot of rabbits around here somewhere, and that they'll probably come back here again one day. So you can wait until the grass gets a little longer and come back to hunt a bunch all at once, or you can take a gamble that one unlucky rabbit will come back and snack some more, and you can catch your dinner."

Alexi nodded, staring at the grass with intense concentration. "You're a good hunter."

She smiled at him. "It was that or starve. I learned around the same age as you are now. I learned to listen to what the woods were telling me. If they were sick, I was going to be sick too. If the food chain was upset by an influx of predators, then my food would be scarce too. It all trickles down from the Apex animal, right down to the mosquitoes."

"The forest talks to you?" Alexi sounded skeptical.

"Not with words. Like how the leaves on this tree are curling and dying already, even though it's not even close to fall. Or the way the ground is hard and dry, because there's no damp rising up. The long grass that itches when it brushes your legs because it grew too well last year and then died off too quickly this summer. These are all whispers from the forest telling you that it's a really dry season and you have to be careful making fires, or using machinery outside. Listen to what the forest is telling you, and you'll be safe."

It was the longest speech I'd ever heard from her, and while her words weren't perfect English, Alexi didn't seem to mind. It was like he understood her—not just her words, but who she was. I guess, in a way, they'd had similar life experiences when it came to their early childhood. I pulled out my phone, snapping a picture of her with the small boy, because it was too perfect not to immortalize.

Finally, she seemed to realize I was there, or wanted to acknowledge I was there anyway. I didn't think I'd actually managed to sneak up on her. She looked over her shoulder and smiled softly in the setting sun, and I wanted to freeze the moment forever. Instead, I took another picture.

Denis wiggled in my arms, and I put him down so he could toddle around the back deck. Unsurprisingly, he went straight to Kitten. When he reached her, he stood with his arms flailing in the air. Kitten just stared at him like he was doing the YMCA.

Alexi touched her elbow. "He wants you to pick him up."

She frowned down at Denis, like he was a puzzle, before grabbing him around his middle and hefting him into the air. He giggled, grabbing her in a head-lock and snuggling his nose into her neck. Cubs could scent the Omegas, and found comfort in their presence.

"What am I supposed to do with him?" she whispered, her eyes wide like he was a bomb strapped to her chest.

"You're doing it. At this age, they're basically spider monkeys. Just hold them however you're comfortable and they'll hang on right back. He'll let you know when he's done with you." I walked over and wrapped my arm around her shoulders, patting Alexi on the head as well. "You're good with them."

"Liar," she grumbled softly, though I noticed her stroking Denis's back unconsciously. Yeah, Kitten might be worried about the whole cub thing, but I wasn't. She was willing to try, and I thought that was more important than any natural skill.

21

KITTEN

There was a knock at the front door of the Packhouse, but I wasn't sure if I should open it. No one else was around, so even though it made my heart race, I answered it.

Tanner the vampire was on the other side, a goofy, lopsided grin on his face. "Kitten! Just the person I was looking for. Howya going?"

I shrugged. "Okay?"

His grin widened, showing off his immaculately white fangs. His eyes were friendly, but those fangs scared the hell out of me. No sooner had my heart rate risen than Corvin was there, standing right behind me.

Tanner quirked an eyebrow. "Alpha. How goes it?"

"It?"

"Life, love, you know? All the good shit."

"Uh, it's good, thanks." I looked between the two Apex predators as they sized each other up.

Eventually, Tanner just shrugged. "I'm here to get that family history and a little bit of blood." He held up his bag, and then frowned. "Ah, bloody hell. Forgot the doppler machine so we can check on your other Omega too. Kill two birds in one visit, you know?" He shoved his doctor bag at Corvin. "Hold this for me, mate? Won't be a minute."

He was gone in a flash, and literally forty-five seconds later, he was back with a handheld ultrasound machine tucked under his arm. He took back his bag from Corvin. "Best part of being a vamp, if you ask me. Would've loved to have superspeed during my hospital residency, but it might have been difficult with all the blood, you know?" he told me with a grin.

I blinked up at him slowly. So many words, and they somehow managed to run altogether with his accent. "Uh, yes?"

"Don't worry, Omega. I've got better control now. Raine has total faith in me. She said so."

I looked up at Corvin, who was frowning but I couldn't tell if it was with worry or because he was as confused as I was. Tanner must have taken his silence as fear.

"I swear, this will only take a few minutes. The Alpha General put me in charge of this, and he's a scary bastard. Your Pack is completely safe with me. I take my Hippocratic Oath seriously, even as a vampire. Do no harm."

Shit, now we'd offended him. I elbowed Corvin, and my lover shook his head. "Sure, come in, Doc Tanner."

He gave us another brilliant surfer boy smile. "Just Tanner will do." He stepped into the house. "Nice place you've got. No wonder you snagged yourself a matching Omega pair."

I scuttled ahead of them into the living room, sitting on the armchair in the corner. I worked on calming my heart rate. Tanner wasn't a threat. No one in Maxton was a threat anymore. At least, theoretically.

Everyone else appeared from the other parts of the house, and I didn't even protest when Cooper came over, picked me up and sat down on my chair, settling me on his lap with a low thrum.

Tanner greeted them all like they were old friends, and I was beginning to think that he was the vampire equivalent of a golden retriever. He pulled out a notebook from his satchel. "I'll do a quick checkup soon just to make sure everything's going okay, but first we might get down to the old family tree. Parents?"

I shrugged, my cheeks a little pink. "No idea. I was about three weeks old when Lorso found me on the border of Packlands."

Tanner frowned as he scribbled. His handwriting

was illegible. "No chance this Lorso could be a relation?"

I thought hard about it. It wasn't the first time I'd wondered, because what kind of person takes in a baby and keeps it a secret for years? Especially a Manix who was basically so ancient he'd become a thing of legend? But he'd never said anything, and I'd never asked. Deep in my soul, I didn't think he was, though I couldn't be sure.

So I shrugged. "It could be possible, I guess, but he never insinuated that we were related. The only time we ever spoke about it, he said he was hunting and thought I was an injured bobcat because I was wailing so hard. I was basically frozen, and he said I was so dirty and covered in filth that either I'd been out there for days or someone hadn't taken good care of me."

Tanner wrote it all out, his face not betraying any thoughts or feelings about my statement. However, despite the fact he knew my history, Cooper's arms tightened around me, and his thrumming got more intense, like he could comfort that abandoned child retroactively.

It was fine. I didn't have any residual boohoos about it. I'd had a happy—if unconventional—child-hood running wild. It might have seemed like a terrible fate to Corvin and Beckett, but I hadn't known anything different. I'd been free in a way very few people ever got to be.

"Considering the fact that your Pack is expecting cubs, if it's permissible, I might draw blood from all of you just to put into my database. I might get some histories from you guys too, though my predecessor was an excellent note taker, so they're pretty up to date."

The scent of sadness flooded through the room at the thought of Doc, and I snuggled my nose comfortingly into Cooper's neck. I watched as Darius rubbed his still flat stomach, lost in his thoughts.

Clearing my throat, I sat up. "Okay." I held out my arm. "I'll go first."

Tanner clapped his hands together. "Excellent! Don't worry, Omega, if there's one thing I'm good at, it's finding a vein for a blood draw."

Corvin growled at his terrible, terrible joke. "Not funny, vampire," he rumbled.

I snorted. It was a little bit funny. Tanner seemed oblivious to the menace of my Alphas as he drew my blood with all the expertise he'd just bragged about. He didn't even seem fussed when he moved on to Cooper, Corvin and then Beckett. He left Darius for last.

He bowed his head. "Omega."

Darius grinned. "Has anyone told you that you look too young to be a doctor?"

"Several people. Luckily for me, I was turned at a time when twenty-three meant you had been working since you were twelve." He quickly took blood. "Shortage of doctors in Australia in the early 1800s. Shortage of everything except blow flies, actually."

He grabbed his doppler ultrasound machine, hooking it up to what looked like a state-of-the-art tablet. He waved them in our direction. "Gift from Raine and the Convocation. She was predicting—or maybe hoping—for an increased need for some fetal imaging equipment." He turned back to Darius. "May I? I've never done this before on a bloke. Or on a Manix, so you'll have to cut me some slack as I work it out. Your biology is different. I'll just get you to lie down."

Darius pulled off his shirt, which led to more growling, though no one protested. Tanner put the gel on the wand thing and waved it around.

"I've studied the notes on male Manix pregnancy, not just from your Doc, but from the ones before him. It's made for interesting reading, but I'm a hands-on kind of guy, you know?" He put the wand on Darius's stomach, and I think we all took a collective breath in. "Alright, let's see if we can navigate this bad boy. So if we go over... Oh, nope that's your bladder. No babies in that one. Okay if I head over here... Ah-ha! There we go. The womb. Hey, that makes sense, that would have been your prostate if you'd been born a human. Now, if I turn on the sound..."

He clicked a button, and my world came crashing

to a halt. Echoing around the room were several fast whooshing noises. Heartbeats. Sweet Goddess.

"Okay, let me see if I can drive this thing. Alright, over here we have one." He handed Darius the tablet, and Cooper scooped me up in his arms so we could all go and have a closer look. A weird black blob shifted around the screen like mercury. Tanner moved the wand and then there was another black blob. "That's two. And if I go just slightly over here to the left, there's three." He looked up at us and grinned, his eyes shiny. "Congrats, mate. You're having triplets."

Darius's eyes looked too wide as he stared at the screen, watching as Tanner positioned the wand so you could see all three sacs at once. And not just that, you could see the definition of three tiny bodies. Each one was curled up, comfortable and safe inside an Omega who wanted them more than anything in the world, and supported by a Pack who thought they were a literal miracle.

"Doc's notes said that the gestation time for a male Omega is half that of a human pregnancy, so I'd like you to come in for regular checkups. Also, if it's okay, I'd like to track their progress for my own notes."

"My Omega and cubs aren't your lab rats, vampire," Corvin growled, and Beckett slapped him on the head.

"Shut it with the growly shit. This guy is gonna deliver a whole new generation of Manix, and the last thing we want is for him to go into it blind."

Tanner smiled. "Thanks, man. Speaking of delivery, you might wanna decide if you are delivering these guys the traditional way, or having me do the C-section, because you don't really have that long to decide."

I frowned. "The traditional way?"

Tanner's face got excited. "One of the Alphas would slice open the Omega with his claws, from sternum to pelvic bone, while the others prayed to the Goddess for safe passage of their young. Then, when the cubs were delivered, you would bind him together as best you could and wait for his Manix healing to knit the wound. Can take anywhere from 2-5 days if you don't use stitches, I hear."

Cut. They wanted to cut him open? With their claws? Chanting and blood and... "I don't feel so good." I went to stand, but the room spun a little. What was wrong with me? I'd gutted all sorts of animals before—why did the idea of Darius being split open and scooped out like a piece of fruit make me feel like this?

The world went a little white, and the last thing I heard was, "So a C-section it is then, I guess?"

Strong arms caught me just before I hit the floor.

22

CORVIN

"Yo, Corvin. The boss wants to see you. The big boss."

"Jeff?" Why the hell would Jeff want to see me? He ran the engineering and mechanics arm of the Legion, and my boss, Crowley, ran the mechanics portion of that. Only time I ever saw Jeff was at holiday Christmas parties or when I ran into him at the bakery.

"Nah man, the Alpha General."

Oh, fuck. I schooled my features into something neutral and reminded myself that this wasn't like being called to the Alpha General's office years ago, where you were either going to get yelled at for forty-five minutes, or get the shit kicked out of you with no recourse.

Courtland was different. He ran things differently.

I put down my wrench and stretched my back. I'd

been working on a busted pump all day, cursing my giant fucking fingers for at least three hours. Maybe while I was there, I could ask Radic if we could fork out for a new pump—there were only so many times you could Frankenstein something back together.

I wiped the grease off my fingers and told Crowley that I'd be back after lunch. Crowley grunted. Honestly, as long as I got my required quota of work done, Crowley wouldn't give a damn if I did it naked in the moonlight.

The shop was just off the main street, about half a mile over from the Legion offices, so it was a bit of a hike, but it was a nice day. I lifted my nose in the hopes I'd catch the scent of Darius or Kitten, but nothing. Maybe after I saw the Alpha General, I could run home and say hello. Maybe make them come a couple of times, and then go back to work smelling like their pleasure.

My dick got hard, and I mentally told him to calm his shit. I could not walk into the Alpha General's office with a hard-on. Probably wouldn't give the right impression.

I waved at the people who yelled greetings and congratulations. The grapevine in Maxton was laughably active, and I would bet that a good portion of the town knew Darius was pregnant before we'd even gotten him home to tell him.

Finally, I swiped my hands on my pants once more

and walked into the Legion Building. When I was a kid, this building had seemed huge and imposing. The kind of building that struck fear inside of you. It had everything to do with the administration inside and little to do with the place itself. Now, I could appreciate the building for what it was: the heart of Maxton. Or maybe the brain.

I walked past the offices of the Legion Generals, and some of the administrative branches of the Legion, before I stepped inside the Alpha General's office.

Radic sat behind his desk, and smiled at me when I stopped. "Corvin! Thanks for coming. How's Kitten settling in?"

I shifted my weight from foot to foot. "Not bad, Rad. Some things take a little more getting used to than others, and she's still not a fan of crowds, but she's pretty fucking resilient. We've done everything at her speed, on her terms."

Radic raised an eyebrow. "Almost everything."

I flushed and set my jaw. "Almost everything. That was an accident. A happy one though. We're working through it and we haven't put any more pressure on her about the cubs. She can be as involved or uninvolved as she wants." I looked at the Beta with hard eyes. "I refuse for it to be an either/or situation. I want the cubs and I want Kitten."

Radic lifted his hands. "Hey, I'm happy for you, Corvin. We all are. The whole town knows that Darius has wanted cubs from the time he was old enough to play families with Cooper. And if we thought for even a moment that Kitten was being coerced into anything, we'd take her out of your house in a heartbeat, whether we were friends or not. This isn't the Maxton of last year, Corvin. Everyone has rights, and no one's life is worth more than anyone else's."

"That's correct, my Beta."

I turned at the sound of the Alpha General's voice, and the weight of his power hit me once more. I could see how they'd had to cripple him to have even a chance in the Alpha battle.

He stared at me with those fathomless black eyes. "Thanks for coming, Corvin. It could have waited, but I had a spot in my schedule which wasn't filled with bureaucracy, and seized it."

Radic snorted. "It's not that bad."

Courtland huffed. "I say the same things over and over every day, Radic. There are only so many times I can reassure senior citizens, cut through the same red tape, and appease the families of the new Omegas, before I need a break. Let's go, Corvin. I'm sure I have some half-decent tequila here somewhere."

He spun and walked back into his office, while I looked at Radic, who rolled his eyes but had a small smile on his face. He gazed after the Alpha General like he was the last donut on the plate. They obviously loved each other.

The Alpha General's office was different now. It had always been austere and masculine, menacing even. All old wood and sharp edges. Now, some of Courtland's Hispanic roots were on display. Bright pops of color were dotted around, and the couch was an unbleached linen, which lightened the whole room. They'd painted the walls a more neutral white instead of the harsh navy blue that had previously been there. It was way less intimidating, and would probably be cozy if it wasn't for the Alpha behind the ornate inlaid desk.

"Uh, I like what you've done with the place?"

He smiled, and even that was an intimidating expression. "Thank you. My sister and Bonnie redecorated it for me. It's much less... over-the-top masculine. I don't need a leather couch to let you know that I could skin you and eat you in a heartbeat."

I blinked. "Uh, no sir. You don't."

He waved a hand. "Please, call me Courtland. I thought I'd call you in because I was talking with Alexi last night, and he had some interesting things to say about your Kitten."

My heart thudded in my chest. "Alexi?"

His dark eyes were like magnets. "About this high, around the age of five? Doesn't talk much?" He indicated about four feet from the ground.

"Oh, from the Sanctum?" Okay, now I was even more confused.

"Yes. While we were eating dinner last night, he told me that the forest was sad. When I asked why he thought so, he said that Kitten had taught him to read the trees. He told me that the forest was warning me of danger." He tilted his head to the side. "I'm not sure if you've spent much time with Alexi, but he isn't a child to waste words, so I'm inclined to listen."

I nodded. "I've known Alexi since he was basically a baby. He's a pretty solemn kid. But I'm confused about what you actually want?"

"Tell me about Kitten."

I froze. The Alpha in me saw threats everywhere, doubly so when it came to my Omegas.

Courtland pulled a bottle of tequila and two glasses from his desk drawer. "Don't panic, Alpha. I mean your Omega absolutely no harm. In fact, I think she could help us. But first, I want to know how an unknown Beta could live on the edges of our society for two decades without anyone knowing."

I shrugged. "What do you know about Lorso?"

He poured two tequilas and moved one toward me. "*Salud*," he said, downing it in one go and pouring himself another one. "I don't know much. His name has been mentioned, but only in passing."

I nodded. Courtland had had an absolute barrage of information thrown at him recently. Folk tales about old Manix would be pretty far down the list.

"A couple of hundred years ago, the Raku-Lorso-

Niles Pack was one of the most powerful Manix Packs on the continent. Back when there were more of us, anyway. They were the last Pack to have an Omega pair —well, until now. Margaux and Timothy were the beating heart of their Manix congregation. They produced over sixteen offspring, and by all accounts, were basically Goddess-sent with their kindness.

"However, the elders of the larger Pack—which included Niles, Lorso and Raku—noticed a trend of less female Manix being born, and decided they wanted to try mating with other species to see if they could reverse the trend. Raku, Lorso and Niles agreed, but they wanted to go and meet with the other shifter Packs, see if they'd be amiable to some political marriages to bond our species together. When our offers were rebuffed, another faction of the elders decided to take a wolf shifter Omega by force and 'test' their hypothesis. That was the beginning of the Manix Wars. The shifters mightn't have wanted an allegiance with us, but they were more than happy to ally with each other against us. Which I totally get."

"Agreed," Courtland said, downing his drink, so I did the same. I waited for the burn, but it was smooth, not getting fiery until it hit my gut. Good tequila.

"You'd think this would've stopped that other faction of elders from continuing their experiments, but it didn't. The more the war raged, the more people we lost, and the more desperate they became to find a solution to our dwindling female problem. However, in the end, they doomed us all. They kidnapped a Lycanthrope female. They assumed that because they were more like us than the two-natured shifters, that our biology would be more amenable.

"Hell, maybe they'd have been right, but they never really got the chance to find out. The Lycanthropes were pissed. Their numbers had been hunted nearly to extinction already, so Lycanthrope females were extremely rare. When the other Manix elders refused to give her back—no matter how hard Lorso, Raku and Niles argued—Lorso decided that his Pack and any who supported them would split off and form their own township. They gathered up the children they had left who hadn't died in the Manix Wars, their friends and supporters, and moved to the mountains in Montana, founding Maxton.

"Which was fortunate, because a week later, the Lycanthropes came and demanded their female back, in person. You see, even the loss of one female would've rendered the Lycanthropes functionally extinct. So when they found out she was dead, they slaughtered every remaining Manix in the old congregation. The Lycanthropes went up and down North America, destroying every Manix tribe they could find until we were almost as extinct as they were. Both Raku and Niles were killed trying to smuggle other Manix Packs into Maxton. It was only because we were hidden away up here that we survived at all. It was why most other supernaturals assumed we were gone from the face of the earth."

"You weren't the only pocket of survivors, obviously, but apparently we all assumed we were the last of our kind," the Alpha General murmured, pouring me another.

"For better or for worse, I guess. It's why everyone freaked out when you brought the Lycans in to save Bonnie. Some fear is just written into your DNA." I shrugged. "Anyway, Timothy was the last Omega male to carry cubs, and when Margaux died, no more Omega females were produced. Most assumed it was the Goddess punishing us for the sins of our elders, and maybe they were right. There's no other way to describe what's happened over the last few years if not divine in nature, right?"

Courtland inclined his head. "It does feel that way. But I do not understand what this Lorso has to do with your Omega in the woods."

I reclined back on the sofa, hoping I wasn't getting grease on the white linen. "We all grew up hearing these stories, like when Margaux died in childbirth and made Lorso swear to treat the remaining Manix like his own children. Timothy died of a broken heart a few months later. It was just Lorso and his Betas, Shelley and Sol, for decades. Then when they died, it was just Lorso by himself, clinging to a promise to his

Omega. Eventually, the Legion rose up as the governing system and Lorso just faded away. We all thought he was dead, gone to be with the rest of his Pack in the afterlife." I grinned, because this was always my favorite part. "Until one day, I was hunting in the woods with Beckett when our rabbit trap went off, and in it was a scrawny, hissing girl..."

23

KITTEN

"Omegas, I'm home. Prepare to be loved up," someone shouted from down below. Corvin, by the scent. Well, it was almost his scent, if his scent was drenched in alcohol. I jogged down the stairs to see a very amused Darius standing in the foyer. Corvin was grinning widely, his eyes shiny.

Beside him were Radic and Courtland. "My apologies, Omegas. We may have had a little too much tequila during our meeting."

Radic shook his head. "You forget that everyone isn't basically pickled like you and Dominic. No one can handle liquor like you two,"

I looked at Corvin again, my lips curled in amusement. Yep, he was sloshed. I'd never gotten drunk; when I'd gone to town, to the human bars, I never had more than one glass of wine. I was a woman by myself, and Manix or not, I couldn't let myself be as vulnerable as the average Joe.

Corvin looked at me intensely. "Goddess, they are so beautiful. Don't you guys think they're beautiful? No, fuck that, you guys aren't allowed to think about them like that because they're mine. I love them. They make me so fucking happy," he rambled on, and Darius laughed.

"Goddess, he's shitfaced. Come on, big guy. Let's go upstairs and put you to bed."

Corvin gave him slobbery kisses on the cheek, all love and not a whole lot of finesse. "Will you come to bed with me?"

"Baby, I can almost guarantee that you'll be snoring and drooling by the time your head hits the pillow." Darius propped himself under Corvin's shoulder, and I went to grab his other side when the Alpha General stopped me.

"Omega, if I may have a word?"

It was a testament to how drunk Corvin was that he didn't even protest. Darius, however, stilled his feet, looking between us. Courtland inclined his head. "I promise Kitten is safe with me, Omega."

Darius continued to hesitate, and I gave him a quick reassuring look. "It's fine, Darius. I'll be up in a minute."

He gave us one more concerned look, and then

Corvin was sucking on his ear. Screwing up his nose, he gave me an imploring look. "I'll be back in a moment."

I had no doubt that Corvin was going to be tossed onto the bed as quickly as possible and Darius would indeed be back in a moment.

I turned back to the Alpha General and Radic. I held myself tense, ready to react. They both noted my stance, but politely ignored it. "What can I do for you, sir?"

Courtland gave me a reassuring smile. "Alexi tells me that you speak to the forest."

I shrugged. "Yes?"

"He also tells me that you said it's unhappy."

I frowned. I was simplifying the concepts for a child, so I guess unhappy would be the right word. "It's especially dry this year. Makes for difficult conditions for the wildlife and the forest."

"Such as?"

"Poor feed, less water, the possibility of forest fires."

"Solutions?"

"Goats."

Radic coughed. "Excuse me?"

I chewed my lip, but Lorso had taught me never to make yourself small in front of a predator. Unless that predator was a bear. Then you had to hope to the Goddess he thought you were a bush or something, because no one wins in a fight with a bear. But Courtland wasn't a bear, so I straightened my shoulders and stood taller.

"Goats. Last year was a good growing season, so the undergrowth is longer than normal. Despite what you'd think, long grass doesn't make for good feed for wildlife. Combined with the dried up waterholes and the general hate of the Manix, all the herbivores have left and nothing will eat the tall grass. Good way for a fire to start. So we bring in goats, let them do what they do best. New growth will form once it isn't being over-shadowed by the tall undergrowth, meaning next year should be better."

Both men stared at me like I'd suggested alien abduction. Finally, Courtland shook his head. "Do you want a job? I'll make you your own position. Forest and wildlife management. There's no pressure, and feel free to talk it over with your Pack first, but I feel as if no one would understand what the forest needs the way you do, yet we live right in the middle of it. So having someone who can understand its language can only be beneficial, wouldn't you agree?"

My jaw unhinged as I blinked at him. My mind was running, but I was struggling to think of the right English words in my shock, so I just nodded. The other men beamed at me.

"Excellent. Let us know what you wish to do, but if you could come down and let Radic know how many goats we may need, we can get that underway as soon as possible." He stepped back toward the door, holding it open for Radic. "And Omega?"

"Yes?"

"Congratulations again on your cubs. It is scary, but they are a blessing for the whole race."

"Thank you, sir." He gave me another soft smile, and then he was gone. I turned as I heard Darius come down the stairs.

"Everything okay? Sorry I took so long—I swear Corvin grows three extra arms when he's drunk. He's like a horny octopus."

"Everything is fine. The Alpha General offered me a job. Forest and wildlife management."

Darius whooped and grabbed me up in his arms. Hugging me tightly, he asked, "Are you going to take it?"

I snuggled my face further into his body, inhaling his spicy scent. It had changed since I first met him, due to the cubs, and if it was possible, it had become even more comforting. "Do you think I should?" I mumbled against his chest, and he rubbed my back.

I'd enjoyed the guys going back to work, although I missed them, because it meant I could spend more time with Darius. With the Alphas, everything was always so charged. But with Darius, it was easy. On days we weren't at the Sanctum, we snuggled on the couch and Darius introduced me to all his favorite TV shows. We ate snacks, talked or napped. It was just nice. The new Omega in me enjoyed being with him. If I was honest with myself, she more than enjoyed his company. She loved him. I loved him. Actually, I loved *them*.

However, there was a little part of me always waiting for something bad to happen, for Lorso's warnings to come true.

"It's up to you, Kitten. You know we'll support you, no matter what you decide to do. But if you want my opinion?" I nodded. "I think you'd enjoy it. It would allow you to continue to do what you love. Allow you to have some financial independence from the Pack too. I know you might need that security."

I wanted to protest that I wasn't going anywhere, but I'd be lying if I didn't think about going back to my cabin whenever things seemed too much. I pulled back so I could look at him. "I don't need money, Darius."

"No, of course not, we'll take care of you. We aren't loaded, but we have enough to live comfortably. But sometimes, your own nest egg can make you feel more—"

I put my fingers over his lips. "No, I mean I'm rich. Lorso left me everything he had, the remainder of his Pack's investments and money. I've got millions of dollars, last time I checked."

Darius pulled back, his eyes wide. "Come again?" He shook his head. "But the guys, they brought you food and clothes and things."

I shrugged, stepping away because I did feel a little guilty about that. "It made them feel better about leaving me out there if they thought they were providing for me. Plus, if they knew I had money, they'd have tried to make me leave and live in town, maybe try to find me a house. I didn't want to do that. Lorso lived rustically, despite his wealth, and raised me to appreciate the things I could do with my own hands, rather than benefiting from someone else's labor. Also, it saved me from having to go to town. I hated going down into the village. How did the guys think I was surviving after they stopped coming?"

He shook his head. "I didn't want to think about it. You survived and now you're here with us, and that's all that mattered." He let out a low whistle. "Wait until we tell the guys. They're going to be so shocked." He chuckled to himself gleefully. "I'll have to set up my camera!"

24

DARIUS

I wasn't sure what stage of pregnancy made your hormones go fucking nuts, but I was definitely there. I should call Raiden, of the Huxley-Grey Pack, and find out how long it would last, because I was going crazy. Every time one of my Alphas walked by, I had to hold myself back from jumping on them. And when Kitten so much as entered the same room, I had a raging hard-on and an urge to grind my dick into her. It was driving me insane. Then, if I thought about how crappy my hormones were for more than five minutes, my eyes would brim with tears and I'd start to cry.

What the actual hell was up with that?

It was almost a relief when the guys went to work. Kitten hadn't officially started her job yet, though she'd accepted it and made arrangements for goats to come later in the month. I didn't understand what she needed goats for, but you know, she seemed happy about it.

She was at home, seductively eating oatmeal with peaches at the breakfast bar. I watched as each mouthful passed her lips, mesmerized by the way her throat bobbed as she swallowed. The way a droplet of peach juice clung to her chin.

"Darius, are you okay?"

The whine bubbled from my throat before I could choke it down. I gritted my teeth. "I'm fine."

She put down her spoon and came over, her brows drawn together in a frown. "You don't look fine. You looked flushed."

She lifted her soft hand to cup my cheek, and I turned my face so I could bite the fleshy muscle below her thumb, making her gasp. "I need you, Kitten. Please." It was a breathy plea, and I was kind of disgusted with myself, but it didn't dampen how much I wanted her. She looked a little shocked, so I grabbed her hand, sliding her index finger past my lips and sucking on it.

"Oh," she whispered, and I moved on to the next digit. "It's okay, Darius. I've got you." She removed her finger from my mouth with an audible pop. Grabbing my hand, she dragged me to the couch. I growled, flopping down on the cushions and grabbing her hips, pulling her down onto my lap. I kissed her hard, trying to suck her down, to feel and taste her everywhere all at once. I was frantic to have her. I'd denied the feeling for too long, and now I couldn't wait any more.

She straddled my lap, threading her fingers in my hair and then tugging hard. "Calm, Omega. I told you I've got you. I'll make you feel better."

My dick throbbed at her authoritative words. She tilted my head back, taking control of the kiss. I gripped her ass, grinding her against my hardness, trying to get some relief. She rolled her hips against me, and I could feel her damp core already. Kitten wanted me as much as I wanted her. Her fingers slid beneath my shirt, and she tugged on the hem until she was pulling it off over my head.

"So pretty," she murmured against my lips. "I always thought Omega men would be tiny and elfin; instead, you're all muscle and so fucking sexy." Yeah, my muscles. Apparently, in my third trimester my abs would separate at the main muscle bands to make way for my bulging womb. I hoped she could appreciate them now, because soon they'd be lost in a giant bulge of belly.

"Darius, why are you crying?" Kitten gasped, leaning back. "Did I hurt you?" She tried to scrabble off my lap but I held her closer, squishing her to my chest.

"Soon I'm going to be huge like a fucking beluga whale and my abs will be gone and I won't be able to see my toes." I didn't mean for it to come out in a pitiful whine, or for tears to leak from my eyes.

Kitten looked at me with a horrified—or maybe panicked—look on her face. "Darius, no. You're amazing. And you'll be as sexy then as you are now." She pulled away so she could push me back onto the couch. "I mean it."

Then she proceeded to show me, kissing down my neck, and over my collarbone. She curled her body until she could get one of my nipples between her perfect pink lips. She sucked it softly, and when I gripped her head, she sucked harder, adding a scrape of her teeth.

Oh fuck, it felt too good. "More. Kitten, please..."

She hummed her assent, and moved to the other nipple and bit down softly. I clawed at her skin, my groan echoing around the living room. She moved from my nipples downwards, her fingernails scraping along my skin, spreading goosebumps in their wake. When she reached my slightly protruding stomach, she laid her cheek there and thrummed softly.

I choked back the fucking hormonal tears that wanted to burst out of my eyeballs like a geyser again. Luckily, she was unbuttoning my pants soon enough, and a whole different emotion took over.

I tangled my fingers in her dark hair, pulling it up so I could see her face as my dick sprang free, engorged and dripping with precum already. She sucked in a breath, and then blew it out, cooling the trails of moisture over the head of my cock. I threw my head back with a groan, but she wasn't teasing me today. No, Kitten put that tongue to work straight away, licking it all up like a dripping ice cream. She pushed the head between her lips, sucking softly as she twisted, taking it deeper and deeper.

I didn't realize I was chanting the word fuck, until someone cleared their throat. I looked over Kitten's head at Beckett, who looked like he'd walked into a pile of presents on Christmas morning.

"I've never been so happy to come home for brunch."

Kitten pulled her head from my crotch and looked over at Beckett, a saucy grin on her face. He was across the room quicker than my eyes could follow. He kissed her, sucking her lip between his teeth. "Don't let me interrupt, Omegas. You look like you're just getting started. Would you mind if I joined?"

I loved that he'd asked rather than just inserting himself into the situation, but quite frankly, I wouldn't mind it if he inserted himself—

"Don't mind at all," Kitten answered, before sliding my cock back into her mouth. Oh shit. Beckett grabbed my chin and kissed me possessively, his tongue sliding between my lips to tangle with mine, thrusting in rhythm with Kitten on my dick. The sensation threatened to make me come in an instant, and I wasn't done wringing out my pleasure yet.

I wanted to be inside her. Or Beckett to be inside me.

I grabbed at Kitten's shoulders. "Come here, baby. I want to feel you around me. I want us both to feel good."

She stood up, throwing off her shorts and shirt until she was gloriously naked in front of me. A couple of months in civilization had rounded out her gaunt edges, and she was soft and feminine and beautiful, not that she wasn't before.

I wanted to be inside her more than I wanted anything else at this moment. She straddled my hips, and I wasted no time pressing the head of my dick against her entrance. I was vaguely aware of Beckett standing, but honestly, my entire focus was on her, on this woman who'd come into my life like a wrecking ball, but together we'd somehow built something amazing from the rubble. I clutched her hips like a lifebuoy as she slid down on my dick. God, she felt good. She felt like mine.

Beckett appeared over her shoulder, his eyes hooded with lust. In his hand was a bottle of lube. "Remember when you said you didn't mind if I joined you? Because that looks fucking delicious, and I'd like to be in there with you."

Both Kitten and I stopped our movements as we

processed his words. "You want both of us to be in her pussy, at the same time?" My eyes flew to her face as I watched the idea process. Shock, lust, desire, fear, lust again. It was a rollercoaster that seemed to settle on desire. Beckett seemed to know though, because his hand stroked down her naked back, making her arch against his hand and her pussy clench hard around my cock. I groaned, my eyes rolling back.

"Our girl can take it." He leaned closer so his chest was pressed against her back. "She likes the stretch, don't you, Kitten? You like feeling so full that you're sure you'll break in two. You like that burn as we fill your body to its capacity." The way she was clenched around my dick, grinding down on me told me he wasn't wrong. She really did want this.

"Just so we're totally clear... You want two D's in the V? Double meat in your taco? Two pilgrims in the cave of wonder?"

Kitten stared at me, and Beckett snorted out a laugh. "Really?"

I shrugged. "I've seen the size of your dick, Beckett. Know it intimately. I'm not sure that's going to fit inside our tiny Omega at the same time as mine. So what do you say, Kitten?"

"Uh, send in the pilgrims?" she said, rolling against me again. She was definitely wet enough, but I reached out and played with her clit a little more to make sure.

Our girl was going to be so wet, she'd feel nothing but pleasure.

As if Beckett read my mind, he spread my thighs wider so he could stand between them, his already hard dick pressed between her ass cheeks but not asking for anything more. He kissed his way down her neck and spine, until she was shivering.

For endless moments, we just pleasured Kitten, and I hung onto my control by a very, very thin thread. Finally, she was mewling and needy, and her wetness was dripping down my dick.

Beckett looked down at me, his eyes bright and excited. "I think you're ready, gorgeous. Lean back a little, Darius, and hold her tight to your chest. You're both going to need the support," he joked, but I think it was one of those jokes that was tainted with the truth. This was a first for me too.

I banded one arm around Kitten's ribs, pulling her to my chest. I curled up a little so I could kiss her— soft, sweet kisses that had four-letter meanings. Despite how wet she was, I heard the cap of the lube come off and felt the cool pour of the liquid run over my overheated flesh. I thrust in and out hard a couple of times to work in the lube, holding her hips and trying my best to hit that G-spot. I wasn't ashamed to admit that I'd done my research about how to make a woman come once I learned Kitten wanted to stay. I wanted her so well pleasured that she would never even dream of leaving. If that meant I had to debauch my Google search history, then so be it.

Kitten was pressed into my chest, Beckett's huge body blanketing us both. "I'm going to slide inside you now, Kitten, and fuck you both. Do you still want that?"

"Yes, please," she begged, and my whole body trembled in preparation for what was about to happen. I felt the press of his cock against mine, and his hands covered my own as he angled Kitten just right.

"Deep breath, baby." And then he slid his cock along mine, sliding inside Kitten, stretching her so wide and tight that I could hardly breathe. How she was still conscious was beyond me. As if there was no end to the blissful torture, Beckett pulled back once more and then slid deeper.

"Oh fuck, oh fuck, oh fuck," Kitten chanted beneath her breath, her body shaking and her nails digging into my chest. It was a mantra I could get behind as our moans created a fucking opus.

An eternity—or possibly just minutes—later, Kitten's body had stretched to accommodate us both, and that's when the real insanity started. Taking control of Kitten's hips, Beckett fucked us both. Slow and steady thrusts that drove me wild, and Kitten's every breath came on a scream of pleasure.

It was like fucking dying in the best possible way.

"Fuck, I'm coming again. Oh god," she whimpered, and clenched down hard, making pleasure shoot right to my balls. They pulled up tight, and she wasn't the only one who was coming as I shouted my release with hers, vision flickering.

I held her so tightly to me that I was sure we were one person now instead of three, Beckett still thrusting shallowly, but soon enough the force of our combined orgasm had him tipping over the edge too. I could feel his knot swell, but there was no way Kitten could take us both and his knot.

He caught himself on the back of the couch as he collapsed, stopping his full weight from crushing Kitten between us. He pulled out gently, the sensation making us all whimper, then kissed across her neck and shoulders. "You did so good, baby. So fucking good." Then he froze. "Can you smell blood?"

I looked Kitten over, but she seemed fine. Oh fuck, had we hurt the cubs? Kitten must have thought the same thing because she jumped off my dick so fast, she almost toppled over.

Beckett sucked in a breath, but it wasn't because the cubs were hurt. No, it was because there, on my chest, was a perfect, Kitten-size bite mark. I hadn't even felt it, so that must mean it had happened while we were reaching climax. That meant...

"Oh shit."

25

COOPER

When I arrived home from work, I could tell immediately that something was wrong. The air felt too electric, too disturbed. And it wasn't just because the living room smelled like a porn set.

"Where is everyone?" I shouted, my heart rate picking up.

"In the nest," came Corvin's muffled reply, and I raced upstairs, taking them two at a time. I slowed as I reached the door, pushing it open hesitantly, unsure what I'd find.

In the middle of the nest, Darius lay completely curled around Kitten, his body almost completely encapsulating hers. She had her face buried in the blankets, and didn't even look up as I entered. Corvin and Beckett looked more solemn than usual, and I was beginning to freak the fuck out.

"What's wrong?"

Darius gave us all dirty looks, but his words were gentle. "Today, we were having an amazing lovemaking session, and Kitten may have accidentally initiated a matebond with me." He waved one hand at a raw bite mark on his chest, as if it was just a cat scratch and not the beginning of a lifelong tie.

I slumped back against the wall. "Holy crap!" Darius threw me another angry look, so that was clearly the wrong response. "Well, you did kind of accidentally steal her eggs, so maybe this makes you guys even?"

Every set of eyes turned to look at me then, even Kit's. Beckett shook his head. "That's not helpful, Coop."

I wasn't getting this. "Why is everyone acting like this is a tragedy?" I walked toward the center of the nest and knelt down in front of Kit. "Babe, I've wanted to bite you and make you mine almost from the first moment I met you. Hell, I barely knew you and I wanted you to be ours. Now that I do know you? I can hardly imagine our Pack without you." She looked up at me with watery eyes, so I grabbed her hands and clasped them in mine. "I can safely speak for all of us when I say we are waiting for you. We'll continue to wait for you. Just because you've initiated the bond with Darius, that doesn't mean you need to bond with us all right now. Or that Darius has to complete the matebond with you. Your Beast had different ideas, but it was an idea that lined up with our own."

I lifted her hands to my lips, kissing each knuckle. I sucked in a breath, because this next part was physically painful to contemplate.

"If you don't want to be mated to us, or to Darius, we can help you find a way to break the bond. It isn't two ways at the moment, which means breaking it will only be painful for you, and not for Darius."

She shuddered, and Darius wrapped that possessive arm around her a little tighter. I could see his Beast burning in his eyes, and I would bet my left testicle that he was straining to keep his teeth out of her skin and his dick out of her delectable-smelling body. His Beast would be riding him to finish the mating.

God, I loved that man for waiting.

Kitten blinked slowly, chasing away the tears that were resting on lashes. "I don't want to break the bond. That's why I feel so damn bad. I took away his choice."

Darius gave a rumbling growl that turned into a low, barely audible thrum, while Corvin let out a relieved snort. "Kitten, pretty sure he would have thrown himself at your itty-bitty fangs if you'd even whispered the suggestion of a matebond with him. We all would. We thought you hated that you were tied to us now." He grinned at her from across the room. "Anytime you wanna take a nibble out of me while riding my knot, you just let me know. Day or night."

We all echoed our agreement, and I lifted my shirt, showing her Darius's matebond mark on my right pec. "There's space for a matching one right here, whenever you're ready." I pointed to the left pec. "Now, can we all stop moping in the nest? I want to make some pasta and eat it off the body of at least one of my Omegas."

Kitten huffed a small laugh, and I grinned at my success. She might think I was joking, but I really wasn't. Not about using her as a pasta bowl and definitely not about the matebond. The sooner she was Pack, the sooner both the man and the Beast would be happy.

THE FOLLOWING DAY, I called off work to take Kitten to see Tanner the vampire. It was hard to call him Doc Tanner when he looked like a frat boy who lived on ramen and surfed instead of studied. Still, the Alpha General seemed pretty happy with him, and the Convocation seemed to have faith in him, so I'd give him the benefit of the doubt.

Tanner had called to say he had the results of our DNA tests, and wanted to talk to Kitten about it. She'd automatically looked nervous, so we decided one of us Alphas should go with her. Actually, we'd all wanted to go, but Kitten had found her pride and talked us down to one.

Then we'd rock-paper-scissored like grown-ups to decide who got to go. I won—those other fuckers were predictable as hell. Beckett always over-thought it, and went with scissors. Corvin went with rock. Every single damn time.

We were sitting in the waiting room, though I couldn't smell the vampire anywhere. That didn't mean much really. Vampires didn't have strong scents; Tanner's scent mainly came from his clothes. Antiseptic wash and other strong medical smells, mostly. And chocolate, which confused me, but he must eat a bunch of it to smell so strongly of the candy.

As if I'd conjured him, he appeared in the doorway. He looked flushed, with his hair more mussed than usual. I breathed in deeply, and a familiar scent filled my nostrils, though I couldn't quite place it. Definitely Manix though, and if I wasn't wrong, horny Manix at that.

I raised an eyebrow at the vampire, and he flushed pink. "Sorry I'm late. I was detained with another patient."

"I hope the patient is doing okay?" I asked, with as much gravitas as I could muster while trying not to laugh.

He cleared his throat. "Yep. Right as rain. Let's go into my office, hey?" He almost sprinted through to the exam room, and I stood, pulling Kit to her feet and holding onto her hand. She squeezed it back, making my heart swell.

Tanner pulled out a couple of chairs and grabbed a file. "Okay, so your results are back and I'm not gonna lie, I was surprised as fuck." His eyes scanned the page, and I groaned.

"Don't leave us hanging, Tanner."

"Well, Kitten, you are fifty percent Manix, which I expected. But your remaining DNA is only partially human. The rest is Griffin."

I blinked.

Kit blinked.

Tanner grinned. "Right? How bloody cool is that?"

I shook my head. "Can you just repeat that?"

"I had the DNA test sent away to a specialist who's contracted by Raine, as the Convocation Member for Endangered Species. You can imagine that it's a service that is often needed." Kit nodded dazedly, though I wasn't sure she was really listening, but if Tanner noticed, he chose not to draw attention to it. "So it says you are 50% Manix, 35% human and 15% Griffin. That would explain why you didn't get the infant sickness that the De Léon cubs suffered from—there wasn't enough of the other shifter in there to cause a dominance battle. But congrats. I thought the Griffins were long dead. Like long, *long* dead. Even before the succubi. Guess this makes you the last of your species, unless your mother is still alive."

"It couldn't be her father's genes?"

Tanner laughed. "Not unless Gatlin Huxley is hiding a bird head and some seriously epic wings."

I choked. "Excuse me, fucking *what?* Gatlin is her father?"

Tanner shook his head. "No, of course not. There's only what, twelve or thirteen years between them? I mean, you guys are remote, but not cult-child-bride remote. Well, not yet," he laughed. "No, they shared a father. All her paternal markers matched with the ones I had from Gatlin's file, when I did his lineage profiles."

"The old Alpha General is Kitten's biological father?"

Tanner nodded. "Yep." He looked over at Kit. "He sounds like a prejudiced cuntwaffle though, so I don't think you missed much not having that Hallmark moment. Not a single person had anything nice to say about him, especially not Gatlin."

"Does Gatlin know?" I asked, and Tanner shook his head.

"Nah, I thought Kitten should know first. It's her DNA test, after all. But I'll have to tell them eventually, considering their cubs and yours will share a bloodline and they'll make up a large portion of the next generation of Manix. The Alpha General—the new one, I mean—made the right decision tracing all this.

Though you guys probably would have already been out of luck, considering your connection to Finlo Grey. So fucking convoluted, right? Your family historians are gonna need a whole ball of red yarn to trace this craziness." He chuckled again. "Do you have any questions?"

Kitten shook her head, but she looked thoroughly shellshocked, making me wonder if maybe I should get Tanner to check her out.

The doctor's face softened. "No worries, Kitten. Just let me know when you think of something. I'm always available. I'm a bit of a night owl, you know? Or a night bat. Ha, get it? Because I'm a vampire. Though we don't actually turn into bats, but that would be awesome." He grabbed a small stack of papers. "Here, this is for you guys. Has all your DNA results in it, and the rough pedigree I mapped out for you." I took the manila folder from him, before helping Kit to her feet. "Tell Darius that he should come in for another checkup soon."

I thanked Tanner, and we headed out the door. I led Kit back to the ATV, refusing to let go of her hand. I wanted her to know I was here for her.

"You okay? Is there something you want me to do?"

She shook her head, but then hesitated. "Could we go back to my home?"

I nodded, trying to keep the disappointment off my face. She still didn't consider the Packhouse her home, which part of me understood. The Beast, however, growled at me to lift my fucking game before we lost our Omega.

"Of course, sweetheart."

WHEN WE MADE it to the cabin, Kitten went in by herself, asking for time alone. As much as I wanted to say no, wanted to bundle her up in my arms and tell her that this didn't change a thing, I respected her wishes.

I paced a track in the clearing around the cabin, messaging the guys to give them the Cliff Notes version of what happened. They all immediately wanted to drop what they were doing and come out here, but I told them no. If Kitten wanted space, I didn't think she'd appreciate the whole Pack crowding around her in an overprotective huddle.

I tried to imagine a little Kitten running around here, catching rabbits, exploring the world, talking to the forest. It wasn't hard to imagine at all. There was still that wildness in her, despite the fact she'd been living in civilization for the last few months.

Finally, I got bored and went to the wood pile behind the house to start splitting logs. I needed something to keep my body active and my mind distracted. Soon enough, I was sweating, there was a stack of logs halfway up the side of the cabin, and the dusk was beginning to settle over the mountains. I laid the ax down and picked up my shirt, shucking it back over my head.

A small hum of disappointment had me whipping my gaze back toward the house. Kitten sat on the back step, her chin on her knees. A small smile curled her lips, but she still smelled sad.

"Kitten! Why didn't you tell me you'd come out?"

She shrugged. "Free chopped wood and a view? Too good to pass up."

If she was making jokes, that meant she was okay now, right? I wandered over to her, sweat making my shirt stick to my skin. I sat down so our bodies were pressed together, but I didn't bundle her into my lap like I wanted to. Instead, I just sat with her in silence as my phone blew up in my pocket.

After the thirtieth text, Kitten raised a brow at me. "Think you should answer that?"

"Probably. The guys are worried about you. I told them to stay away, but that was basically like a wounded deer cry. They want to be here more than anything."

She sighed and rested her head on my shoulder. "Sorry. I just needed to be out here. To try to go back to a moment when everything made sense."

I kissed her head, giving in to the urge to wrap my arm around her and pull her even closer to my body. "Things still make sense, Kit. They're just a little more complicated. You're still Kitten, the same girl who ran wild through these forests, who hunted and survived like a badass. Lorso still loved you—enough to protect you from the greatest threat to the child he thought of as a cub. Enough to ostracize himself from society and paint his people as monsters.

"You still have us, and we still love you. Yes, you have a new half-brother, if you want, but that's not a big deal either. Half of Maxton is fucking related, which is why Tanner had to undertake that ridiculousness anyway. In a few more months, we'll have cubs, and they'll be a little part of you too. None of these things are confusing; they're only facts, and it's just how you feel about them that might be confusing. But you won't find answers in the past, Kit. The past has no bearing over your future."

We sat in silence for a little longer, until finally she shifted beneath my arm. "We better go home. The others will be worried."

I kissed her temple. "Okay, Kit." I gave her one more squeeze. "You know I'm hopelessly in love with you, right?"

She tilted her head, looking up at me with her face washed in the dying red of the setting sun, and she smiled. "I know. I love you too, Coop."

26

KITTEN

I'd spent the afternoon reassessing every single aspect of my life. I started with the fact that I had a half-brother who lived less than ten miles away, a man that I had met once before who shared half my DNA. A month ago, when I'd met him on the street, had I known deep down in my soul that he was related to me? Had he smelled familiar?

Nope, though I do remember not being as fearful of him as the other Alpha, Wilkie. But that was because they were as different as night and day. Gatlin seemed nice, if intense. Wilkie was everything Lorso had ever warned me about. At least, that's what I'd thought Lorso was warning me about, but maybe he'd had a particular Alpha in mind.

Despite the fact that none of this shit really mattered—and quite frankly, being a motherfucking

Griffin was way more interesting—my brain kept coming back to a day about fifteen years ago, when Lorso had yelled at me, like *really* yelled at me, for the first time ever.

He'd caught me on the edges of Maxton, watching the normal people get in and out of their cars, bringing out bags of pastries from the bakery, and kids playing on the sidewalk, doing normal people shit. I remembered thinking that it all seemed so easy and not scary at all. Not like the boogeymen Lorso had painted them to be. But then Lorso had busted me and dragged me back to the cabin. He'd made me sit in the corner while he first ranted in English to himself, because at the time, I didn't understand English at all.

Finally, when he'd calmed down and ran out of steam, he'd squatted down in front of me, his face more serious than I'd ever seen it. That was saying something, because Lorso was a really reserved kind of man.

"You can't do that, Girl. If the Alpha General of that town caught you, he'd take a little Beta half-blood like you and make you a chew toy for the upcoming Alphas. He'd punish you for your very existence. For what you represent. You cannot do that again. *Swear it!*"

That was when he'd yelled, in fear or maybe frustration; I couldn't tell then and I still wasn't sure now. I'd sworn never to go back, of course. Lorso had never yelled at me before that day, and it scared the crap out of me for years after. I never went even close to Maxton ever again, and didn't set eyes on another Manix until Corvin and Beckett stumbled over me when they were teens.

Now, I wondered if it wasn't all Manix Lorso was trying to keep me away from, but the Alpha General in particular. The same Alpha General who'd preached racial superiority. Maybe having two half-breed mistakes would have been too much?

I'd never know now.

There was a knock at the bedroom door, and I called Beckett to come in. I knew his scent intimately now. I could pick him out of a crowd of a thousand with my eyes closed. They'd been good about leaving me alone after we returned from the cabin, even Darius, but I guess twenty-four hours of processing was all I got.

Beckett appeared, carrying a plate with toast and a glass of juice. He set them on my nightstand, and hesitated before sitting down on the edge of the bed. "Want to talk about it?" I shook my head. He squinted at me. "Not even about being part Griffin? Because holy hell, that's cool. Like the coolest thing I've ever heard. My mate, the half-Griffin."

I let out a rough laugh. "It's more like fifteen percent. But I guess it's pretty cool."

"When you told us last night that you were a

smidge Griffin, I did a bit of research. Did you know that they were revered for their incredible strength, bravery and protective instincts? That's why they're on all those fussy nobility crests."

"I'm only fifteen percent of all that. I'm fifty percent power-hungry sociopath."

Beckett winced. "Man, now I wish we'd never described the old Alpha General to you." He lay down next to me, pulling the blankets up over him too so he could spoon his body in next to mine. "You might be half-Manix, which I'm so happy about because it means you can be mine in every way possible. But you aren't just the same DNA as Alpha General Huxley—who was a psycho, I'll grant you that. You also share that DNA with Gatlin, who is arguably one of the best Manix I know. Maybe he has a bit of Griffin in him too, because he's always stood up for those who are weaker than him. Both Ellar and Seven, his Betas, were considered rejects by proper Manix society. And he tore down the world for Naja, his Omega. He's a good person, and so are you. Screw what your DNA test says."

There was another knock on my door, and Darius poked his head in. His eyes softened when he saw me. I could see him physically struggling not to bound across the room and wrap me in his arms. Or maybe I felt it, through the half-bond we now shared.

"How are you feeling?"

I shrugged. "Better, I guess? I've come to terms with

it, anyway."

He gave me that smile that did crazy things to my heart. "Well, that's good, because Gatlin Huxley and his Pack are downstairs."

I froze. I looked at Beckett, who was frowning at Darius. Then he looked back at me. "You don't have to go down. They can come back. It's not like they live on another continent—they're only twenty minutes down the road."

I sucked in a deep breath, steeling my spine. "No, let's go down now. Better to get it over with, right?"

Beckett kissed my lips. "Such a brave little Kitten."

They left me alone to get changed and brush out my hair. I put on a white sundress that made me feel pretty and feminine, but left my feet bare. Stepping out of my doorway, I pushed my shoulders back and lifted my chin. I'd met Gatlin before. He wasn't any more scary now than he was then.

I strode down the stairs, toward the hubbub of voices. The living room was teeming with adults and children. Darius was holding a squirming baby, while its siblings were power-crawling around the floor. A little girl, who can't have been much more than a toddler herself, was crawling around after them while a pouty-looking Beta watched on with eagle eyes. The big blond Alpha—Finlo was his name, I remembered —was talking to Cooper, and when they were standing side by side, I could tell they were related.

Corvin broke away from the group, bounding up the stairs to me. "Is this alright? They decided that it would be better if this seemed more like a festive thing than the end of the world. Darius had already wanted to talk to Raiden about the whole pregnancy thing. In the end, it was just easier for them all to come, and this way you can be introduced to the rest of the Pack too. Rip it off like a bandaid. But say the word and I'll send them all but Gatlin home."

The tone of the room changed, even though everyone kept speaking. They'd heard Corvin's words, and no one protested. They'd leave if I wanted them too, and for some strange reason, that was enough.

"No, I'll be fine."

Corvin nodded and wrapped a possessive arm around my hip as we finished descending the stairs. I could feel the eyes of my Alphas on me, watching for any sign that I was uncomfortable so they could whisk me away.

Corvin put his lips close to my ear. "Be brave. We'll do the hard part first." He nipped my earlobe, making me gasp, and then directed me to stand in front of Gatlin. Beside him, Naja smiled brightly, a baby in her arms.

We stood awkwardly opposite each other for a moment. I looked at the man in front of me, cataloging his features. They didn't look even remotely similar to my own.

"So…" he said, and cleared his throat awkwardly.

Naja shook her head. "He'll fight armed gunmen and insane cartel bosses, but faced with a half-sibling, he loses the ability of speech." She stepped close to me and wrapped her arms around my shoulders. "Welcome to the family." She dropped her voice to a whisper. "He won't say it, but he's excited to have some blood kin. For so long, the only family he had was your father, and to say he was a fucking asshole would have been an understatement."

I just patted her back. I didn't know what to say. I'd grown up believing I was alone in the world too, but I had Lorso, and then Beckett and Corvin. Then I had no one.

I looked at Gatlin, his gaze intense and his Alpha power close to that of even the Alpha General. "I don't know how this works. I don't know what to say."

He inclined his head. "I don't know what to say either. I'm glad you exist?" He sighed. "Do you drink? Because I feel like this is a conversation that would be infinitely smoother with scotch."

I grinned. I definitely drank. Lorso had shunned the ways of humans, but the man loved whiskey.

Corvin let out a relieved breath. "I'm cracking open the thirty-year-old bottle I got as a mating present. If there was ever a situation that deserves good liquor, it's this one."

I couldn't agree more.

The babies had all been fed and gone down for a nap early—which quite frankly, seemed like a small miracle—and everyone sat around the living room. Kitten was grinning goofily, probably just on the line between tipsy and drunk. She was keeping up with the drinks admirably however, considering she had approximately half the body weight of the rest of us—not including Naja, who wasn't drinking at all.

"So you don't remember your—I mean our—father mentioning any woman at all? Any hints who my mother might be?" Her words were slightly slurred, and she kept slipping into Latin, but honestly it was kind of adorable.

Gatlin shook his head. "There's what, eight years between us? By the time I was eight, I was beginning to exhibit my power, and my father did everything he could to distance himself from me. I wasn't sad about it, because by then I realized what a psycho he really was. You're better off just meeting his headstone. He would've fucking sold you to Wilkie or some other backwards fucking Alpha Pack in a heartbeat if it suited him."

Naja muttered something under her breath in Spanish, but I didn't need a translator to know she was cursing the very existence of the former Alpha General. She chewed her lip. "Courtland did say that he inherited a bunch of ledgers and diaries when he, you know..." She shot a quick look between Gatlin and Kitten, then grimaced. "Anyway, maybe there'll be something in there. I'm sure Courtland would be happy to let you flick through them, see if there's anything in there around the year you were born."

Kitten grinned goofily again, and honestly, I loved her so damn much.

Ellar, Gatlin's sweet Beta male, nudged me with his elbow. "I know that look, Beck. You're one more scotch and a few layers of clothes away from bringing her into the Pack," he murmured softly, and I gave him a lopsided grin.

"You know it."

The longer the Huxley-Grey Pack stayed, the more comfortable Kitten felt. Maybe it was just the booze, or maybe it was the Pack themselves. While we'd gone to school with Raiden, Finlo and Gatlin were a little older than us, but we all got along. Maybe it was because both Packs had male Omegas, or because Finlo and Cooper were cousins. Either way, if Kitten was going to have some long-lost family member, I was glad they came from this Pack.

Finally, the cubs woke, and Finlo suggested it was time to go home. We waved them goodbye, and Kitten was still smiling. "They seem nice. I want that."

I wrapped an arm around her waist. "To be nice?"

She slapped at my shoulder but leaned against me. "No, to be a Pack—properly. I want you guys to mate me. I want to take your knots and complete my bond with Darius."

You could have heard a pin drop, or the sound of all the blood whooshing through my body to my dick.

I wanted to say no. Not tonight, when she was drunk and recently had some life-altering news thrust upon her. But the words refused to pass my lips.

Luckily, Darius had more fucking sense than me. Or better control over the howling Beast that demanded we take her right now, fill her with our seed.

Darius stroked her cheek. "Not tonight, sweetheart. This isn't a decision you make with a belly full of scotch."

I huffed but didn't argue. I appeased myself with the fact that at least it was on her mind, and soon enough she'd make that decision sober as a judge and with love in her eyes. Then I would make love to her until she clenched around my knot and I could make her mine forever.

She flopped against Darius, giving him nipping little kisses along his jawline. "You're so handsome. Don't you think he's handsome, Beck? Now I know why you guys left me. I'd leave me too if I met someone as sweet and sexy as Darius."

I clutched her tighter to my chest. "We didn't want to leave you, baby. Remember? We wanted you too. You were always meant to be part of our Pack; it just took us a while to get where we needed to be."

She sighed heavily, letting her eyes close softly. "So much wasted time. I'm mad at Lorso. So fucking mad at him for convincing me that this town was the gateway to Hell, and that all Manix were bad, when he only really meant one Manix was evil. I could have lived with you. Been a part of a Pack, instead of being alone. I was so fucking lonely."

Darius tilted her chin up so he could kiss her lips. "Lorso was right though. You heard Gatlin—if his father had known about you, you would have been forced into a shitty mating and been miserable. You definitely wouldn't have been allowed to be with us."

She rested her lips against his, squishing their faces together, and for a moment I thought she'd fallen asleep. "Maybe you're right. Maybe I was meant to wait until I turned Omega. Goddess's plan." She reached down and rubbed his stomach without opening her eyes. "So I could be a mom. A mom better than mine was, anyway." She pulled away with a sleepy smile. "I want a nap now."

I kissed the top of her head. "Okay, Kitten." Scooping her up in my arms, I carried her up the stairs. By the time we reached the landing, she was sound asleep. I laid her down in the bed and crawled in after her, keeping a firm hold on my Beast.

Soon. Soon she'd be ours forever.

THE FOLLOWING DAY, I took Darius to his checkup with Tanner. Darius wasn't some weakling Omega who needed his Alpha for everything; I just wanted to go. There was a chance that one or two of those cubs were biologically mine, and I wanted to see them any chance I got. Plus, you know, Tanner was a vampire and he made my Beast wary, even though he didn't throw up any red flags.

Darius, being the sweet guy he was, didn't even protest about my overprotectiveness. He'd definitely popped more in the last week, his stomach protruding enough to be noticeable now. Which meant every person in Maxton was gawping at him like he was a sideshow exhibit, and it was riling my Beast.

"Stop growling, Beck. They aren't going to leap out

and attack me, and I honestly don't care if they look. This is magical. I'm not going to hoard it for myself."

"I wish we could," I grumbled, but did my best to rein it in.

We stepped into the doctor's office, but there was no one around. "Hello?"

A squeak from the back room, some hurried whispers, and the sound of the back door shutting told me that the doctor was in. The door to the exam room opened, and a whoosh of pheromones wafted out. Omega pheromones.

"It smells like a sex den in there," Darius said to a flustered-looking Tanner.

It was undeniable that the good doctor was fucking one of the new Omegas, though I wasn't sure which one. If the rest of Maxton found out, there'd be hell to pay though—regardless of who it was.

Darius obviously thought the same thing. "Best be careful, Tanner. This place might have a brand new Alpha with some pretty open-minded ideas, but this town is still populated by the close-minded assholes who let the old Alpha General get away with his bullshit for so long. Too many people see Omegas as a commodity, and they won't like you trying to steal one. Not me, of course. I say as long as everyone is willing, let there be fuckfests for all. But my Pack isn't in the majority."

Tanner bowed his head respectfully. "Thanks for

the warning, Omega. I know you're right, but I can't help it. She's like a bloody addiction that I can't give up."

I knew he was Australian, but when he used the word bloody, it always threw up the worst mental images. Still, I felt sorry for the poor bastard. I shrugged. "Then don't. Just be prepared."

Tanner nodded again, before tilting his head at the exam room. "Give me two minutes to, uh, clean up and then come on back."

He disappeared back into the exam room, and Darius raised an eyebrow at me. He didn't have to say the words for me to know he was wondering the very same thing that I was—who was the Omega? There still weren't that many, but Tanner had been in contact with all of them to undertake his genealogy assignment. The new Omegas all smelled different from their old scents, so it was hard to pinpoint exactly who it was.

But you know what? My own life had enough mystery in it, so I was going to let this go. Tanner seemed nice, and I trusted him with Darius—I could trust him with one of the random new Omegas too.

We decided that the vampire had enough time to clean at superspeed, and I knocked on the door once before opening it. Tanner was sitting in his chair with Darius's file open in front of him, the very picture of professionalism, like we hadn't just busted him *in flagrante.*

"So you should be about ten weeks along now, and from what I understand, that's just over halfway?"

We both nodded. Well, at least that's what we'd guessed. Raiden had gone about eighteen weeks. It was only male pregnancies that had the shorter gestation, an evolutionary quirk probably due to the propensity for litters. Female Manix had regular gestation periods akin to those in humans. Honestly, if humans found out about us, about how different we really were, we'd be studied for generations.

The idea scared me like it never had before. My cubs could face dangers long after I was dead and buried, no longer around to protect them. Was this what parenthood was? Constant worry?

Eesh, that should have come in the Pack Life Starter Manual as a warning.

"Let me grab the doppler. Darius, if you wouldn't mind getting up on the exam table, we'll check out these cubs."

Darius grinned. "I don't know, Doc. Did you wipe it down after the previous patient?"

Tanner turned red at Darius's teasing. "Of course I did, you cheeky bastard. Get up there before I convince you that you're giving birth to bird-lions instead of babies. No one can actually tell on these things anyway, not without a trained eye."

Oh shit, I hadn't even thought about if the babies could be Griffins. I assumed not, because if Kitten was only fifteen percent, then the cubs would be even less. But what if one had a recessive gene or something? Not that I would be upset if one of them was a Griffin. It would be amazing. But the only Griffin in existence? It would be in for a lifetime of being hunted.

"Beck, are you catastrophizing over there?" Darius gave Tanner a scolding look. "Now you've freaked him out that they'll all come out baby Griffins."

Tanner laughed, not looking even remotely sorry. "Nah, mate. Chances of them being a Griffin is extremely slim, and then the chances of the Griffin animal being dominant are even less. I think you're pretty safe, at least according to the research of that kid doctor who was here before me. The one who worked out all your Betas were changing to Omegas." He lifted Darius's shirt up and whistled. "Gotta spit out those watermelon seeds, Omega. Looks like you're baking a dozen buns in that oven."

I had no idea what any of that meant, but Darius snorted. "Lesson one, Tanner. When you see a pregnant Omega—or Beta, for that matter—do not mention how fat they're getting."

"Eesh, sorry Omega," Tanner said, picking up the wand and putting some gel on it. "My bad. I did suck at my obstetrics rotation, so I guess that's why." He looked up at me. "The medicine part was fine. I promise, I'm real good at delivering babies." He went back to looking at the ultrasound machine. "Ah, here we are. Look at those big boys growing."

"Boys?" Darius squeaked, and Tanner shook his head.

"Just a figure of speech. They're a little too small to see just yet, I think. Probably the next scan though, given the rate they're growing." He continued along, taking measurements and making notes, and the whole time I stared at the screen like it was a crystal ball.

Finally, he was done taking measurements on all three cubs, as they moved and squirmed out of the way of his probing. "Cheeky little buggers," he laughed, when he finally got the head measurement of the last cub. "They look great. Growth is in line with what I think it should be, they're active and their heart rates sound good. Congrats, Dads."

Dads. Holy shit.

28

KITTEN

I'd made the guys all go to their own jobs today. I'd been here over two months now—I needed to grow some lady balls and get out and do things myself. This was a good first step.

I sat in the waiting room of the Alpha General's office. Radic had brought me some coffee, which I sipped gratefully. Non-instant coffee and pastries from the bakery were just a few of the happy bonuses that came from moving into town. If I focused on these small things, and not the fact I hadn't watched the sun rise in months, or run through the woods in my human skin beneath the moonlight, I wasn't as homesick.

Courtland opened the door to his office with a smile. "Omega," he said, bowing his head in respect.

"I'm surprised to see you today. Ready to start your new job?"

"No, uh, well yes. I'd like to start if I could. I've gotten my bearings and I think I'd like to do something that contributes back now. But that's not the only reason I'm here."

"Can you push my next meeting back, Rad? Actually, reschedule it altogether. I'm sure we'll think of some way to fill the extra thirty minutes," Courtland said to Radic, in a voice that was little more than a rumble.

Radic flushed, but that was the only sign the Alpha was flirting with him. His expression remained purely professional. Courtland grinned, and then let his own face slip into something more neutral.

"Come in, Kitten."

Once upon a time, the very idea of walking into a room and being alone with the most powerful Manix in existence would have made me break down into an anxious mess. But as Courtland indicated the wide couch, taking a seat in the single seater opposite me, I felt pretty damn comfortable. His power was like a heavy blanket, but it was comforting and not suffocating, to the point I was sure he was tamping it down to make me feel less threatened.

That was the mark of a real leader.

"What can I do for you, Omega? Are you being treated well?" The small edge that crept into his voice led me to believe he'd rectify any ill treatment in a rather permanent manner.

"Yes, sir. The Wiley-Fletcher-Reid Pack treats me like I'm made of the most precious material on earth. I'm very happy with them."

Courtland smiled. "I'm happy to hear it. Let me know if you run into any troubles though. I won't tolerate ill treatment of Betas or Omegas by anyone, let alone the people who vow to love and protect you. So did you want to sign your employment contract now? Maybe write out a report on what you think needs to be done to maintain the forest and wildlife within the borders?"

I nodded. "Thank you, sir. Actually, um, I was coming to see you about another issue, though I guess it's kind of related. Have you spoken to Doc Tanner?"

Courtland shook his head. "No, your medical records are private, even from me. I have, however, spoken to my sister Naja. I hear you've inherited a new branch on your family tree. I think that makes us extended family also." He smiled. "She insinuated you might want to look at your father's diaries and ledgers from around then, so I had someone dig them out of the records room this morning." He stood, and grabbed a small cardboard box from beside his desk. "I got them a couple of years either side of your supposed birth year, just in case."

My eyes might have welled with tears, which

seemed to send the Alpha General into something that might have resembled panic.

"No, don't cry," he said in his Alpha voice, which just made me whimper a little and try to suck the tears back in. "Ah fuck, no, I didn't mean for that to be an order. Fuck. RADIC!"

The good-looking Beta burst into the room, his eyes ping-ponging between the panicked Alpha General and me, with tears streaming down my cheeks.

"What the hell did you do, Court?" He hurried over to me and wrapped me in his arms. "Hey, it's okay. Tell me what's wrong?"

"You guys are so nice." I hated that my voice was wavering. "You were all meant to be evil and mean, people who just wanted to subjugate me and feed me to the Alpha Manix. I missed out on so much. And I can't write reports because I never learned to write, because I couldn't come to town to go to school. I feel like I've missed out on half of my life already."

Courtland blew out a breath. "Kid, you're barely more than a child in our world. You'll have decades, maybe even centuries to figure all this out. There's time to learn anything you want. This isn't a problem. But you can always talk to any of us if you have any issues, and we'll do our best to fix it. For now, you can dictate your reports into this." He went to a filing cabinet, pulling out a cellphone. "It has a dictation function.

Get one of your Alphas to give you a crash course on how it works."

He pinched his nose. "I want to tell you that the opinions fed to you during your upbringing were wrong, and I hate to echo what so many others have probably already told you, but your guardian wasn't wrong about the nature of the Manix, at least back then. I met your father. He almost refused treatment for my cubs because they were half-bloods. They were this big"—he held his hands about twelve inches apart —"and he was willing to let them die because they weren't pure enough for him. What would he have done to you, do you think? Is that why you want these diaries, to understand the man better? Because I'm not sure you'll find what you're seeking in there."

"I'm part Griffin," I blurted out. Courtland's mouth fell open, and even Radic's arms dropped in shock as he jumped back. "On my mother's side, I guess. I'm looking for clues about who she was. I thought..." I swallowed hard. "I think I'd like to meet her. But I don't want to take my Alphas or Darius. They don't say it, but I think they're mad that she just left me out in the woods, waiting for me to die. She couldn't really have known there was an ancient hermit out there, could she?"

They were silent as they let me have my stream of consciousness meltdown, then Radic patted my arm. "I don't know, Kitten, but whenever you're ready, let us know and we'll send our two best Legion members with you. But talk to your Alphas—they'll want to know what's going on with you." The phone rang, and he eyed his Alpha. "Can you go five minutes without making her cry?"

Courtland frowned and gave him the finger. "Away with you, Beta, before I fire you."

Radic snorted. "Couldn't survive without me, and we both know it."

As soon as he was out of sight, Courtland grinned. "He's not wrong. I love that man." He sat back down in his chair. "Now, where were we? Ah yes, the diaries. Return them when you're done. He might have been an asshole, but he was a damn good record keeper." He shuffled a few more papers. "Ah, actually it's fortunate you came down here. Your goats arrived last week. I'll put out an edict that no one is to eat them, or they can go out into the woods and chew on the grass themselves. Also, I found you two goatherds, assuming you won't want to do it yourself?"

As much as I loved the woods, I wouldn't want to be out there herding a bunch of goats every day either. I shook my head. "I think I'll pass."

Courtland snorted a laugh. "Understandable. Mean bastards, goats. No wonder Satan is always shown to have goat feet. Which is why I've gotten you two equally mean goatherds. My younger sister, Rosa, has recently been getting into fights at school. I'm not sure you've met her?" I shook my head. "Sweet kid. But she's a product of her own upbringing, and she's taken it upon herself to fight the battles of every beaten down half-blood in the school. Teenagers are mean—you should be glad you skipped that part. Still, no matter how noble her cause, she can't fight every battle as a tiger."

"She's a tiger shifter?" I gasped. I'd never met a tiger shifter before.

Courtland nodded. "Way too comfortable in her tiger form too. So, to solve both our problems—and with a little fortuitous timing—Rosa, and the so-called prince of the high school, Eris, will be your new goatherds over the summer. We should figure out a program for clearing the undergrowth, and they can start tomorrow."

For the next thirty minutes, the strongest Manix in North America deferred to me on something I felt passionate about, and honestly, I'd never felt more powerful.

29

CORVIN

"How many damn meetings did they need to have just to decide to do fucking nothing?" Beckett grumbled as he went through one of the former Alpha General's diaries. "Listen to this: '*Nest mother from the Sanctum set meeting about increased resources. Told her that she was breeding warriors and that knowing desperation would encourage them to be ruthless.*' Honestly, I know he's your dad, but I think we should dig him up and piss on his corpse."

We'd been at this for three days, so I could understand his frustration.

Kitten let out a little shocked laugh. Then her face fell. "That would have been me in the Sanctum, struggling to find food."

I pulled her onto my lap and pressed my cheek between her shoulder blades, thrumming softly. "But it wasn't. Anyone got anything that isn't further proof Alpha General Huxley was a cunt?"

"Umm, no. A lot of meetings, a lot of scrimping. He went to town a lot during February of the year that we think Kitten was born. Supply runs, according to this ledger," Coop added. "Only thing he seemed to bring back was a shitload of moonshine though."

I frowned. That seemed wrong. "Moonshine?"

"Yep, from Ol' Sam's Bar and Grill. You think Sam was running a distillery down in the basement?"

I scoffed. "Wouldn't surprise me, wiley old fuck. Pretty sure he waters down his whiskey too." We didn't often go into the neighboring town, but sometimes we liked to let loose, especially when we were younger, and we'd always end up at Ol' Sam's. No one asked questions; pretty sure they thought we were lumberjacks or some shit up here. Or maybe they just knew better. Either way, we went down for supplies sometimes, or to pick up odd jobs.

"Is there mention of a party or a gathering or something in the diaries?"

Beckett went back. "What date?"

"Sometime around the twenty-second of February."

Beckett flicked through. "Nah, nothing that I can see. Considering he wouldn't even give the Sanctum money for food, I doubt he was bankrolling a party."

"Well, that is weird," Darius added from where he

was lying on the couch. They'd brought home a print out of the ultrasound, and those first photographs were now stuck on our fridge. I got choked up every time I looked at them.

"Can't hurt to check it out. We have no other leads so far." Kitten sounded dejected, so I spun her on my lap and kissed her.

"We'll find her, sweetheart."

She shook her head and leaned in so her lips were a breath away from mine. "You can't promise that."

"You're right. I can't. But I promise you we won't stop trying until you have some answers or until we reach a dead end."

She rubbed her cheek on mine. "That's all I can ask." When she rested her head on my shoulder, I squeezed her tightly to my chest. She was soft and warm, her skin glowing and her brown hair so shiny that I wanted to bury my fingers in its curling silk.

"Corvin?"

"Mmm."

"I'm sober right now."

"Yep. Me too, babe."

"Do you think, maybe, we could do the matebond thing now?"

The breath in my lungs refused to exhale, and everyone around me stilled. "You want to perform that mating ceremony? Right now?"

She pulled back on my lap until she could see us all. "Is there some ritual we have to observe first?"

Beckett was half out of his seat. "No. Just mutual consent. Are you sure?"

She leaned forward and kissed me softly. It was tender and loving, and expressed her feelings better than words ever could. Still, she replied, "Yes."

All the air that was burning my lungs whooshed out at once. I launched at her, capturing her lips with mine. I poured my own emotions into that kiss. That love that had simmered in my heart for years, that I'd buried beneath my devotion to Darius and Cooper. The happiness that I felt about her choosing us now.

Hands grabbed at her, and I choked down my growl. I had to share her with my Packmates, these men I loved with the other parts of my heart.

Beckett plucked her off my lap and into his arms. She wrapped her legs around his waist, kissing him just as fervently as she'd kissed me. Beckett had been completely lost when Kitten ghosted us. For months, he'd held onto the hope that she'd come around. His arms banded around her back as he crushed her to his body, walking her slowly to the wall so he could rest her there and continue to kiss her.

I looked over at Cooper and Darius, whose eyes were wide. Fuck, I was a shitty Pack Alpha. "Is this... Do you guys want this still?"

Darius looked at me like I was stupid. "Of course I do. Coop?"

"More than I want my next breath."

I grinned at them both. "I love you guys. Beckett, take it to the nest!"

Apparently, he managed to hear me in his lust haze because he started toward the stairs, stopping to kiss Kitten on each step. Cooper grunted, overtaking them and pulling Kitten from Beck's arms, right there on the stairs.

"Sharing's caring, Beck," he teased. "Come on, baby, I'm going to make you come at least seven times on my knot."

Darius let out a little moan. I looked over at him, my Omega. I took a moment to kiss him, and just like with Kitten, I poured out my heart in the kiss. "I love you, Darius. I loved you from the moment you turned up to our date, dressed like you'd walked out of a magazine, and your eyes locked with mine. I knew then that you were mine, and that I wanted to spend the rest of my life with you. Nothing will ever change that."

He nipped my lip. "Alpha, I love you too. And I love her. You don't have to convince me that you have the capacity to love us both. I go to sleep every night knowing you'd march into the very bowels of Hell for me. As I would for you. And Beckett and Cooper, and now for Kitten." He kissed me softly. "Let's go bond the newest member of our Pack, shall we?"

"So fucking cocky, Omega. You're going to take my knot tonight too—you know that, right?" I growled, and was rewarded with a shiver rolling across his skin.

He stepped away, then grinned back at me over his shoulder. "If you can catch me first, Alpha." He raced away from me, and my Beast howled with happiness.

Tonight, my Pack would finally be complete. Tonight, my Beast would have what he'd longed for all this time.

I chased after my errant Omega. I could hardly wait.

30

COOPER

I walked Kitten into the nest, dropping her gently in the center of the cushioned floor and diving down after her. In between kisses, I started peeling off her clothes. We needed to be naked, stat.

If I could just stop kissing her. I traced her lips with my tongue, then sucked her pillowy bottom lip in between mine until it was big and swollen. Her hands roamed over my body, nails dragging as she explored me with the same ferocity as I was her.

Beckett appeared beside me, and I moved down her body so he could kiss her again. See, I was a good Pack member; I knew when my skills were needed on a different set of lips.

"You're making me the happiest man in all of Maxton tonight, Kit," I whispered when I reached her navel. Grabbing her shorts, I pulled them down her creamy white thighs. Delicious fucking thighs. As I threw her clothes over my shoulder, I dived between those thighs, nipping and sucking at their prettiness. She squealed as I bit a little too hard, leaving a small mark. I grunted an apology, but if I had my way, she'd be covered in my marks by morning.

She gripped my hair, holding me tightly as I traced my tongue higher. "Need you nice and wet for my knot, beautiful. I want you to ride my face like you're about to be the bull riding world champion, okay?"

She laughed, but it quickly turned into a moan. God, to think I'd get to hear that sound every day forever now. And I meant *every* day. I intended to taste her as often as possible until we were old and gray.

It was good that we were doing this now, not during the heat, or after the birth of the cubs, when all our emotions would be running high. Just on a regular Tuesday evening, after eating way too much pasta and having a bit too much wine, content with each other's company. It just seemed... right.

I moaned as I tasted her juices on the tops of her thighs. Delicious. Flicking my tongue out, I ran it through her folds, and just like I asked, she ground herself against my face.

I pulled back enough to look up at her, meeting her eyes. "Good girl."

There was no more time for words though, as I stroked my tongue against her clit before sucking on it a little. She curled against my face harder, and if I wasn't so busy, I would have sighed with happiness. I wanted to die with my face buried in her pussy.

I sucked and licked at her until she was coming over my cheeks, her grip on my hair a delightful kind of pain. I lapped up all her cum, not wasting a drop. Maybe once more, then I was going to pull her down onto my knot where she belonged. I put both of her legs over my shoulders so I could tilt her at just the right angle for my fingers to do half the work. Curling them like I was trying to call for her orgasm, I grinned as her legs flailed a little and her moans got wild. Yes, this was exactly where I wanted her.

Someone cleared their throat, and I looked up at a very naked Darius. "Hello, Omega," I said smugly, knowing my face was shiny. He just grinned down at me.

He was fucking gorgeous too, my Omega. There was a reason I'd decided back when we were four that he was going to be mine. Before I even knew if I liked men like that, I knew I was going to be Darius's Alpha, and everything else would just have to work itself out.

He had this sharp, stubborn jaw, and these huge, expressive eyes, and back then his hair had been as red as a sunburn, though it had darkened to a deep brown now. Honestly, there wasn't a Manix—or human— alive who could have resisted him.

"This is the fucking hottest thing I've ever seen, but

I think perhaps I should work our new Omega up first, hmm? Before you go locking her into one position for the next thirty minutes," Darius teased, tangling his fingers in my hair.

I buried my face back between Kitten's thighs, nudging her clit with my nose, and letting his hand tug at my hair. What can I say—I didn't mind the pain. I blew a raspberry on her clit, and she bucked against my face with a gasped, "Cooper!"

I chuckled low, and her thighs clenched around my ears. Giving her one more hard nip on the thigh, I pulled away. I was still fully dressed anyway, and our girl was wet and ready. I could wait.

Moving up her body, I gave her a sloppy kiss, letting her taste herself on my tongue. "Soon, Kit. Soon."

Rolling off to the other side of her, I looked around the room. Corvin was down to his boxers, his dick a solid outline beneath his palm. His lips were swollen, and I guessed he'd been kissing our other Omega. Lucky bastard.

Beckett was completely naked, stroking his dick with hooded eyes. He was going to blow before he got a chance to be inside her if he wasn't careful. Man, I would give him shit about that for years, though secretly I wouldn't blame him.

I sat up on my knees so I could watch the two pieces of my heart together. Darius had lifted her up and pulled her into his lap so he could kiss her. He was whispering soft things between sipping kisses, and whatever they were, they made her eyes big and shiny.

They looked glorious wrapped around each other. Darius was a lithe guy, slightly smaller than me, but not as small as Omegas usually were. By comparison, Kitten was tiny for a Manix female, and her skin was this beautiful ivory where it hadn't been kissed by the sun. Together, they took my breath away.

Between them sat Darius's protruding stomach, the evidence of how miraculous they really were. He slid his hands down her back, and then took two handfuls of an ass that was soft and round, lifting her up so his dick could find her entrance. He let her slide down his cock, and I wasn't sure who moaned louder. Darius, Kitten, or one of us Alphas on the sideline.

She threw her head back and Darius took the opportunity to kiss along her collarbones as she rode his dick. Fucking hell, Beckett wasn't the only one who wasn't going to last. I could already feel my knot beginning to ache. I stroked it hard, trying to relieve a little of the pressure without making a sound.

This moment between them? We may as well not have even been in the room. There were only the two of them, and they were in their own bubble of pleasure. But right now, I was happy enough to be on the outside looking in.

31

DARIUS

"You're going to be ours forever, Kitten. Mine and Cooper's. Beckett and Corvin's. Family and lovers," I whispered in Kitten's ear as I slowly slid her up and down my aching dick. It took a bit of maneuvering around my stomach, but I made it work. Kitten's heels pressed into my back, but I couldn't go as deep as I wanted. I leaned back and let her take control, her body pressed around mine like we were custom-made to fit. I held her hips as she moved up and down my cock, and god, just watching her with her wild hair and pouty pink lips made me want to come right now.

But I held out, because I knew this was a moment we would remember forever. I lifted my hands to cup her breasts, pinching her nipples between my fingers gently as they bounced so gloriously.

"So fucking beautiful," I murmured, more to myself this time than to her. Because she was. She was everything I could have ever asked for and more. "Come for me, Kitten. Come for me and I'll make you mine, just like you made me yours."

"Yes," she breathed, and I pushed up so I was on one elbow, wrapping the other around her back. I wanted to bite those beautiful breasts. Wanted to leave my mark on them forever. The position made me shift inside her, hitting new spots, making her mewl. "I'm close," she whined and that was it. I leaned forward, sucking her nipple into my mouth hard, making her squeal before I bit down, piercing her skin with my teeth.

The moment her blood hit my tongue, I came in pulsing spurts, filling her with my seed. She clenched around me hard, her moans echoing through her chest and against my lips as I held her still, her own bond in my chest throbbing as we completed the connection.

Then she was there, a burning presence in my mind and in my heart. My Omega. My Kitten.

As her body stopped milking mine, I slowly released my bite. I didn't want to hurt her; the bite should be feeling like pure bliss right now. It would ache a little later, but I'd lick and kiss it until it felt better. I tongued at the wound, tasting her blood like it was the elixir of life.

Pulling her back to my chest, I lay back down,

snuggling her tightly against me. The Alphas would only give us a moment to rest—they'd all be just as eager to bond with this beauty—but I was going to soak this in for all it was worth.

"I love you, Kitten. You're my heart." With our bond, she'd feel how much I meant those words. I felt the overwhelming pulse of her love back at me, and I smiled. This was so, so right.

"I love you too," she whispered against my lips before kissing me softly. Then she grinned at the vibration of heavy footsteps coming toward us. Yeah, Kitten knew what tonight entailed, and there was a shining light of excitement in her eyes.

She was still a little feral, our Kitten.

Beckett was there, and he bent down, scooping her up easily. The combination of our juices slid down her thighs, and someone made a hungry noise. I looked over at Cooper, who was looking at the same thing as he sucked his bottom lip between his teeth, like he was imagining the taste.

His eyes met mine, and I winked. Whoops—wrong thing to do, because suddenly he was eating up the space between us. He dropped to his knees in between my thighs, and then licked my cock from taint to tip. I groaned, tipping my head back as my whole body shuddered.

Once he'd licked and sucked every trace of Kitten's

and my combined taste from my dick, he climbed further up my body, his knees bracketing my hips as he kissed me hard. His tongue delved into my mouth, and I could taste the slightly salty essence of our releases.

He pulled back, looking down at me with so much lust in his eyes, I swore he was about to combust us both. "Tastes better from the source, Omega," he growled, and I could tell his Beast was so close to the surface that it was a wonder he hadn't already shifted. "The night has barely started for you, D. It's not an orgy unless everyone's having fun, hmm?" He kissed me hard again. "I love you, Omega. So fucking much that it hurts."

I lost myself in the kiss, in the feel of his hard body against mine. At some point, he'd shucked his clothes completely, and I could feel the hard press of his cock against my stomach.

"Omega, I need you." It was as close as an Alpha would ever come to an Omega whine, but man, it made me feel powerful.

"Then take me, Alpha." Yeah, Coop's Beast wasn't the only one this close to the surface.

He kissed me hard again, his dick rubbing against mine as he thrust softly against my body. Even though I'd just come like I'd never come before, I was getting hard again. This was bringing back memories of the time we'd created our bonds as a Pack. The

pheromones—or maybe it was the situation itself—
pushed your body past its normal limits.

Cooper climbed off me, rolling me onto my hands
and knees. He positioned me so we could see Beckett
as he fucked Kitten against the wall. Beckett always did
like to have sex on his feet. Guess mating wasn't any
exception to that.

Corvin tossed the lube to Cooper, and I winked at
him appreciatively. "Love you," he mouthed, and I
whispered it back. He'd been so worried that I'd think
he was replacing me with another Omega, when that
couldn't be further from the truth. He was completing
us, and quite frankly, I could use the help during group
sessions like this.

I felt the cold wash of lube run down the crease of
my ass, and the press of Cooper's thumb against my
hole, sliding in and out as he prepped me. Then he slid
in two fingers, stretching me further and making me
bury my face in the cushioned floor with a moan.

"Please, Coop," I groaned, and he replaced his
fingers with the head of his dick. Slowly, he pushed
past the ring of muscle, sliding inside me and turning
my moan into a whine. A few short, shallow thrusts got
me used to the size of him, then he sank down further
until I felt his balls slap against me.

"Head up, Omega. Watch as we complete our
Pack," he growled, and I did as I was told. I lifted

myself up in time to watch Beckett growl low, burying his teeth in her left shoulder and slowly pumping his knot inside her. The noise she made was pure Omega bliss, that high-pitched gasp making me hard and aching all over again. Then, quick as a rattlesnake, she bit Beckett's bicep that rested beside her head. That would hurt, but Beckett just hissed through the pain, his ass flexing as he rubbed his expanding knot inside her.

Oh fuck, it was too much. "Harder, Coop. *Please.*"

My Alpha provided, fucking me with hard thrusts until I was a fucking mewling mess too. His hands gripped my hips as he buried himself inside me, over and over again, before pulling me upright—still balls deep—and stroking my cock. It was his signature move, the one he used when he was close to coming and wanted me to come first.

He wrapped one hand around my dick, the other around my throat, his thrusts shallow and fast, hitting that good place inside me until I was coming in hot, uncontained ropes onto the cushions and over his hand. He came with me, his knot swelling, though he kept that to himself. He needed his knot for something tonight, but it wasn't to lock inside me.

Finally, he withdrew, and we collapsed to the side. Kitten looked like a wrung-out mess, her hair beginning to stick to her forehead and our combined essence locked inside her body. I wished her IUD the best of luck withstanding that.

"Two down, two to go," Cooper whispered in my ear, and I huffed a laugh. Poor Kitten—she wouldn't know what hit her tomorrow.

32

CORVIN

I vividly remembered the moment I knew I wanted Kitten to be part of my Pack. It was about four years after we met her. We'd always been protective of her, but one day, we'd gone to this natural waterfall just outside the Packlands to the north. The wards were shittier back then, so no one knew we'd snuck off, plus there was nothing to that side but more mountains. Maybe a shifter Pack or two a hundred miles away, but no real threats to our safety.

Kitten, of course, had been the one who showed us. She'd spent her whole childhood exploring the crazy wilderness that most of us didn't care about. If she went north, there was little chance she'd be discovered by other Manix, and the whole world was her playground.

This waterfall was amazing though. It fell over a

natural rock shelf, so you could stand under it like it was a shower, just letting the water pour over your body and wash away the world. We'd packed a picnic with some of the food we'd delivered to her, and spent the half of the day running wild up to this small waterfall and rockpool.

When we got there, Beckett and I had stripped down to our swim shorts, but not Kitten. She'd gotten completely and utterly naked. Beckett had almost choked on his tongue, and we'd both turned away, but Kitten's confused laugh had made us turn back. We'd had to explain to her that it wasn't right to see someone naked, to which she just laughed and dived into the water. She was fucking gorgeous.

Somewhere along the way, the Manix—despite being shifters—had gotten a little more puritanical about our human flesh bags. In our Manix form, shit just hung out in the wind. But lose the fur and suddenly we became all shy? It didn't make sense, but it was what it was.

Beckett and I kept our shorts on, but we swam around in the water with Kitten for hours. When she'd climbed up and stood beneath the waterfall, with the water sluicing over her bare skin and her hair like its own midnight waterfall right down to the top of her asscheeks, that was the real magic.

That moment took my breath away. I'd wanted her before, but that was the moment I realized I might actually love her. That I wanted her forever, not just until I found my own Pack.

Now, as Cooper lay behind her, kissing the bond-mark he'd left on her shoulder over and over as his knot deflated, I realized that she was just as carefree and unencumbered by our Manix bullshit now as she was back then. She didn't need elaborate proposals or fancy mating gifts. She just wanted us.

And for that, I would cherish her for the rest of my life.

Darius was asleep, wrapped in Beckett's arms, his head pillowed on his chest, and I smiled at them. I walked over, lying down in front of an exhausted Kitten. She'd had more orgasms than a body had any right to have, and her eyes were barely open slits.

I wanted her so much that my dick was painfully hard.

"Hey baby. Are you too tired now? We can take a break, have a nap, and finish this later," I told her softly, and she frowned.

"No. Now. I want us to all be a Pack now." She reached for my shoulders with a smile, pulling me closer. I couldn't hide my own smile as I kissed her, gentle because her lips were swollen and red. I kissed her cheeks and her eyelids. I worshiped her, because that's what she deserved.

I met Cooper's eyes over her shoulder, and he was gazing at her with such love, even though she couldn't see him. He pulled out of her body, and she gave a weak little cry at the loss.

"Don't worry, Kitten. You won't be empty for long. I plan to fill you right back up." I pulled her onto my chest, stroking my hands soothingly up and down her back. I worked out the kinks in her muscles with my hands until she purred against my chest. Precum dripped from the head of my cock, and it grazed against her core as I ran my fingers over every part of her body. Slow and easy, that was how this had to be. No matter how much I wanted to slam my cock inside her, that wasn't what my Kitten needed right now. She needed softness, and I was going to be whatever she needed me to be.

But Kitten wasn't a wait-and-see kind of woman. She was stubborn and strong, and when she wiggled down my body, reaching between us to grab my dick and push me into her hot pussy, I audibly gasped like a nineteenth-century virgin spinster.

I slid inside her with a moan that was part me and part her, and my balls pulled up tight. I could swear I was going to blow my load right then and there. Knowing I'd never live it down, I gritted my teeth and pushed back my release. Fuck me. I needed to be superhuman. SuperManix, even.

Slowly and steadily, I moved inside her. Not hard and deep, just shallow, easy movements, grinding her sensitive clit against my pelvic bone. She sighed blissfully and just held on as I did all the work, more like a massage from the inside than fucking. Still, it did its job and soon enough, her pussy was fluttering around me as she gasped against my chest, her body jerking slightly as she came again.

"Are you ready to be Kitten Wiley-Fletcher-Reid?"

She looked up at me, all come-drunk. "Sounds like a mouthful."

I laughed, kissing her hard this time. "I'll show you a mouthful, you minx." I thrust harder, making sure to hit that good spot. I was going to drag this orgasm out until she could hardly see. She'd be sex-blind. I groaned as my knot began to swell, before burying myself inside her, drinking up her moans as it stretched her inner walls, filling her until she was squirming to accommodate me. Finally, I thrust hard, pushing my knot as deep as it would go, locking myself inside her.

I groaned as I came, shooting my seed inside her, making her mine inside and out. I put my forearm to her lips and she bit down hard, her teeth piercing my skin and making me hers. It also made her head tilt to the side and I knew where I wanted my mark. Right there, where her slender neck met her shoulder. It would peek out when she wore those pretty dresses, or when she was in a shirt, and everyone would know that she had a Pack who loved her. That she was *mine.*

She hissed softly as I bit down, so I pumped a little

more vigorously, making her hiss turn to a moan as my knot pulsed against her G-spot. Score one for evolution.

Eventually she released my forearm, and I released her neck, licking it softly to ease the sting. She collapsed against my chest, her eyes already closed, and I buried my hands in her hair.

Mine.

33

KITTEN

I was dead. I couldn't move my aching body, and everything felt all glowy and amazing, so that could only mean I was dead. I was in horny Manix heaven. Except in my soul, there were four shiny new presences, each thrumming with a happiness similar to mine. Around me, they were all passed out in a heap. A leg here, someone's arm there, a dick poking into my hip. I couldn't tell where one of them ended and the other began, and I don't think I'd ever been this happy.

However, I did know I had my head on Darius's chest, my arm wrapped around his stomach. I scooted down a little further so I was face to, um, belly button. I rested my cheek there and could feel the small fluttering of tiny bodies against my cheek. It felt... magical.

"Hey guys. I'm sorry I was a bit weird about you

being born. It was just a little bit of a shock." I pressed my lips softly to the roundness. It was firmer than I'd thought it would be. I'd kind of imagined pregnant bellies would be like... I don't know. A jolly fat man like Santa Claus or something. But it was hard, especially so given Darius's former physique.

"But I promise I'll be a good mother. I have no fu—uh, flipping idea what I'm doing, but I like to read, so we'll figure it out. These guys will help."

Ugh, this was probably stupid. They couldn't understand me, but it felt good to make a vow to them as well, after spending the night debauching their fathers in the name of bonding.

A hand stroked my hair, and I looked up into Darius's eyes. Damn, he was so handsome. "You'll be a great mom, Kitten. I have no doubt."

I smiled, because the sincerity in his voice boosted my own confidence. It might be false confidence, but I'd fake it til I made it.

"Darius?"

"Mmm?"

"I'm sticky." Sticky everywhere. Like literally there wasn't a part of my body that wasn't covered in sweat or cum. It was actually kind of gross.

Darius snorted a laugh, and Corvin stirred, but didn't wake. "Come on, sweets. Let's go and shower together. I'll wash your back. And probably your breasts. Let's face it, I'm going to wash any part of you that you'll let me."

I pushed up onto my knees, and my arms were as shaky as a newborn deer's legs. It was going to be a wobbly trip to the bathroom. "Only if I get to wash yours too," I said, winking as I stood on two aching legs. Oh my Goddess. It felt like my vagina had been hit by a hailstorm.

Darius saw me grimace, and frowned right along with me. He nudged Beckett with his foot, until the Alpha opened one eye. "Our Omega is hurting because you guys battered her poor pussy last night. Can you run down and get her an ice pack while I wash her off?"

Beckett reached out and grabbed my ankle, rolling over to kiss my calf muscle. "Of course. I'll make breakfast too." He uncurled himself from around Cooper's back, and stood quietly. "How about I run you both a bath first though? That'll make you both feel better."

He scooped me up in his arms, carrying me out of the nest and across the hall to the bathroom. Setting me on the counter, he then leaned over to turn the taps on in the tub, dumping in some bath salts. He met Darius in the doorway and kissed him softly.

"I couldn't have dreamed I'd be this lucky," Beckett whispered, though I wasn't sure he was actually talking to either of us, because he disappeared down the stairs in the next breath.

Darius shook his head as he watched him leave, still completely naked. Then he turned his smile to me. "Come and wash off in the shower first, while we wait for the tub to fill."

The water pressure was bad, but it didn't matter, as Darius scrubbed my body with a soft wash cloth, and then I did the same to him. I took my time too, memorizing every dip and plane of his body.

By the time we were done, the water in the tub was perilously high, and filled with bubbles as well as salts. I stepped straight into the bath, but as Darius went to hop in the bath, he looked at his stomach and then at me.

"That's going to be uncomfortable if I sit behind you."

I grabbed his hand and tugged him toward the bath. "I don't mind being the big spoon. I kind of like it, actually. It lets my hands explore in their own time." Normalize women being the big spoon—that was my mantra. Well, my brand new mantra anyway.

Darius huffed a laugh but slid into the bath in front of me, and I wrapped my legs around his waist. He rested his head back against my chest and sighed. "Oh, this is nice. I mean, the guys are often the big spoon, but this is so much better. Softer. Not so itchy with all the damp chest hair," he said conspiratorially, like one of our Alphas would appear and steal his little spoon rights forever.

I rubbed my fingers through his damp hair, and he actually purred. Maybe I was the one purring. I wasn't sure, but right now I was deliriously happy.

There was just one more thing I needed to do. My new mates weren't going to be happy though.

"OMEGA, that bondmark looks fresh. Are your Alphas going to tear us to pieces? Because I've seen Corvin in a fight, and I'm quite attached to my pretty face."

The steady pulse of my bonds let me know all the guys were disgruntled but okay. I'd been correct; they hadn't been happy with me this morning, but this was something I had to do before I could settle into Pack life.

I couldn't explain why I didn't want them with me when I went to Ol' Sam's Bar and Grill, but I really just didn't want to sully my future with the past. What if they saw something in the woman who'd tossed me away like trash and, I don't know, regretted their decision?

Irrational bullshit. I knew that, logically. But some things didn't respond to logic, and apparently that included my abandonment issues.

The Alpha General had come through and given me two Alpha escorts: Merrick and Murphy. He didn't mention that they were mated, but he didn't have to. It was in every inch of their demeanor. They operated in unison, the touches between them casual but familiar.

"They know I'm with you guys, and that I'm here. They aren't happy about it, but they respect my choice."

Murphy grinned as he aimed the car toward a parking space out the back of the bar. The day was ridiculously hot, and I was sticking slightly to the leather seats of their SUV. "I wouldn't expect it any other way. Darius has had them wrapped around his finger for years, and I *know* they'd be soft for you too. You chose a good Pack, Omega."

I knew it. I sat and stared at the giant fading Coors sign painted on the side of the bar. I should have waited and thought this through, but I doubted that time would help me come up with the right words to say.

Merrick—who was apparently the more staid of the two—turned to me. "Ground rules, Omega. Stay with one of us, preferably both of us, at all times. If you feel uncomfortable at any point, just say the word and we'll get you out. If I feel like you're in danger, I'm getting you out of there without any negotiation. Agreed?"

I resisted the urge to roll my eyes. "Does that tone work on your Omega?"

Murphy burst out laughing, and Merrick gave me a

mock stern look. "We haven't been blessed with an Omega yet."

I felt bad, but my nose twitched. I'd been working on filtering scents with so many new people around, and there was a scent on them that was definitely... sweeter than theirs. Smelled like Naja and Bonnie. Sweet.

So I just raised an eyebrow. "Okay, Alpha."

Murphy was still laughing in the back. "I can see why they call you Kitten. You have the sass and the claws." He climbed out and opened my door. "Let's go before you draw blood."

I looked over at Merrick, who shook his head with a small smile. But as soon as he was out of the car, he was one hundred percent military. His senses were on high alert, and even though he was slouched casually, his eyes darted around, looking for threats.

Murphy tucked my hand in the crook of his arm. "It's best if people think you belong with us, Shorty." He leaned down conspiratorially. "Besides, a little bit of a scent exchange is going to ensure we both get laid tonight," he added with a laugh.

As soon as we pushed through the bar door though, all mirth left him. He was just as businesslike as Merrick. All eyes turned to look at us, which I could understand, really. Merrick and Murphy were pushing seven feet, well above the average human height. And they were abnormally attractive. Most of the Manix were. I guess they were a condensed version of Darwinism—only the strongest and most attractive got Betas and Omegas. So generationally, their offspring just got better and better looking.

Just because I couldn't write, didn't mean I was stupid.

We walked straight up to the bar, and as Merrick talked to the bartender, I was squished between the two Alphas. I wasn't mad about it either, as I felt the eyes of the bar patrons on me. Not because I was scared of them, but because I didn't want to run into anyone I'd—

"Kate?"

Ah. Fuck.

I looked over at Garth... Fuck, I didn't even know his last name. I hadn't kept company with him for long enough to get his last name.

I pasted a smile on my face. "Oh, hey Garth."

He got off the barstool and strode toward me, frowning. "Where have you been? I was worried you'd fallen off a cliff and died."

Garth was a nice guy—it was why I'd decided to give him my virginity a while back. Yeah, definitely glad I'd left the guys at home.

"Just busy. You know how it is."

Garth reached out to... I don't know? Grab my arm? Hug me? Who knew, because Merrick deftly put himself between us. "Come on, *Kate*. Sam retired and lives around back, according to the barman. Let's go."

"Kate, who is—"

I smiled brightly at Garth. "Nice seeing you, Garth. Bye now."

We strode through the bar and down a dark hallway, which deposited us in the back alley. Across the road was a rickety old log cabin, and Murphy dropped my arm to go knock on the door. When no one answered, he knocked again.

"Hold your fucking horses!" There was a bang and some muttering. "Fucking younger generation. We'll see how quick they feel when they're eighty and can barely take a piss anymore because of an enlarged prostate. No hurrying then," a man grumbled from the other side of the door before wrenching it open. "What do you wan—"

His mouth fell open with such force that his dentures fell out and hit the porch, bouncing away.

"Leandra?"

34

BECKETT

I t was hot, I was sleep-deprived, and my Omega had left Packlands with two other Alphas. To say I was testy would be an understatement. But I still had to go to work or I'd drive myself absolutely insane.

"Beckett Reid."

I winced at the voice calling to me from the sidewalk. Oh shit. I was in trouble now. Turning slowly, I pasted a smile on my face.

"Hey, Mom. How are you doing?"

She shuffled toward me quickly, so I couldn't even run away. I mean, I was a grown-ass Alpha, but I would still run from my mom when she had that look on her face.

"How am I doing?" She patted my cheek, and I grimaced. Yeah, this was going to be bad. "How am I *doing?*" she repeated. "Well, you called me ten weeks ago to tell me that Darius is expecting cubs, and then I don't hear a single peep from you. Then this morning, Cooper's mother called to congratulate me on having a new daughter-in-law. Now, why would I have to hear from Linda Wiley that my only son has bondmarked another Omega, rather than from my son himself? What could possibly be so important that you couldn't take five minutes to call me yourself?"

It was all said in her stern falsetto voice, but I could hear the hurt underneath. "I'm sorry, Mom. It wasn't intentional. I didn't know Cooper had told his mother." I wasn't surprised though; Coop loved his family, and his mother could almost have been trained by the CIA with her skill at getting information out of people.

"You haven't even brought her around to meet me. Are you ashamed?"

"Mom, no. I'm not ashamed at all, of either of you. Kitten is amazing, and you'll love her. She'll love you too. It's just..." Fuck, how did I tell my mother that I'd kind of adopted a wild girl in the woods when I was a teen and now she was my Packmate and Omega? "There's history there, and she didn't trust new people in the beginning. It was a whole thing. But I promise, I wasn't hiding either of you. In fact, we were thinking about having a party to celebrate our mating. Nothing huge, just immediate family."

I snorted internally. Between Cooper and Darius's

large families, plus Kitten's newfound relatives, it was going to be one hell of a get-together.

My mom still looked disappointed, so I wrapped an arm around her shoulder. "Actually, it might be best to bring her around to meet you first." If for no other reason than we could break the news that Kitten was the daughter of the man my mother hated with a fire so hot, it had threatened to burn us both when I was younger.

My mother narrowed her eyes at me slightly, but nodded. "Okay, Beckett. Call me." It wasn't a suggestion.

I leaned in and kissed her cheek. "Love you, Mom."

"Love you too," she huffed, and then we parted ways. My dad's death, and then that shit with the Alpha General, had really messed my mom up. She wasn't the same mother as before, back when she was happily mated and had a son she adored. She was now disillusioned with the world, and the Manix in general. Honestly, she was going to get along fine with Kitten, as long as she could get past the DNA connection.

The sun beat down as I headed to the school. It was going to be hell, because teenagers were moody enough, but hot, sweaty adolescents were in a league of their own. Normally I would've walked, but instead I drove the ATV up the road and parked it in the parking lot behind the main building.

Kids were already languishing under trees and in

the open air seating area. For once, I didn't have to break up an early morning fight, because apparently vendettas went on hold once the mercury hit a hundred in the shade.

I was glad that Darius was at the Sanctum, which was one of the few houses in Maxton that had air conditioning. Though that was only because Bonnie had summoned up the cash for it; it hadn't been provided by the Legion offices, that's for sure.

Terra appeared on my other side. The Maxton school had five teachers—two for the junior school, three for the senior school. The junior school was supported by volunteers, usually retirees who were happy to come and read books and demonstrate how to hold scissors. Surprisingly, very few people volunteered to be teacher's aides in the senior school.

Terra was the main teacher for the junior school. The main teacher for the senior school was an Alpha who was about to hit retirement age and took zero shit from the kids. I didn't always agree with his methods, but usually he was firm and fair.

"We should have called today off. They're going to be restless as hell and teaching them anything will be useless," Terra grumbled.

I just grinned. "And good morning to you too, Terra."

"Why are you so chirpy?" she grumbled, and I pulled the neck of my shirt aside, showing her the pretty little matebond on my neck. "Holy shit? You guys and the new Omega?" When I nodded, she squealed ear-piercingly loud. "Congratulations!" She leapt at me and wrapped me in a hug. "I'm so happy for you guys!"

I patted her a few times on the back and stepped away. It was too hot for hugs. "Thanks."

She punched me in the arm. "What the hell are you doing here instead of at home in a sweaty sex pile? I didn't emerge for like a week after my matebonding."

I winced, both at the idea of Terra having sex—because the woman was basically like my sister—and at the idea of being in a mess of bodies in this heat. Still, I'd probably have done it if Kitten hadn't run off this morning. I wasn't going to lie, I was a little hurt that she hadn't taken one of us, but she had her reasons. I didn't want to start our Pack life by being a domineering prick.

"We've just been through a heat then matebonding, Terra. If I have any more week-long orgies, my dick will fall off."

"Mr Reid said dick!" one of the younger kids yelled, and I looked over my shoulder to see a gaggle of junior schoolers.

"He did, and if you say that word again, Hunter, I will put you in detention and call your mom," Terra yelled back.

I shook my head, walking into my half of the building. I looked out over Maxton, toward town. Terra was right; we should have called today off. But people still had to work, and then there'd be teenagers roaming around Maxton in this heat, getting up to mischief.

What I really wanted was to head out to the waterfall we'd gone to years ago with Kitten. Take the whole Pack and just spend the day out there, cut off from the world. The idea made me smile. Maybe one day soon, before the cubs were born.

The bell rang, and kids started piling into my classroom, but they were languid and slow. They already stunk of sweaty teenager too, and I sighed. Hopefully my sense of smell would switch off soon.

"Who just wants to make paper fans and watch *Die Hard 3?*"

The resounding chorus of yeses had me wheeling out the ancient TV, and pulling up the movie on my phone to stream. I'd make them do the water jug challenge at the end, and call it educational.

As John McClane filled the screen, I propped my feet on my desk and relaxed. The day was heavy with heat, but when Kitten got back tonight, I was going to fill up the hot tub with cool water and make love to her until we were both pruney.

I smiled at the thought. Maybe today was going to be a good day after all.

35

KITTEN

"Leandra?" the old man gasped. "Fuck, am I dead? Have you come to guide me to Heaven?" He grimaced. "Okay, maybe not to Heaven, but you were far too sweet to end up as a Hell demon."

I frowned, because I thought maybe he was drunk, but I couldn't smell any booze on his breath. "Who's Leandra? Is she around?"

My heart was pounding. It was more than I could hope for, and given the shock on his face, I was pretty sure I'd found a name.

"Who's askin'?"

I didn't know what to say. I stood there, just staring at the grizzled old man who was in sweats that sagged in the crotch and a shirt covered in ketchup stains.

Luckily, I wasn't alone. Murphy gave the man what most would consider a disarming smile. Disarming, if his whole countenance didn't scream predator. It was like a smile on a crocodile.

"Can we come in? We just have a few questions we thought you might be able to answer."

Ol' Sam gave Murphy the stink eye. "I'm an old man, boy. I've been here a lot of years. Enough years to know you two come from up in the mountains, and I don't want nothin' to do with your lot."

He might be a slob, and probably a bit nuts, but he wasn't wrong about that. But I didn't want to go in there alone, and I didn't want to miss this chance. I couldn't risk the old guy having a coronary in his bed tonight while I was searching for the world's only non-threatening-looking Manix to accompany me.

"Sir, I'm just looking for the woman who might be my mother."

Sam indicated two shabby lawn chairs on his porch. "Sit down, girly. It's hotter than Satan's flaming ballsack today." I went over and sat, and he dropped himself down in the seat next to me with a groan. "You better start at the beginning."

I bit my lip. "I was, uh, adopted over twenty years ago, and had no idea who my birth parents are. The only lead I have to go on—and it's a bit of a long shot—is this bar and you."

Sam nodded. "No doubt in my mind you belong to Leandra. It's like looking at her twenty years ago, that's for sure."

"Does she have a last name?" Merrick asked, and I shot him a grateful smile.

Sam scowled in his direction. "Adler. Leandra Adler. Sweet girl. Sassy. She rolled into town one year, asked me for a job, and was the best bartender I ever had. She kept the patrons all in line—some because she took no shit, but mostly because they were all a little in love with her. She had a way about her, Leandra."

"Does she—"

"Just wait, girl. I'm tellin' a damn story here." I mimed zipping my lips, and he continued. "Anyway, the best bartender I ever did have. Don't know where she came from, but I appreciated her anyway. Paid her good too. Then one of you turned up." He looked at Merrick and Murphy, curling his lip. "Turned her head, he did. She went from being the best employee I had, to the worst. Always late for shifts. Always tired. None of her old pep. Then, all of a sudden she stopped turning up for work at all. No 'hey Sam, I'm moving on,' or 'Sam, I'm in trouble,' 'cause I would have helped Leandra in a heartbeat. But there was no nothin'." He sucked in a deep breath.

"Do you know where she is now?" I asked quietly, my breath burning in my lungs.

Sam looked at me sadly, and that tiny flicker of hope that still burned inside of me flickered out. "Didn't hear from her for months. Then one Sunday morning, I was heading in to open up for the after-church crowd. Noticed a couple of big trash bags beside the back door. Was getting ready to chew out the new bartender for being lazy, but they just seemed... wrong. When I opened them, I found Leandra. Pieces of her, anyway."

I bolted out of my seat and threw up over his porch rail. Hands reached out and stroked my back soothingly, but I wanted my Alphas. I'd been vain and stupid to come here without them. My stomach continued to roil, and someone handed me a handkerchief. I wiped my mouth, and stood up. Sucking in a deep breath, I composed myself and looked back at the old man.

Sam now looked older somehow, and he'd already looked ancient before. "I've seen some shit, girl, but that will haunt me to my dying day. They launched an investigation, of course, but they couldn't find any evidence. Just became another cold case, and I paid for her to be buried over at the cemetery on Fifth and Main. Don't even know if that's what she would have wanted, but I had bought an extra plot for my wife as a weddin' present, then she left me for Dan Hickey. Thought I may as well put it to use. If I have to have a grave neighbor, well, Leandra would be the best sort."

I stood up straighter and wiped my hand across my mouth. "Sorry about that."

Sam snorted. "Nah, girl. Not the first time someone puked over that rail. Though normally it's me." He gave me a gap-toothed smile, and I realized his dentures were still on the porch. I picked them up and handed them back, watching as he just stuffed them back in his mouth.

Well, that was a little gross.

"She's buried over on the boundary line at the graveyard, if you wanna go visit. No one's been there for a good while. Guess that's my bad." He frowned. "How old did you say you were?"

Now it was my turn to smile sadly. "Twenty-three."

"She disappeared to have you? Damn it, Leandra. She shoulda known I woulda helped. I mightn't have had any kids myself—hell, I'm not the paternal sort—but I liked the girl. I wouldn't have thrown her out on the street for getting knocked up." He shook his head. "If you ask me, it was one of those guys who killed her." He pointed to Merrick and Murphy, making Murphy growl near silently, until Merrick elbowed him. "Soon as she started seeing him, she changed. Made herself less. Got real skittish. Once, I saw him putting his hands on her, and me and the boys made to get my fucking shotgun and teach him a lesson, but he was gone by the time I got back. Lucky, since I woulda put a pound of lead in his giant ass."

I let out a shaky breath, giving Sam a tight smile. "Thank you for answering my questions." I had no doubt in my mind that he was right. That my father had her killed. Seemed like just his kind of thing, though no one had ever said he was a murderer. Just that he was a fucking psycho. But Lorso had always been wary of him for a reason.

Sam stood, and his whole body creaked. "No worries. I'm sorry I couldn't have given you the happily ever after you probably wanted." He frowned again. "What'd she name you?"

I shook my head. "I don't know. I was adopted as a newborn. My friends call me Kit though." Well, at least one did.

"Well, Kit. Come back if you ever wanna hear stories about your mama. I have enough of those, at least." He paused. "Were you raised alright?"

I nodded. "I was happy."

"That'll help her rest easier then. I'm glad a little piece of her lived on." He let out a wobbly breath. "Now, you better get outta here. Jeopardy's about to start." He sounded gruff, but I saw the shine in his eyes.

We said our goodbyes, and I promised to come back and visit one day. He looked... lonely, and as the only person who seemed to give a shit about my mother, I almost felt duty-bound to check on him every now and then, which was ridiculous.

But I'd still do it.

Merrick and Murphy stood close to me as we walked back to the car. "Do you want to head over to the cemetery?"

I shook my head. "No. I'll come back down with my Alphas later." It felt like something I would need them for, rather than two perfect strangers, no matter how wonderful they'd been.

It hit me then that both my parents were dead. I'd never really know what happened in the past, if it was my father who had killed Leandra Adler, or even if she was really my mother. But it felt true in my soul. It all fit too perfectly that it was hard to find a shred of doubt in there.

The guys left me with my thoughts on the way home. Maybe I'd take the cubs to her grave after they were born. I didn't think her soul would be lingering around or any of that crap, but it felt like a tribute in its own way. I could feel the rush of warmth and love from down my bonds, all of them easing my pain as much as they could from far away.

We were almost to the border of Packlands when I looked out to the north. Near where my cabin was. I thought about asking Merrick and Murphy to drop me off, maybe take a bit of time. But the more I stared, the more something looked... wrong.

"Can you stop the car?" I called, then thumped the back of the seats. "Seriously, stop the car!"

Merrick slammed on the brakes and I climbed out, tipping my nose to the wind.

Cold fear slithered through me. Oh no.

36

DARIUS

I wasn't ashamed to say I was lying under the aircon like a beached whale.

"Stop being so dramatic, D. I'm fairly sure I have a bigger stomach after too much Mexican food," Bonnie teased, rubbing my exposed belly like I was some kind of good luck charm.

"Yeah, but your burrito doesn't spend its time kicking you in the bladder," I grumbled, making her laugh. Jerk.

The kids were down for their nap, and it was one of those random times when Bonnie and I just got to hang out. Usually, we were passing like ships in the night, especially lately with the whole Omega thing— me getting a female one, Bonnie becoming one. But sometimes, I just missed my best friend.

"Bonnie, there's something I've been dying to

know…" I gave her a serious frown. "Dominic has all that big dick energy. Does he have the goods to back it up?"

Bonnie snorted, but waggled her brows. "I'll never tell," she said with a wink. I laughed, and my whole stomach jiggled with me. That wasn't something I'd ever get used to.

"Have you thought about what you're going to do when I have the cubs? You can't run this place by yourself."

She shrugged. "Courtland has talked about just subsuming them into our household and adopting them all."

My jaw literally swung open. "He wants to adopt *all* the kids?" My respect for Courtland went through the roof, but on the other hand, I also thought he was insane.

Bonnie smiled. "He's a lot softer than people think. The kids come over for dinner a few nights a week anyway, so they're all comfortable. We have the space, we have a whole houseful of kids anyway, and they all get along. It makes sense. Taylor will probably want to move out soon, and we'll help him get an apartment, if that's what he wants." She looked at me. "Will you be sad without the Sanctum? You can come and babysit anytime, I promise."

Would I be sad without the Sanctum? Absolutely. I loved this home that we'd built for the kids, but what Bonnie was offering them? That was a family, and I wanted that for each of them more than anything else.

"Sad, yes. But happy as well." I sighed. "I guess I'll be busy too though."

She grinned, patting the belly again. Definitely an Omega trait, the touchy-feely stuff.

I lay back and reached for my connection with Kitten. She'd been sad earlier, which had torn at my heartstrings. Either she'd found nothing, or what she did find wasn't what she'd hoped. I'd ask her about it tonight, hold her while she cried the tears I could feel her bottling up inside.

I was dozing off when a sudden jolt of her fear had me rocketing upright. Bonnie jumped to her feet. "Darius? What's wrong? Is it the cubs?" She was in front of me, looking me over for injuries or pain.

"No, it's Kitten. She's panicked. Scared." I scrabbled for my phone and called her, but she didn't pick up. Fuck. I tried Merrick, but it was Murphy who answered.

"Darius!" he yelled, and it sounded like he was panting.

"What's wrong? Is Kitten okay?"

"She's fine, but we have a massive fucking problem. A wildfire's started just outside the north-western border of the Packlands. Fuck, this wind is bad. Darius, I need you to start getting the Sanctum ready to evacuate. I'll get your girl back to you as soon as possible. I have to go."

"No, wait—" But he'd hung up.

Fear like I'd never known spread through me. Bonnie stood in front of me, her face pale. She would have heard all of that. She shook her head, the panic being replaced by cool determination. "I'll call Courtland. Or Radic. Let them know if they don't already, and find out the fire plan." She froze. "Oh no. Rosa is out with the damn goats, clearing undergrowth. Shit." She pulled her phone out and started frantically calling.

Fuck, we needed to get shit together. I raced to the hall cupboard and pulled out a couple of suitcases. We needed to pack supplies for the little ones. Everyone's documentation would be needed from the office filing cabinet. All the car seats, blankets and some pillows, just in case. Food and water.

I punched in Corvin's number, and he answered immediately. "Darius, the bond is going crazy—what's wrong?" I tried to keep my voice steady as I told him about the wildfire. About Kitten being out there, and about possibly evacuating the Sanctum.

I needed Kitten to be here with me right now. I needed her close and safe.

Corvin swore softly under his breath, though he sounded entirely calm when he said, "It'll be okay, Omega. Stay there at the Sanctum, and leave with

Bonnie if you have to, okay? I'll check everything out, and if I can, I'll come and get you. Don't do anything dumb. I'll find Kitten and bring her home, but you have to protect the cubs first and foremost, Darius. They are your focus."

"Yes."

"Good Omega," he purred down the phone. "Now, take care of your charges and I'll keep you updated. I'm ringing Cooper and Beckett now. If I can, I'll send Cooper to you." He paused. "I love you."

"I love you too."

Then he was gone. Beckett would have to evacuate the school kids if it came down to it, and I knew that was why Corvin would only send Cooper to me, but selfishly, I wanted them all right here.

Instead, I got back to work. I started with the blankets, taking them out to the Sanctum van and laying them on the floors. Now that I was outside, I could smell the smoke and see it in the distance. It was close, but didn't seem too threatening. But the heat of the day was already unbearable, and a breeze was beginning to pick up.

I began loading all the supplies, glad the children were still sleeping so I could let my panic run free for a little longer before I had to be someone else's rock.

Bonnie was off the phone, and she looked as freaked out as I felt. "Courtland confirmed it. He said the fire's growing and almost inaccessible by land at the moment. We have to wait for the humans to mobilize their resources, because we can't get water to it from the ground. He said we should prepare to evacuate. He's sending over Dominic now."

I wanted to tell her that I was scared too. Scared for my brand new Pack, for my cubs, and for the woman I might lose before I even had a chance to love her properly. I hoped Merrick or Murphy had manhandled her back to town, because I knew Kitten. The cabin would be the first thing to go if that fire started moving toward Maxton. She'd fight it with a bucket and her bare hands if she had to.

"Let's get the kids back from school if we can," I told Bonnie, kicking us both back into gear. I picked up the phone and called Beckett. There was no time for panic now.

37

KITTEN

For the first time in my life, the Beast who shared my soul roared in frustration that I couldn't shift. If I were Beast, I could run faster, be more protected, be *more*.

"Kitten, where the fuck are you going?" Murphy shouted from behind me.

"Wildfire!" I yelled back, pointing at the haze to the west of us.

Murphy sprinted a little faster, getting in front of me so he could run backwards, looking at me. I took back all my good opinions of the man. Fucking showoff.

"Are you sure?"

This time, I stopped dead. Murphy tried to brake, but stopping suddenly while running backwards was harder than it looked. He stumbled backwards and landed on his ass. Merrick caught up, and didn't even laugh at the fact that Murphy had just gone head over heels in the dirt.

"I'm sure. Smell the air? You can taste the smoke. Feel it. Hear it. The animals are disturbed—they're running to find shelter already. That hot wind? It's going to pick up this evening, or maybe even sooner, and with it the fire will rage."

Merrick nodded. "I believe you. But what are you going to do running toward it? We have no water, nothing we can use to put it out."

I shook my head as my heart raced. "The kids are out here with the goats. It's their third day as goatherds. They should be in the western quadrant."

Murphy swore. "Let's go. Merrick, call the Alpha General," he grunted, and we started running again.

Ten minutes later, I stopped, looking for the telltale signs of a large herd of goats. "We're in the right place, but they could be anywhere within a six mile radius. ROSA! ERIS!"

A shout sounded in the distance, and we took off in that direction. The smoke was getting thicker, and my heart began to sink. I was still hoping that we could maybe figure out a way to put out the flames. But the thickening of the smoke meant it was picking up speed and burning harder.

"Over here!" Eris yelled again.

We raced toward the sound of his voice, and soon

enough I could see the red of his shirt. The world went silent as I saw the unconscious girl in his arms. Around him, one or two goats lingered, but there was no sign of the rest. Too close, I could hear the crackle of fire. Birds were fleeing overhead, and I could see deer scattering through the trees.

Merrick stepped close to Eris, who was pacing and pale. Merrick's Alpha power swelled until it encompassed us all. "Be calm. What happened?"

"It was an accident. Everything was fine, we had lunch, and then walked the goats a little further into the woods, but when we came back, all our stuff was on fire. I don't even know..." He trailed off, shaking his head over and over again.

I put my hand on his arm. "It doesn't matter right now," I said slowly. "What happened to Rosa?"

Eris swallowed hard. "I told her we should run and get help, but she said we couldn't leave the goats out here to burn. She'd named them. I told her she shouldn't name the stupid animals. You get attached," he choked out, his voice growing tight. "She was trying to herd them back toward town, but they were panicked and one knocked her and she tripped and hit her head on a rock and now she won't wake up."

Shit. I checked her head, and there was a pretty big lump and a gash right on the side of her skull. Fuck. "She needs to see Tanner right now."

Merrick took control again. "Do you have an ATV out here?"

Eris shook his head. "We herd the goats out here on foot, then herd them back to their pen in the evening."

"Fuck." Merrick fished his keys from his pocket. "Give her to me and shift. Now, Eris!"

The boy gently passed her over and shed his clothes, shifting into his Manix form immediately. I grabbed his shirt, twisting it slightly and wrapping it around Rosa's neck to support it. It was an old field medicine trick Lorso taught me, like setting a nose. I'd never had to use it before though. I didn't think she had spinal damage, but couldn't be sure.

Merrick passed her back to Eris. "Go quickly, but don't jolt her around. My car is on the road south-east of here. Take her straight there and then drive to the new doctor, Tanner. *Do not stop*—do you understand me?" It was an Alpha command, and though Eris was an Alpha too, he was still just a kid.

Eris nodded, cradling Rosa's head to his chest, his arms holding her like she was a doll. He moved smoothly and quickly through the trees, and I ran in the other direction, further into the woods. The fire wasn't far away now. I could taste it on the air, like a demon coming from Hell to destroy everything in its path. We needed to see though. Needed to judge.

"I'm going up to look," I called, scaling the closest tree. I ignored their shouts and climbed faster. I'd climbed hundreds of trees in my life; I wasn't going to fall. When I got to the top, I hissed out a breath. The fire was bigger than I thought, acres of flames spread out on the horizon.

There was nothing I could do. Absolutely nothing. Trees were already alight, and I could feel the wind picking up. We had no chance, as the embers would float on the breeze.

I looked down and spotted the remaining goats running around frantically, but not in the right direction. To the left, I could almost spot my home. Tears flooded my eyes, but I blinked them back. No time. I climbed back down quickly, landing in a crouch.

"I see where you get the nickname now," Murphy said jokingly, but it was weak. I gave him a tight smile.

"There's nothing we can do. Call Courtland and tell him to get onto the human authorities. There aren't even any fire trails out that side. They're going to need to do aerial drops." I took off running again.

"Stop, Omega!" Merrick shouted, with his Alpha voice again, making my feet slow and my teeth grind. "You're going toward the flames."

"I'm aware of that, *Alpha*. But the goat herd is just there, and if we can push them south, they'll have a better chance of surviving." I didn't keep the venom from my voice. I wasn't a fucking inept child. I knew these woods better than these men ever would.

Murphy whistled at my fierce expression. "Go, Omega." I ran, grabbing a big stick, but not before I heard him tell his Packmate, "I'd sleep with one eye open until she forgives you, Rick."

The goats bleated in a circle about three hundred feet away, and I got behind them easily. "Hyuh! Come on, you hairy dumbasses." Waving my stick, I sent the panicked beasts off at a run in the right direction. I'd do what I could, but then they were on their own.

By the time I got back to Merrick and Murphy, the goats were running at a good speed. "Keep driving them back toward town," I shouted at Merrick over the increasing crackle of the fire, before turning and running further north.

"Where the fuck are you *going?!*"

"Home!" I shouted, and I heard them swear.

Soon enough, Murphy was right behind me. "I'm going to assume you don't mean Maxton?"

I shook my head. I needed to get my memories. My things. Everything that made me Kitten was in that cabin; what little history I did have was locked up tight in an ammo box. Everything that was left of Lorso. I had to try and save some of it.

Murphy shifted between one step and the next, and suddenly there was a fully grown Manix beside me. "Let me run, I'll carry you. It will be faster," he growled in a voice an entire octave lower than his human voice. He didn't need to put Alpha power into it

—it was already there, like a blanket that flowed over your skin.

I wasn't going to argue. I quickly climbed onto his back, and he took off toward the last remnant of the person I used to be.

38

COOPER

Everyone was panicking. I was panicking. Corvin's phone call had made ice-cold fear seep through my veins. I still couldn't get hold of Kitten, and the panic in our bond was driving me crazy.

As soon as word got to us that there was a wildfire, we'd dropped everything at the job site and dispersed. Some of the guys would head to the Legion offices to defend against the fire, but guys like me and Finlo, who had Packs and families? We would be useless. The need to be with our Omegas would overrule every other rational thought. There was only one thing the Beast wanted in an emergency, and that was the safety of the Pack. As far as my Beast was concerned, the rest of Maxton could rot, as long as my Pack was safe.

People were swarming everywhere, making the

roads busy. We lived in the mountains, so the town itself had a fairly decent wildfire plan, but sometimes even the best plans meant nothing. I swung into the driveway of the Sanctum and was off the ATV before it had even rolled to a full stop. I burst through the front door and the relief I felt at just seeing Darius threatened to make my knees give out.

"Cooper." His voice was wobbly, and I had him wrapped in my arms in seconds.

"It's all good, D. It's going to be fine," I soothed. I looked around the Sanctum, noticing that Pryce— Bonnie's Omega mate—was there with his cubs strapped to his chest, as well as Dominic, who was her other Packmate and Courtland's second-in-command.

"What do you need?"

Bonnie shook her head. "Nothing, really. The SUVs are loaded up with everything we might need, as well as some of Tanner's first aid supplies. Courtland says they've got a couple of buses on standby to ferry everyone out if a full evacuation is needed, because ATVs will only get us so far. He said he's managed to secure an entire town about four hours away, and if need be, we can all relocate there until the danger has passed."

I nodded, because it all sounded reasonable to me. I just felt useless. "Do you need us?"

Bonnie shook her head. "Go home. Find your mates. Get prepared."

I gave her a serious look. "Don't wait, Bonnie. You should go now. You guys have been through enough already."

She pinned me with a soul-piercing expression. "Take care of them, Coop." The 'or else' was implied, but she didn't need to say that to me. If anything happened to any of my Pack... I couldn't even think about it.

"Call us if you need any help. We're here if you need us." I hustled Darius out the door and onto the ATV. "Any word from Corvin? Beckett?" I swallowed hard. "Kitten?"

He shook his head. "Beckett is contacting parents and he'll have to go with the kids whose parents can't collect them. Corvin is searching for Kitten."

I raced toward our Packhouse. We'd pack what we could, but the rest was up to the Goddess to protect. We rounded the corner, and came face to face with an SUV. "Fuck!"

I swerved, skidding out on the shoulder of the road, and the SUV swerved too, ending up in a ditch on the other side. I hit the brakes, and looked over at Darius.

"You okay?" I yelled at Darius, checking him over. "The cubs?"

"We're fine, Coop. Who the fuck is that? Isn't that Merrick's vehicle?"

I leapt out of the ATV, sprinting to the car in the ditch. Ripping open the passenger door, my heart stopped at the sight of blood and a woman's body on the back seat. "*Kitten?*"

As my brain caught up, I realized it wasn't Kitten, but Rosa, the Alpha General's little sister. In the driver's seat was Eris, one of the young Manix Alphas.

"What the fuck happened?"

Eris looked pale. "She hit her head. They said I had to get her to Doc Tanner. I don't fucking know how to drive!" The panic in his voice was nearing hysteria.

I sucked in a deep breath and calmed my tone. "It's all good, kid. I'm here now; we've got this." I looked over my shoulder. "Darius!" I called, before looking back at Eris. "Scootch over, okay? I'll get you both to the Doc's office in one piece."

Darius pulled open the back door, and he gaped at the girl in the back. But not for longer than a breath, because then he was sliding in beside her and slamming the door. I quickly backed the SUV out of the ditch and drove back toward town, looking in the rearview mirror at Darius, who was checking her pulse.

"How long has she been out?" he asked Eris, pumping those calming Omega hormones out into the air like they were Vicodin.

"About fifteen minutes? She woke up halfway to the car, but then fell unconscious again."

I frowned. That was a long time, but hopefully her shifter nature might protect her a little more.

I pulled gently to a stop in front of the doctor's office. "Go get Tanner and the spinal board, okay?" I told the boy loudly. If he could hear it, Tanner would too. The vampires had some crazy good hearing. "D, call Bonnie and tell her Rosa's here. Someone needs to be here with her."

Darius nodded, his phone already out. Tanner appeared, Eris in tow, along with a spinal board. I was right. He could hear us out here.

"Slow down, mate. Now, start from the beginning. Where did she hit her head?" As Tanner slowly pumped Eris for information, I helped him maneuver Rosa from the back seat with as little movement as possible. Though, if she did have spinal damage, that horse had probably already bolted, considering Eris had apparently sprinted with her to the car and then nearly crashed her into a ditch. I didn't say that though; the kid was already panicking. If she did have any major injuries, hopefully her shifter healing and Tanner's surgery skills could fix them.

I carried her into the doctor's office, then helped Tanner shift her to the bed. Eris didn't leave her side, and after the second time Tanner had to tell him to move, I pulled him back to the waiting room. "Stay here, Eris. Call your parents to come and get you."

Eris shook his head. "This is my fault. I'm not leaving her until she wakes up." I could have argued with him, but the set of his jaw told me that it was no use. He was in shock too, and no amount of logic would break through the haze right now.

"Okay, but call your parents anyway, because they'll be freaking out." I paused. "The Omega with Merrick and Murphy—where is she now?"

Eris shook his head. "They were still in the forest. I think they were trying to herd the goats back or something."

Fuck. Fuck, fuck, fuck. "Where's the fire?"

"North-west, over by the Fucking Tree."

Damn, I'd forgotten about the Fucking Tree. It was the name high school kids had given a particular tree formation, where a tree had fallen over but remained rooted. Another trunk had grown pressed up behind it, making it look like they were doing it doggystyle.

The Fucking Tree was reasonably close to Lorso's cabin. Kitten might be herding goats toward home, but she'd head to the cabin as well. I knew it in my bones.

I looked at Eris. "Call your parents. Do not move from here unless they tell you to, or unless we have to evacuate, understand?" He nodded.

I ran back outside, and slid into the SUV, with Darius now in the passenger seat. What the hell did we do with Merrick's car now? Fuck it. I was going to kick their fucking asses for letting Kitten run headfirst into a goddamn forest fire.

"Call Corvin. She's at the cabin. I know it," I told Darius.

I listened as he told Corvin everything that happened, and heard Corvin swear.

"She'll be going back to save Lorso's stuff. That old box she used to keep under her bed," he muttered. "I'll get her. Don't worry, Omega. You just get home and take care of yourself. Cooper, pack up our shit. If this goes pear-shaped, I won't risk Darius and the cubs."

"Already on it, Corvin. You just bring her home."

39

KITTEN

By the time I made it to the cabin, I knew I was being an idiot. The smoke was thick and beginning to burn my lungs, but it didn't make me stop. I ripped open the front door, knowing where I was going even with the blinding smoke. I could have found my treasure box with my eyes closed. I could have drawn a picture of every single thing in there with intimate detail.

I dived beneath the bed, grabbing the handle of the box. It held my last remaining memories of the man who raised me, the last vestiges of the girl I once was. This might have been a gamble, but it was one I had to make. I should have brought it into town earlier, but it felt like it had belonged out here. I was such an idiot.

I took one more look around the cabin that had been my sanctuary, my home, for as long as I'd been alive. I knew that come tomorrow, even if they held the fire back from Maxton, my home would be gone.

I tucked the box under my arm and went back to an anxious-looking Murphy. His eyes were bouncing around the cabin, taking it all in with the eyes of a well-trained soldier. I coughed a little on the smoke, and his eyes darted back to me, his brow scrunched in concern.

"We really need to go." I nodded, and his face softened. "This was your home? The place you grew up?"

I stepped back onto the porch, then leapt down to the grass. "Yes. Lorso is buried over there. Maybe I should dig him up so he finally gets the cremation he wanted."

It was a dark joke, and Murphy was looking at me like I'd gone nuts. "Lorso? *The* Lorso?"

Ah, he didn't know. "Yep. Old as hell. Crotchety. The best Manix I may ever know, though you only remember nice things about the dead, right?"

"Holy shit," he muttered, taking the box from me. "Jump on, Kitten. We need to get the fuck out of here before we all get cremated."

I leapt onto his back, but we didn't make it far when an ATV pulled into a clearing by the trees. Corvin jumped off, racing toward me, and he looked furious.

Murphy made an *uh-oh* noise and promptly dropped me back onto my feet. "Your Alpha looks pissed that we're out here in the middle of a fucking forest fire," he whispered under his breath.

"Kitten, are you insane? It's a fucking wildfire! One shift of the wind and you could've been trapped and burnt to a crisp." Corvin turned to Murphy. "I'll have words with you later."

Murphy snorted. "Don't threaten me with a good time, Corvin Fletcher. But if it's all the same to you, I say we get the fuck out of here."

Corvin bent down and picked me up bodily, sprinting back to the ATV. I could feel the wind picking up, blowing smoke and embers ahead of the flames. Murphy was right; we needed to get out of here, so I didn't protest being manhandled like a sack of potatoes.

Corvin stuck me on the back of the ATV, and Murphy dropped my treasure box in my lap. He climbed up the front beside Corvin, and we roared away. I watched the one place I felt like me—truly and one hundred percent like Girl, the person I'd been before Kitten—disappear into the distance. That girl would burn with the building, and I was the only person who'd mourn her loss.

We made it back to Maxton well ahead of the fire, but if I was right, the late afternoon breeze was about to pick it up and turn it from a lazy forest fire into a ravenous, insatiable beast.

"You have to drive us to see the Alpha General. He

needs to know to evacuate. There'll be no fighting this once the wind changes. The whole forest will go up like a tinderbox."

Corvin gritted his teeth but drove toward the Legion building. "Fine. You go in, deliver your warning, and then we get the fuck out of here, okay? No arguments."

He must have taken my silence as an agreement, and I didn't disabuse him of the idea. If he thought he was getting an Omega who blindly took orders, he was going to be sorely mistaken. But I didn't want to hang around either. Not really.

We dropped Murphy off at the Legion building too. "I have to go and find Merrick and... Yeah. Kitten, I'd like to say it was a pleasure but honestly, it was an emotional rollercoaster." He grinned at me. "If you ever want to leave this growly fuck..."

Corvin bared his teeth, and I swallowed down a laugh. Murphy tipped an imaginary hat, then ran off.

I sat there holding the box of memories, unsure if I should take it with me or not. Corvin took the decision from me, taking it and tucking it under his arm like it weighed nothing. He knew I wouldn't want to leave it behind or lose it.

Tears welled in my eyes, and he pulled me close to his chest with his free hand. "I'm sorry I was snappy. I was worried."

I sniffed softly. "I know. I'm sorry for worrying you."

I pulled back. "She's dead. My mother. Murdered and stuffed into a trash bag."

I saw his heart break for me, and eventually, I knew that's how I would feel too. Once I had time to process that there was nothing else for me to find. No more answers out there, waiting for me to uncover them. No mother who'd wrap me in her arms and tell me she was sorry for abandoning me in a fucking forest.

Okay, there were some serious issues going on here, but I'd unpack it all later. I took the stairs three at a time, and the inside of the Legion building was a hive of people. Things were being moved around, people yelling on the walkie-talkies. Everyone was going nuts.

I walked quickly through to the Alpha General's office, and found a slightly pale but calm Radic.

"Kitten! It's good to see you safe."

"How's Rosa? Is she okay?"

Radic gave a worried nod. "Tanner says she's fine, just a nasty concussion. Might have been a different story if you weren't out there though."

Courtland appeared in the doorway. "Indeed. We owe you a debt."

I waved a hand. It had been my fault they were out there anyway. "Eris should get all the thanks. He was well on the way to rescuing her when we arrived." I stepped closer to them both. "Alpha General, it's my opinion that you evacuate the town now. Don't wait. It'll burn through hard and fast if the wind changes."

Courtland let out a low growl that might have also been a sigh. "They are resistant to leaving. Most want to stay and defend the town."

Corvin snorted. "We don't have the resources for that. The reservoirs would only hold maybe two or three hours of firefighting."

Courtland shrugged. "I can force the elderly, the children and those more susceptible to smoke inhalation. The half-bloods. I can make them all go. But there is very little I can do to persuade each and every Alpha to leave their home. By the time I got to the last one and used an Alpha command to make him go, the town would be up in flames anyway." The frustration in his voice was searing. "It is better to live than defend some bricks and mortar, but they don't see it like that."

Corvin shook his head. "Most won't. I won't take a chance with my Pack though. We'll be gone as soon as we get back to the Packhouse and collect everyone."

Radic grabbed a piece of paper and handed it to me. On it was an address for somewhere called Moonburst, and the phone number of a person. The name didn't look familiar, but then I didn't know many people.

But apparently Corvin did. "Holy shit, Loren survived?" he gasped.

Who the hell was Loren?

Sensing my confusion, Courtland addressed me as well. "Loren is a witch and one of my oldest friends. He helped secure Maxton with me during both the Alpha fights, and we thought he'd fallen saving my Beta from an assassination attempt." He looked over at Corvin. "My men found him eventually, though we thought we would be burying him. Instead, we found him convalescing with a coven of witches up near the border." Courtland smirked. "He seemed... content." His face lost all its mirth. "I called about our predicament, and he talked with the coven. They've offered us refuge for the time being, should we need it. Do you truly believe we'll need it?" he asked me softly.

"Yes."

I didn't have an attachment to this town the way that the rest of my Pack did, or even Radic. But I was beginning to form attachments with some of the people here, not just my Pack. I really liked the De Léon Pack, especially Bonnie. I had a brother and nieces and nephews here now. I wanted everyone to be safe. And if that meant being a pessimist, then so be it. I would cry doomsday and either everyone would live, or it wouldn't matter anyway.

"Okay, we'll head to Moonburst now and coordinate from there."

"Go with Dom, Pryce, Bonnie and the Sanctum kids. Dom knows what to do at the other end, and I'd appreciate any help with keeping everything calm and in order, Omega."

Shit. I didn't really know how to use my Omega

vibes for anything other than crazy sex, but I guess there was no time like the present to learn. "I'll do what I can, Alpha General."

Corvin cleared his throat. "Be safe—we're kind of used to you now. You aren't a captain, and this isn't a ship; you don't have to go down with it. If they won't leave, you don't have to stand guard over their stupidity."

As another frantic-looking Manix burst in, Courtland just nodded to us both. "I'll keep that in mind, Alpha. Now go."

40

CORVIN

Despite what I'd said to the Alpha General, it wasn't as easy to leave my home as I thought. All our Pack firsts had happened in this house. I wanted our cubs to be born here. But in the end, they were just things, and my real home was not a place, but the four people in front of me.

We had to leave on the ATV, at least until we got to a nearby town, where we could get a hire car. But this meant we could only take as much as we could carry. Unlike Kitten, whose memories fit in a small metal box, ours were spread all across our house. Framed photographs of us as a pack, ticket stubs from the first concert we saw together. The table where I made love to Darius for the first time.

The hardest thing was dragging Darius from his nest. He was so close to term that all he wanted to do was nest and prepare, and I was dragging him into unknown territory with a bunch of witches we didn't know. Normally, he was the most level-headed of us all, but some things were ruled by instinct, not logic.

My own instincts rebelled at the idea of leaving safe territory to go anywhere near an unknown—and probably pretty powerful—group of paranormals. But the urge to protect my Pack overruled everything.

"Let's go, D," I said softly. He'd wrapped up one of the soft throws into a garbage bag to keep the scent in, and had it pressed close to his body. Kitten was still out the front, watching the horizon, and I wondered if I should call her in here to try some of that Omega soothing. But Darius just nodded, clenching his jaw and heading toward the stairs. At the bottom, a small pile of duffle bags encapsulated our entire life.

Beckett hung up the phone and looked up at Darius. "You okay?"

Darius nodded, adding his bag to the pile. "Your mom?"

Beckett's mom had never remarried or gotten a Pack. She was alone, and it worried us all in emergencies. We'd offered to move her into the Packhouse once, and while she was grateful, it had been a resounding hell no.

"She got on the first bus out of here. They're doing a run around the town, collecting people, and then they shouldn't be far behind us. I put all the kids who hadn't been collected on that bus too. My mom will keep them in line, and I need to be here with you guys." Beckett's mom had been a teacher as well. He picked up a few of the duffles. "There's a car waiting for us in the town; I've organized to swap it for the ATV. We'll just have to get a new one when we come back."

It wouldn't matter really. If the mountain burned like Kitten was convinced it would, there'd be no reason to have an ATV anymore. Besides, we'd need a car for the cubs.

I nodded. "Let's go then."

Cooper was standing behind Kitten, who was looking at the trees in the distance like she was having a silent conversation with them. Her face was pinched with worry, and when a gust of wind blew at her dark hair, I knew why.

She looked over at us. "Wind is picking up. We need to go."

We all loaded into the ATV, with the bags tied onto the back. It was actually considered a UTV, but we'd been calling them ATV's for so long that it stuck.

Then we left, leaving it all behind. All we could do was pray to the Goddess that it would be there when we got back.

Something told me that this was goodbye though.

.   .   .

THE GUY we were buying the car off had rolled up with a look on his face that said he was ready to screw us, but by the time Beckett and I had uncurled ourselves to our full height, his face had changed pretty damn quick.

We'd left Cooper, Darius and Kitten on the edge of town, because a pregnant man might have been too much for the townies. The trade had been quick—the SUV was actually not bad—and we were on our way to Moonburst. If I hadn't already known it was a witch colony, the name alone would have given it away.

Soon enough, we'd caught up to the De Léon Pack —probably because they had so many small children, which meant six million toilet breaks. According to Beckett, behind us was the first busload of Maxton residents. Kitten also mentioned that Gatlin and the Huxley-Grey Pack had intended to stay and defend the property, but Naja had convinced them it was better to leave, so they were just coming down off the mountain now.

Kitten was taking the whole thing surprisingly well, but then again, this wasn't her first upheaval. She'd already left her home and started somewhere new. It was Darius who was worrying me the most. He seemed forlorn and listless.

Kitten and Cooper sat in the back with him, and even I felt zen with the amount of Omega happy pheromones Kitten was throwing out. But they didn't seem to be working on our other Omega. I had no platitudes that would help either, so silence reigned throughout the car.

After a little while, Kitten fell asleep against Darius's shoulder, and he nodded off as well, his head resting on hers. They looked peaceful together, these two beings who were worth sacrificing everything for. I would lay down my life for either of them in a heartbeat.

"Did Murphy say anything about how she went at Ol' Sam's?" Beckett asked softly, and I shook my head.

"No, but her mother has gone to the Goddess. In quite a brutal way, if what she said in passing was true. Murdered," I whispered back.

Cooper sucked in a sharp breath. "The old Alpha General? Her father?"

I shrugged. Without knowing the details, I couldn't confirm anything. I felt so bad for my Kitten. Not having the answers would drive her mad. I'd just have to keep her so busy that she wouldn't have time to dwell on the past.

It was nearly midnight when our convoy finally arrived in Moonburst, Montana. The streets were barely lit, and from what I could see, it looked almost abandoned. Shopfronts were boarded up, driveways empty. It had a stillness about it that screamed ghost town.

"Kinda creepy," Coop muttered, as we drove through to the only lit up building in the town.

Parking out the front of a little cottage, I could see three people standing on the porch. One was Loren, and I recognized him immediately. I'd talked to him a few times when he lived in Maxton, and I liked the guy. I'd been sad when we thought he'd died during the coup.

Beside him was a small woman with long, silver hair, though she looked young. On the other side of her was an older woman with salt and pepper hair that sat almost straight up like she'd been electrocuted, and had tiny beads strung through it. Honestly, her hair seemed to defy gravity, or like she was trying to be the Halloween stereotype of a witch. She smiled broadly, and one gold tooth glinted in the headlights.

Dominic got out first from the vehicle in front of us, and I slid quietly from our car too. I looked at Cooper. "Stay with the Omegas," I said softly so they didn't wake. They were exhausted, and I wanted to just wrap them up in cotton wool to keep them safe and happy forever.

Beckett climbed out from the other side, and we went to stand near Dom. The group looked harmless, but you could never be sure with witches.

Dom didn't seem to have the same hesitation though, because he ran at Loren, wrapping him up in a hug that would have cracked a lesser man's spine. "It's so, so fucking good to see you, brother," he whispered, slapping his back. Then he pulled back and punched him hard in the gut.

The woman beside Loren gasped, her hands clenching and the feel of magic in the air making my skin tingle. I stepped forward, growling low, and Loren straightened up, wheezing and laughing at the same time.

"I fucking thought you were dead. You sent me back through that fucking portal and I thought you were *dead!*" Dominic hissed, then hugged him again.

"I'd do it again," Loren told him, coughing a couple of times.

Dominic shook his head. "I know you would, you self-sacrificing bastard."

"You can talk," Loren sniped back. "Dominic, this is Electra. She's who your Goddess sent me when I was dying. Lucky too, because I was about to be food for the coyotes and the worms." He indicated the pretty silver-haired witch. Then he pointed to the one with the crazy hair. "And this is the leader of the Moonburst coven, Wilbur."

"Wilbur? No offense, ma'am, but isn't that a man's name?" Dominic said curiously.

Wilbur shrugged. "I had an accident in 1973, and just went with it. Easier to have tits than to summon an *Averialati* demon to turn me back—trust me on that. If you want my advice, don't do magic while you're downing your weight in shrooms, kids."

I blinked. Then I blinked again. The woman—I think?—was grinning a little wildly, so maybe those shrooms did a lot more damage than just one spell gone bad.

The silver-haired girl, Electra, rolled her eyes and sighed, while Loren looked like he was having a hard time holding back his laughter. He looked past Dominic at me and Beckett.

"Hey guys, it's good to see you." His face fell, all mirth gone. "Sorry it's not under better circumstances though. Come on, we'll get you all settled. Courtland gave us a heads up, so we've spent most of the day with the coven, cleaning out some of the houses." He wandered down the steps. "Used to be a big oil refinery out here, but eventually the well dried up and the workers all left. Place is basically a ghost town now. Electra and Wilbur live out here, along with a couple of others in the coven, but all the humans left a decade ago. The places still need some work, but they're liveable."

Loren looked over our shoulder, and I could see the lights of the bus in the distance. He fanned his fingers, and a small blue orb that flashed like a sparkler appeared in front of us. "Follow the blue orb and it'll take you to what it decides is the best house for you.

Like the sorting hat in Harry Potter, but with real estate."

"Okay..." Beckett said incredulously.

Witches. They were so fucking weird. Still, we climbed back in our car and followed the bright blue orb down the street. Luckily, it traveled pretty slowly. It led us past five cross streets to the aptly named Sixth Street, and then to the third driveway down from that. Every other house around us was dark, so I assumed this wasn't one of the witch-inhabited areas.

The house in front of us was a double-story one, with a wraparound porch and large front windows. A tree with a tire swing stood in the front yard, and it had a large barn shed out the back. It was pretty damn picturesque, even in the darkness.

It wasn't perfect, of course. Even from here I could see that the porch roof was sagging, and the paint was peeling from the cladding. There was a missing step, and we hadn't even opened the front door yet.

But it gave me a good feeling, and when Darius woke up, he smiled at the sagging house. That was enough for me.

41

BECKETT

I sat on the second story landing, watching tiny glowing orbs race around the town of Moon-burst. They were every color in the rainbow, and they adapted their speed to the people they were assigned to; if you were walking, it would plod along in front of you at a reasonable pace. If you were in a car, it traveled a solid ten miles per hour to get you where you needed to go. It was a pretty awesome piece of magic. My mom had messaged me and said she'd been put in a sweet little row of cabins on Third Street, and I was glad she wasn't too far away. The orbs really were like the sorting hat.

"It's pretty magical, isn't it? But I've never seen a place with so few trees," Kitten said, coming to sit beside me on the deck. It seemed pretty structurally sound when I stepped out here, but Cooper was going to have a good look at it in the morning.

I pulled Kitten onto my lap, and she snuggled against my chest. "We're in part of the Great Plains. Not many trees out this way. Does it make you unhappy?"

She shook her head. "No. I'll learn to listen to the plains the same way I listened to the forest."

I stiffened. "Has anyone heard from Courtland? About what happened to Maxton?"

We'd been watching the news, but as far as the human world was concerned, the only thing up in those mountains was an abandoned logging village. How we'd gotten away with that for so long in the age of satellites was a mystery.

She shook her head. "No, but the orbs moved the De Léon Pack right next door. And the Huxley-Grey Pack the next street over. Guess they wanted to keep all the Omega Packs together." She shrugged. "Anyway, Darius and Cooper are over there helping settle the children, so maybe they'll have news when they come back."

The human news mightn't mention Maxton by name, but the fire was now big enough to warrant television coverage, and it didn't look good at all. Half the mountain was on fire.

I rubbed my hands up and down her arms. "This isn't the life we promised you. I'm sorry." I breathed in her scent, drawing it right into my lungs.

"Beckett, this was exactly what you promised. That you'd take care of me, love me, and be there when I needed you most. I don't blame you for natural disasters." She kissed me softly, and for just a moment, I leaned on her too.

We fell silent again as another bus rolled into town. Those little orbs would be exhausted by the end of the night.

We watched until the sun was just lightening the sky. The horizon seemed so far away when it wasn't impeded by trees or mountains. It looked like a wide expanse of nothingness, and I found it both daunting and comforting. There weren't even any other towns nearby, which was probably why the humans had moved away.

The door downstairs banged shut—you had to bang it since it was warped and wouldn't shut properly otherwise—and I scented Darius. More specifically, his tears. Kitten was off my lap and through the door into the house before I'd even twitched, but I wasn't far behind her.

When we made it to the foyer, the rest of our Pack was huddled in a tight circle. Darius's eyes welled with unshed tears, and Cooper looked pale.

"What happened?"

"It's all gone," Cooper whispered.

I reared back. "All of it? Courtland? Rad?"

Darius sniffed. "They just arrived. Rad said they

fought until the wall of fire was too great. Still, we lost five Manix. Some wouldn't leave, others got trapped behind the lines. Courtland looks... devastated."

He'd feel every single one of those losses, even though it wasn't his fault. He'd given everyone an opportunity to leave. Stayed and fought the fire beside them. But it wouldn't help with the guilt, I knew that in my soul.

"Who?"

Darius shook his head. "I don't know."

In a population as small as Maxton, it was likely we knew them. Would I be missing the faces of friends or neighbors tomorrow?

"Let's go upstairs and get some sleep. You need to rest, D," Corvin said quietly, lifting our Omega into his arms and carrying him back to the ground floor bedroom where we'd put all the mattresses and given him the beginnings of a nest, just in case the worst happened. Which was looking more and more likely that it had actually happened. Now, we'd have to thoroughly add our scents to the room, find him things he could use to furnish it before the cubs came. And then...

And then what? What would we do now? Go back and rebuild?

Exhaustion pulled at me, and I only managed to remove my shirt and jeans. I couldn't be bothered bending down to remove my socks. Kitten snuggled against my chest, her fingers curled in mine where they rested on Darius's stomach. Cooper lay further down the nest, his body curled around Darius's hip, his head just beneath Kitten's breasts. Corvin was on the other side of Darius, closest to the door. Our last line of defense.

"I love you guys," Kitten whispered into the darkness. "I'm sorry."

"We have each other, and these guys," Coop said, rubbing Darius's stomach, "who are already getting brownie points for staying where they are for the duration of this damn saga."

I huffed a laugh, my eyes slowly closing. He had that shit right. No matter how precarious things were right now, I was still the luckiest man alive.

TWO DAYS WERE SPENT JUST... adjusting to the new normal. This was aided by the fact that Cooper gave us a list of things that needed to be done to the house, just to make sure it wouldn't fall down around us. It wasn't anything major—just adjusting a screw here and there, propping up the front step, taking the door off the hinges and planing down the edges so it would close softer.

While we still hadn't decided what to do, it was generally assumed we would be here for a little while at least, and if this helped keep our mind off the fact our home had burned to the ground, then I was all for it.

When our place was done, I went around to my mom's to make sure it was okay. Which was an awkward way to introduce my mother to my new Pack-mate. Kitten wouldn't say it out loud, but she was nervous. I could see it in the way her hands moved restlessly, the way she paced around all morning.

"Should I make something? I don't know how to cook," she fretted to Darius, who seemed to appreciate someone else being the emotional basket case for a moment.

Darius shook his head. "No, Beckett's mom will have spent all morning cooking. Where we've had all this to keep our mind off it, she'll have baked. Wear your stretchy pants."

The witches had dropped off baskets of food, from who knows where. I had to respect Loren; he'd taken us all in without so much as a word, and the rest of the witches had embraced us. I think it was their brand of witchcraft. They were green witches from what I could tell, or as the elders used to call them, fae-touched witches. They had an affinity with nature that went beyond the general witch obsession with Mother Earth.

It meant that a lot of the fresh fruits and vegetables had probably been grown with magic, but I wasn't worried. I'd take their offerings thankfully. The ones who had dropped off the food had been two young men with big smiles and a demeanor that made me instantly at ease. Which was suspicious in its own way, but I didn't think they meant it maliciously.

When we'd asked for tools, they'd happily directed us to a workshop on Main Street which had been dusty and empty of people when we arrived. Except for an old Mustang that had made Corvin nearly come in his pants.

My job was secure, since all of the children had made it here. I'd made sure of it. I had purposefully not called a few parents who I knew would stay against advice, risking the lives of their kids. So I hadn't called them until the bus was well and truly on its way to Moonburst. Unethical? Probably. But my students meant more to me than their pigheaded parents, and I wasn't risking a single one of them just because they believed being fifteen made them old enough to fight a raging fire alongside their fathers. I wouldn't lose sleep over it, anyway.

Even Cooper's job would be easily transferred to Moonburst. But Corvin's job was gone, since there was no Legion machinery left to be maintained. It was all gone.

I wondered if I could talk Courtland into letting us use the workshop so Corvin could work on cars and small engines. He'd enjoy that; he always liked to be working with his hands. Something to think about, or maybe I'd ask at the meeting tonight. We'd know more afterwards, and we could make better plans.

Now, as we walked over to my mother's house, I had my arm around Kitten's shoulders to stop her from bouncing away. She looked beautiful in the only dress she'd packed when we'd evacuated.

"She already loves you, Kitten, because you make me happy. This is just a formality."

She nodded, but I had the impression she wasn't really taking my words to heart. I guess she'd see soon enough.

42

KITTEN

I was so fucking nervous. This was important, and I was convinced I was going to screw it up. The guys were equal parts amused and consoling, which in short, meant they were no damn help at all.

We found the right cabin, and it was cute as hell. These must have housed single workers at some point, because there were seven in a row and they were all skinny and long, with little porches out front, complete with swings. I could almost imagine them with little flower gardens on the small square of lawn.

I tucked myself behind Beckett's back as he knocked on the door. Corvin ran his hand over my spine, giving me a reassuring smile.

Darius leaned over and kissed my ear. "Baby, I had every reason to hate your guts, and you wooed me in seconds. This is nothing."

I frowned at him. "I wooed you with the power of my vagina, Darius. That doesn't apply here."

Beckett cleared his throat as I heard his mother chuckle on the other side of the door. My face flushed bright red.

"Fuck," I mouthed silently, while Cooper hissed a laugh at the back of the group like he was about to die. I was tempted to help him along. Instead, I painted a pleasant smile on my face and hoped to god I was wrong.

Beckett's mom was beautiful. She had Beckett's dark hair and huge eyes, but her face was more dainty and slightly rounder. She grabbed Beck, pulling him into a tight hug. "It's so good to see you, son. I know you made it here before me, but I just kept waiting for someone to tell me that you'd gone back and something had happened..." She trailed off, and I could tell there was pain there. Old, festering pain. Shaking her head, she stepped back and nudged his arm. "Introduce me, Beckett Reid."

"Kitten, this is my mother, Tia. Mom, this is my Omega and Packmate. The mother of my cubs. This is Kitten."

"You mean the poor girl you kept secret from everyone for nearly half a decade?" she chastised lightly, stepping onto the porch and dragging me in for a hug. Oh shit. What did I do? Did I hug her back?

That seemed right. I wrapped my arms around her back and squeezed.

Finally, I pulled back. "It's okay, ma'am. I asked them not to. They were just respecting my wishes. I think everything turned out how it was supposed to in the end."

Tia pulled back and cupped my cheek with her soft hands. So soft. I wasn't sure I'd ever felt skin that soft. Was this what women's hands were supposed to feel like? Mine were calloused and rough, from hunting and chopping wood and generally just surviving for so many years. The guys' hands were equally as rough, though Beckett's and Darius's were slightly less so.

I realized I'd been sitting there staring at nothing with my cheek in Tia's hand for too long and pulled away, clearing my throat. But the older woman didn't seem weirded out. In fact, her eyes were big and filled with something warm. Empathy, maybe? Or compassion.

She gave a tight nod. "Come into the house. Darius, I wanna hug you tight and you can tell me all about how my grandbabies are cooking in there." She kissed him as he entered. "Corvin." She just said his name like it was a term of endearment. "I'm happy for you too, son. So happy. Your mama would have been proud."

"Thanks, Tia," he said, kissing her cheek.

Last was Cooper, and he gave her a big smile, wrapping her up in a hug and kissing her loudly on the cheek too. "It's good to see you, Tia. I told Beckett we needed to get our shit together before you kicked all of our asses. But does he listen?"

Tia snorted. "No. Stubborn like his father, that one. Now, everyone go into the kitchen—I made banana bread. There's not much room, but it'll fit you guys and my grandbabies well enough."

We were hustled into the kitchen that actually opened into the living room too. It was barely enough space, but it just seemed cozy.

Tia spent fifteen solid minutes fussing, filling us with cakes and coffee, and then more cakes, until my stomach bulged. But between all that, we just talked. We talked about what had happened in Maxton. It was the first conversation on everyone's lips, because it had irrevocably altered all our lives. But once we got past all the gossip—including everyone guessing who was dead and who just hadn't shown up in Moonburst—we settled onto a sweeter topic. The cubs.

"Are you feeling okay, Darius? Is there anything you need me to do?" She'd fussed around us both all afternoon, which would normally make me feel claustrophobic, but with Tia, it just made me feel wanted.

"Not unless you want to carry them for the last few weeks. My back is killing me."

I made a mental note to give him a massage tonight. Rub out some of those knotted muscles. Then maybe I could get one of the guys to knot my muscles back up again.

"And you, Kitten? Any luck finding your parents?"

Beckett looked stricken. I guess he thought I was still fragile about the subject. But it was okay; I liked Tia. We were family. "Mom—"

"Yes, the former Alpha General. Gatlin is my half-brother, which was a surprise. And my mother was a..." I looked at Tia's gray face. "Are you okay?"

"Mom—" Beckett started again.

But Tia cut him off. "Your father was the former Alpha General?"

I frowned, but nodded slowly. "Yes?"

"Oh." She turned to Beckett. "I'm feeling a little off, Beck. I might just go and lie down." She stood and left, and I gaped after her. What the fuck had just happened? I looked around at the guys and caught the expression that passed between Corvin and Beckett.

"What just happened?"

Silence. Everyone avoided my eyes, until Darius sighed and threw them an angry look. "You two—go make this right with Tia. Come on, Kitten. It's a story better told outside under the warm summer sun."

Cooper and Darius led me out of the cabin and back toward our temporary home. We walked silently for a moment, before Darius grabbed my hand and held me closer. "Beckett's dad died when he was young. He was the love of Tia's life, and they'd been destined for each other like the stars themselves had written it. Unfortunately, he died in an accident, leaving Tia a widow with a young son."

My heart constricted at the idea of losing any of my guys, so I didn't want to imagine the pain Tia must have been in.

Darius continued. "Tia was respected around town, being one of the few teachers, and she was beautiful as well. The former Alpha General Huxley decided that Tia needed to remarry and have more cubs, for the good of the Manix. He harassed her about it for years. When she rejected every suitor put forth, the old Alpha General decided it was because she had been waiting for him. He came around one night when Beckett was out with Corvin and Raiden, and tried to, uh, present his suit. Tia rejected him, but rejection wasn't something the man took well..."

"Did he?" I gasped, horrified.

Darius shook his head. "Beckett and Corvin arrived home just in time, with Raiden in tow. Raiden was the son of a Legion General, and an Omega at that. He was harder to manipulate into silence than two preteen boys. So the old Alpha General left, and Tia moved in with her brother's family so she was never alone and vulnerable again. Huxley let her be after that, but the whole thing changed Tia."

Holy shit. I was spawned from absolute evil. "And no one thought I should fucking *know* this before I walked into her goddamn living room and ate cake?"

Okay, I might have screeched that last part. How could they have been so damn insensitive? Needing to get away before I said something I regretted, I turned and ran in the opposite direction.

"Kitten!" Cooper shouted, but I dead-eyed him over my shoulder.

"Do not follow me or I will kick you in the balls, Cooper Wiley," I yelled, sprinting off.

I was so fucking mad. So. Fucking. Mad. I jumped the unused train tracks and just ran some more. It was flat, wide grassland, and I felt like I could run for a hundred miles before I hit a mountain. It was the exact opposite of what I was used to but somehow still comforting. I only ran a little more before flopping down in the grass, staring up at the wide, cloudless sky and cursing my bad luck.

How would she ever be able to look at me? At our cubs? I was the reason her tormentor's DNA would live on. I let the tears slide down my temples as I wallowed in self-pity. I hated this man I'd never met. I was mad that I couldn't meet him and tell him that he was a waste of space and emotion. Mad that he was the reason I would never have a mother. I lay out there for hours, letting the bitterness swirl in my gut until it churned to acid.

Crunching grass was my only warning someone was close by. I sat up, and I was surprised to see Gatlin.

"Your mates thought you might respond better to seeing me than to them right now."

"They'd be correct."

He sat down in the grass beside me. "For someone who's so good at tracking, you left a trail like a bull-dozer through the grass."

I narrowed my eyes at the man who was suppos-edly my brother. Who shared my tainted bloodline. I guess we could both lament together. "I wasn't trying to be stealthy."

Gatlin grunted. "I'm shit at this talking thing. You should have seen Naja's face when they all suggested I come and talk to you. She thought it was funny as hell. I don't do... feelings well."

I snorted. "Maybe that's hereditary too."

"That man gave us nothing. We are who we are *despite* the taint of his blood. He had less than nothing to do with your upbringing, so he didn't foist his bull-shit ideals onto you. You can't inherit bigotry—that's a choice, and it isn't one that either of us will make." He paused. "Tia has her own demons that have nothing to do with us. It was probably just a shock. She knows you aren't your father's daughter, Kitten. You're nothing like that asshole who made us, and I know that for a fact."

He stood up, rubbing grass from his butt. "Now, stop wallowing, and let's head back. Courtland is holding a meeting in twenty minutes, and I have a feeling that it's going to shift all our futures."

43

DARIUS

The cubs were practicing their choreography for a flash mob in my womb. I was sure of it. I rubbed my stomach in an attempt to soothe them, or distract them.

The recreation center we were using as a meeting hall was packed with Manix. Dispersed amongst us was a handful of witches. Some seemed wary, some were fascinated—especially once they spied me—and some just looked bored as hell.

A female witch, who was probably in her fifties, walked up to where we were sitting with a smile. She seemed non-threatening, but my Alphas were still on guard. "So it's not a myth? The males of the Manix species do give birth to the young?" Her eyes were sparkling with mirth. "I gave birth to triplet boys over twenty years ago now, and I would have sold my soul to have my husband carry them around for even a day!"

I winced as one of the cubs got a rib, and the woman winced right along with me.

"I remember that feeling well. Don't worry—there's not long to go, but actually..." She reached into a pocket and pulled out a handful of rocks. Picking a shining white one, she handed it to me. Corvin began a rumbling growl, but I put a hand on his knee to calm him. She gave Corvin an understanding, if slightly nervous glance.

"It's a moonstone. There's a river of them here, below the town, which is why the coven grew here. When I was having my sons, resting a moonstone on my stomach seemed to calm them for a few moments so I could just breathe. It may work even better with shifters, given your affinity for the Moon Goddess. It won't harm the cubs, or you. It's a feminine energy stone, but is also good for insomnia and balance. I figure it can't hurt to try?"

I clenched the gift in my hand, inexplicably touched by her thoughtfulness, whether I believed in this stuff or not. "Thank you. And thank you for opening your home to us. I'm Darius, and this is my Pack." I indicated my Alphas and Kitten.

"I'm Jeziya. And you are welcome here in Moonburst. I half hope you stay. What is the point of being in a coven that nurtures life and nature, if you are surrounded by empty buildings and a ghost town barely hanging on? This is the most energy the town has had in years."

I gave her a sad smile. "We are here for as long as you'll have us, I think. There's nothing to go home to now."

Jeziya's eyes welled with tears, and she rested her hand over mine. "I am very sorry about your homes. The Goddess is mysterious in her workings. But sometimes in nature, everything has to burn in order for new growth to happen."

Courtland stood up in front of the crowd, and Jeziya ducked back to the rest of her coven with a quick wave. Courtland looked somber, his face pulled into stressed lines. "The Manix thank the Moonburst coven for allowing us to stay in their homes and for making us feel so welcome. The Manix owe a great debt to you all." He tilted his head at Wilbur and Electra, who were sitting in the front row.

"My fellow Manix, our home is gone. I returned to Maxton yesterday, and only the foundations of the Legion building remain. The fire went through fast and hard. We lost five of our brethren." A sad noise flowed through the crowd. "It is a time for mourning what we have lost. However, it is also a time for decisions to be made." I could see him square his shoulders, so this next part was probably going to hurt.

"It is my opinion that the Manix shouldn't return to

hiding. The feuds of the past are over. We are no longer living in secret to protect our numbers. In fact, this hiding has become detrimental to the Manix species as a whole."

Noise exploded throughout the room. I looked over at my Pack, trying to judge how they were taking the idea, but they weren't giving me much.

"Everyone, a little silence please. I'll have time for questions in a moment." Courtland waited until the noise was back to a reasonable level. "You all have autonomy. When it comes to your safety, the Legion Generals and I will do what is necessary. But when it comes to your future, and where you would like to reside, that is entirely a decision for you to make. However, we have had discussions with the Moonburst coven, and they have offered us homes here in Moonburst."

"At what cost?" someone yelled from the back.

Electra stood up. "Witches work with the energy around us. Some energy comes from nature, some comes from the coven, and some comes from the people who surround us. Since the oil refinery closed and the workers left, our coven has been starved of energy. Many of us are expelling far more energy than we should be to keep our crops alive in winter, or to perform simple spells. By breathing life back into Moonburst, we would live symbiotically. Fully energized, we can protect you from outside forces, and provide for large numbers such as your Pack. In return, you have to do nothing but live. Provide the skills we are currently lacking in town. We will give you homes and buildings, out of which you can run businesses. Together, we get Moonburst back."

She sold it well. Courtland nodded to her. "I should warn you that it is the intention of my Pack to stay in Moonburst. The children of the Sanctum will also remain here. If you return to Maxton, we would essentially split into two separate townships." More gasps, and maybe one of those came from me. "The Maxton group would have to elect a new Alpha General, or adapt to a new leadership structure. It is my hope that this will be the beginning of a new era for the Manix, one out of the shadows, where we can properly flourish as a species." His nose flared, the scent of anxiety in the room almost noxious. "I'll take questions now."

Thus began two torturous hours of Courtland essentially answering the same questions on repeat. The other Legion Generals answered some questions, including whether they would return to Maxton, of which they were almost split in half. There were more questions about the coven, including their numbers, why they didn't all live here in Moonburst, whether they were minions of the devil. Wilbur laughed uproariously at that last one.

But there were also more thoughtful questions, like

how we would be able to shift into our Beast forms here where there were no trees to shelter us from prying eyes? Would our cubs be safe if we were so easily accessible? All of these were completely valid concerns.

It was Electra who assuaged these fears. She held out a hand to Courtland. "Alpha General, if I may?" He put his hand in hers, and then they disappeared. Like, fully gone.

"Holy shit," I whispered.

"We are still here—we are just mirrored with magic," Electra's voice told us. "This would be cast over the whole town at certain times of the year, and over a particular portion of the grasslands. This would allow you to run and, uh, do whatever it is Manix do in their fully shifted form, without worrying about humans accidentally spotting you. Once cast, this magic tethers itself to the unique geological features of Moonburst. So long as there is energy in the town to maintain the illusion, it will stay. Also, we will set up alarm systems to alert us to outsiders entering the town. It will be as safe and secure as we can make it, perhaps even more so than your mountain home. There's always a chance a rogue hunter might see you there, no?"

"Where do you think the Bigfoot legends come from?" someone shouted from the back, causing a ripple of laughter.

Electra dropped the illusion, and they both reappeared. Courtland smiled at the heckler and nodded. "You can all make your own decisions. The Manix's financial assets will be divided between the two townships, so you will have something to start with. I would ask for your decisions soon, so we can get reconstruction plans for Maxton underway, as well as Alpha General elections held, and for those of you staying in Moonburst, we will be organizing permanent jobs and resources you'll need to start your lives again. And again, if you just want to talk, my door is always open."

With that, we all began to disperse. Beckett helped me to my feet, and I stood with a sigh. I felt huge. That was my other worry. The unknown factor of when I was about to give birth was sending my Beast into anxiety overdrive. I couldn't live like this. We needed to make decisions and we needed to make them now.

But it wasn't just me in this Pack. Cooper loved his family, and I knew he'd be unsettled if they chose to go back to Maxton and rebuild. Gatlin and the Huxley-Grey Pack had always been loners—would they go home, taking with them the chance for Kitten to have kin?

So many moving pieces. We had a week to decide, otherwise the cubs would decide for us.

LIKE MOST THINGS, my Pack turned the life-altering decision of where we should live into a game, but with a pro-con list. Every time you listed a pro or a con—for either staying or leaving—and it got shot down by someone else, you had to remove a piece of clothing. For instance, when Cooper said that Maxton had been where we'd lived for generations, Beckett replied that while we'd been happy there, Maxton had always had its share of problems, mainly because it was so steeped in the old ways. This was a chance for a fresh start.

If you made a point that no one could argue with, you got to nominate who had to get naked.

Needless to say, we were all pretty nude after a while, but the pro list for staying in Moonburst was considerably longer than that for rebuilding in Maxton. Kitten had been pretty ambivalent about either option, but I'd seen her heart swell when Beckett had suggested we could rebuild our Packhouse where her cabin had once been.

Beckett's mom had basically said she'd stay wherever we were. We still hadn't talked about what had happened with her, but we'd have to eventually. Cooper's parents had also insinuated that our choice would have a bearing on their decision, but they were leaning toward Moonburst too.

Finally, Kitten was naked, Corvin was down to just his boxer shorts and socks, and Cooper had been butt ass naked for most of the game. Only Beckett and I maintained our clothes, and that was because we were both arguing hard for Moonburst. Hell, maybe we all were really, but someone had to play devil's advocate.

We looked at the piece of paper in front of us, splashed with beer and guacamole from the nachos we'd eaten halfway through the game. It was unanimous really.

The Wiley-Fletcher-Reid Pack would stay in Moonburst, Montana. Our cubs would be the first to be born outside of Maxton since Naja. It was both exciting and terrifying, all at the same time.

44

COOPER

There was some serious drama when Merrick and Murphy turned up a week after the fires. It wasn't that everyone had thought they were dead. No, it was because they turned up with Susannah and Quinn in tow. Without Wilkie or the rest of his Pack.

If that wasn't dramatic enough, no one had seen Wilkie since the fires. Courtland was pretty sure he hadn't stayed to fight the flames—it wasn't Wilkie's jam to be heroic—but he hadn't turned up in Moonburst either. Most people thought he was just lying low somewhere else, because the man was a fucking bigot. He hated everyone who didn't stare back at him in a mirror every morning. On the list of beings he thought were inferior were witches. So everyone had assumed that he'd taken his Pack elsewhere to weather the storm, so to speak.

But Susannah and Quinn rocking up with two other Alphas? That was a scandal.

Doc Tanner finally reappeared too, though everyone knew where he'd been. He'd remained in Maxton to move his equipment down the mountain and treat any of the injured Manix who'd stayed behind. When Maxton had burned, he'd been recalled by Convocation Member Baxter—or Raine, as she made everyone call her. But apparently, he was still our doctor despite not being in Maxton anymore, and I breathed easier knowing he was nearby, just in case Darius went into labor.

The witches had been less impressed. Apparently, there was no love lost between the vamps and the witches, but somehow Courtland had sorted it out. Honestly, it was probably due to Tanner's general golden retriever energy too.

Like the split in the Legion Generals, the split in Manix staying and going was also quite even. I wasn't surprised that a lot of the older generation wanted to rebuild and return back to the mountains, because they were just too old to adapt. They were a generation lost to the way things were. But a lot of the younger Manix had chosen to return too, which was a surprise. Almost all of my peers back in high school had complained about being stuck, but I guess whining about wanting a new life was easier than having to build one for yourself.

I knew some of them were tradespeople, and that made sense too. There would be oodles of work rebuilding, and the old guard weren't going to accept outsiders building their homes. Even Finlo was going back temporarily, to oversee the rebuild. His Pack was staying in Moonburst though, which was a relief. My parents were also staying.

Actually, everything was going okay, which was a weight off my chest.

I could hear Darius muttering to himself in the nest he was building in the house, the same one assigned to us by the glowing witch orb. That orb had been right; it had been the right house for us. We'd settled in just nicely. We'd gotten all the supplies we needed, including new tools for my job as town handyman and for Corvin's new mechanic business on Main Street. We both worked out of that dusty garage, and honestly, it was amazing.

Courtland had taken a convoy of SUVs and a truck down to the largest town nearby and bought out essentially everything in the place. I'm sure we raised a few eyebrows, but we didn't care. We even drove up to Canada for things, and although we were scrutinized crossing back over the border, we followed all the rules so no one said anything. We all had basic driver's licenses given to us when we came of age, though none of them listed Maxton as an address. You couldn't live in a modern society without identification, but we kept it as basic as possible.

It meant that our house was reasonably ready for the cubs to arrive, which was getting closer and closer every day. Darius was beginning to look exhausted, and Kitten hovered nearby at all times. She was the only one Darius would let fuss for longer than five minutes, so they spent most of their days napping or watching television. Both the nursery and nest were almost complete, and then I'd start on the rest of the house, in between fixing small things for the rest of Moonburst, including the witches. Apparently, while they were attuned to nature, they weren't very attuned to a hammer.

I poked my head into the nest, seeing Darius still wandering around, fluffing cushions and blankets, a scowl on his face. Kitten sat cross-legged on the floor, frowning at him.

"Is everything okay?" I said softly. Loud noises, the expression on my face, the water stain on the foyer wallpaper, global warming—all had pissed Darius off over the last few days. I just wanted to wrap him in my arms and make it all better.

"He seems uncomfortable," Kitten murmured, and Darius threw us both an irritated glare.

"I'm pregnant, not deaf." He winced, and that made me frown too.

I strode into the room. "Are you in pain, Omega?" I used my Alpha voice so he wouldn't blow off my question.

"Yes," he admitted through gritted teeth.

Kitten was on her feet in an instant. "Why didn't you tell me? Is it labor? Something else?"

Darius let out a shaky breath, and I saw it then. Saw it in the whites of his eyes and the tight line of his lips. He confirmed it with his next words. "I'm scared."

Hell, I was fucking petrified, and I wasn't the one who had to be sliced open to have the three children who'd literally been growing inside my body removed. I could only imagine what he was feeling.

Kitten wrapped him in her arms, and I put my own longer ones around them both. Holding them all tightly, I sent up a small prayer to the Goddess, before pulling back and kissing Darius softly. I could feel the thrum of his heart against my chest.

"It will all be fine, D. I know it in my soul." I looked over at Kitten. "Get him to the bedroom. I'll get the guys and Tanner." I paused, looking at Darius. "You still want Tanner, right? If you want to have a more traditional birth, I could... or Beckett or Corvin?"

Please say you want Tanner. Please say you want Tanner.

"Of course I want the damn doctor, Cooper," Darius grumbled, grabbing his stomach. "You might need to hurry though."

Kitten shoved my arm. "I got this, Coop. Go." She stroked Darius's back. "Let's go, baby. Have I told you lately that you're fucking amazing?" she crooned to him, and it was a testament to how much he loved her that he just purred. If I'd tried to say the same thing at that moment, he would have eaten me.

I ran out of the house, grabbing my phone on the way. I tried the guys first, but no one was answering. Beckett would be teaching, but Corvin should have his phone on. Fuck it. Instead, I ran straight to the new doctor's office. Bursting through the front door, I halted when I saw Tanner kissing—

Fuck, it didn't matter. "Darius is in labor."

Tanner spun around, grabbing his bag. "I'll be right there," he told me, then he paused. He glanced over his shoulder at the Omega behind him, then gave me a cool look. "About this..."

I waved a hand. "I couldn't fucking give a shit." I looked at the Omega. "Good for you. You deserve this. Now, *my* Omega is in pain and about to give birth in an extremely dangerous manner, so let's get the fuck out of here. Your kinkery can wait."

After leaving the doctor's office and telling Tanner to head straight to the house, I ran to the garage. I knew immediately why Corvin hadn't heard his phone, since he was blasting pop music. It was the funniest fucking thing, this giant, burly Alpha with a love of pop music.

He was underneath the old Mustang, and I could hear him singing along. I stopped, just for a moment, to appreciate how much I loved this man. He was going to make a wonderful father—I knew that in my soul.

I grabbed him by the ankles, pulling him out from beneath the car. He frowned at me, but one look at my face had him scrambling to his feet. "What's wrong? Is it time?"

I nodded. "It's time. Tanner's on his way over already, and Kitten's with Darius. Get over there. I'll go collect Beckett."

But he was already gone before I finished my sentence. I locked the front doors of the garage and ran to the school. I was beginning to really regret loaning the car to my parents today.

The school was basically just a large, open storage shed, and instead of having the school segregated into upper and lower classes, they were all together in one room. Terra was still in Moonburst, but she was going to return to Maxton with her Pack to ensure they'd still have a teacher there. I was eternally grateful to Terra; she was selfless and one of the best people I knew.

I wrenched open the door, and fifty faces turned toward me.

"Cooper? Is everything alright?" Terra asked, stepping toward me quickly.

I gave her a tight smile. "I'm just looking for Beckett."

Her eyes went wide. "Oh. Oh, yes. He's out back doing gym class with the older kids. Stephanie! Run out and get Mr. Reid. Knees to chest, child, knees to chest," she shouted after her as tiny little Stephanie ran like the wind out the door. Terra turned back toward me. "You'll give Darius my love, won't you? I'll send up a blessing to the Goddess when I get home."

Beckett returned with a pleased-looking Stephanie in tow. "I ran so fast, the world went blurry," she crowed, and I laughed.

Terra rolled her eyes at me, but then turned and smiled at the girl. "That makes you the student of the day, Steph. Go put your picture on the board." She shooed the girl away, turning back to us. "Go, Beckett. I'll call in Trace to make them run laps until they whine. Go have some babies."

Beckett hugged her tight. "Thanks, Terra," he said quickly, then we raced from the room.

Much like Stephanie, we ran so fast the world was a blur. Our future awaited.

45

KITTEN

Darius groaned loudly, rolling onto his hands and knees. "For the sweet love of the fucking Goddess, they need to hurry up. These cubs are doing their best impression of Tasmanian devils on my insides."

I rubbed his back, pouring every ounce of Omega pheromone I could muster into his body. He was a lot more relaxed than he'd been earlier, but he was still in pain and there wasn't any amount of good vibes that could help that.

Tanner finally showed up, but as soon as Darius saw him, he scrabbled to the other side of the bed, growling low. Shit, that sound was way more Beast than man.

I crawled across the bed after him, pulling him softly into my arms as I thrummed. It didn't sound quite the same as when the males did it, but hopefully it was comforting nonetheless. "It's time now. We have to meet our cubs, but you've got to let Tanner work. We trust him—he wants what's best for both you and the babies. But if you really don't want him here, the guys will be back soon. They can deliver the cubs, but it will be more dangerous: for you, for them, and for our Alphas. They love you. The last thing they want is to do surgery on you when they've never held a scalpel in their lives." I cuddled his head close to my chest, the tension in his body making him stiff.

"I need my Alphas," he whined, and I swallowed back my panic. Okay, we could make this work. "But Tanner can deliver the babies." The relieved whoosh of my breath ruffled his hair.

Tanner was still moving quietly around the room, setting up everything he needed. "That's a bloody relief," he whispered under his breath, and I whole-heartedly agreed. "Get him to lie on his back, Omega. Sit up there by his head and keep him calm. Your Alphas shouldn't be too far away now. I don't think there's time for an epidural, but I'll give as much local as I can, to try and numb the pain. It might still be uncomfortable though."

I stroked a hand down Darius's back as he let out a pitiful sound, and I could feel the cubs moving around in his body. When Darius had first gotten pregnant, I'd done some reading. Without the help of their Pack to cut open the womb, the cubs would eventually claw and chew their way out of an Omega, though the mortality rate for all of them was nearly a hundred percent. Seemed like an evolutionary fuckup.

"Come on now, Omega. You heard the doctor, onto your back." I moved away but he let out a low keening sound that tore at my heart. "I'm not going anywhere. I'm here for you forever, my love," I crooned, and when he rolled onto his back, I scooted behind him, my legs either side of his shoulders, so he could rest his head on my thighs. I looked down at his face. "We've got this, Darius. You and me. I love you."

His hands gripped my ankles, anchoring himself to me. "Love you," he grunted, and from this angle, I could see just how much his stomach was rolling around. Jesus, it looked like an alien had crawled in there and was doing a jig.

Tanner stood over us both, and my Beast went on guard. The human part of me trusted Tanner, but the Beast saw another type of predator in the room while Darius was at his most vulnerable. We'd protect Darius at this moment, even knowing we didn't stand a chance against a vampire. Neither love nor the Beast were logical.

I almost shuddered with relief when I heard the front door bang open, the scent of one of my anxious mates preceding him down the hall. Corvin burst into the room, a growl already on his lips.

Tanner sighed. "This is going to be rough, isn't it?"

I nodded. "Sorry, Doc. It's instinct." I looked at Corvin. "Come here—your Omegas need you."

Yeah, I included myself in that, because I was freaking the fuck out on the inside. Corvin was across the room and on his knees beside us in an instant.

"I'm so proud of you, D," he whispered in Darius's ear. "We're going to be parents today because of you."

Tanner was talking us through the whole process, which was probably safest. "Okay, I'm just putting antiseptic on the skin to kill any bugs. I know Manix aren't susceptible to infection, but better safe than sorry, amiright?"

With a big sponge thing, he turned Darius's stomach yellow with some kind of liquid, then threw the sponge in a trash can he'd made appear from somewhere. I looked at the rest of the things he had set up. There was a weird metal tray which held a range of scissors and scalpels, as well as other things I had no clue about but assumed were necessary.

The front door opened and closed again, and then Beckett and Cooper were there. It was going to be crowded in here, but we'd make it work. Darius needed us all.

Tanner looked between all the broad shoulders and wild eyes. "Well, this is going to be a tight squeeze. Now, I need clean blankets to wrap the babies in, and I need for everyone to stay as calm as possible, for your Omega's sake."

He wasn't Manix, but the doctor's cool confidence in this situation was authoritative in its own way. Beckett nodded, his eyes lingering on a writhing Darius, before he disappeared into the hall. He reappeared moments later, laying a stack of blankets down on the dresser.

Tanner sucked in a deep breath, and cut. "I'm just making an incision through the first three layers," he said softly, and I wasn't sure if he was repeating it to himself like a recipe or if he was keeping us informed. Maybe a little of both?

Darius whimpered, and I put my hands on either side of his head, pushing as much of my newfound Omega calm at him as I could. Actually, for once, I wasn't really pushing it. It was flowing out of me naturally, like it knew now was its time to shine. The new Omega inside of me knew that this was the moment she was needed most, and I almost wept when Darius's body unclenched.

"Woah, Omega. I get why everyone says you guys are like a Xanax now. Even your Alphas look more chill," Tanner pointed out, a goofy grin on his face. "Moving the muscle and cutting the peritoneum now. Alpha, if I could just get you to put on those gloves and hold this open for me, that would be great."

He motioned to Cooper, who looked like he was

going to pass out at the suggestion. Even so, Cooper didn't hesitate, putting on gloves and holding the instruments that Tanner indicated.

"Okay, now I just need to cut here. And now here." Cooper made a groaning sound, making Tanner look up sharply from what he was doing. "If you're going to puke, don't do it into his abdomen, mate."

Cooper pressed his lips closed, and Darius started to look down. Yeah, that wasn't a good idea. I gripped his chin, tilting his head up to look at me.

"Are you ready?" I whispered. "You're amazing at this. You're going to be the best father. You all are." I held his eyes with mine, because while I'd dressed my fair share of meat, it was hard to watch a knife slide through someone you love.

I stroked my thumbs over his cheekbones, mouthing "I love you," until Tanner gave a small grunt.

"Alpha, come here. Bring a blanket. Take off your shirt too."

Beckett leapt forward, literally ripping his shirt open. Tanner pulled out the first baby and I... It was beautiful, curled up into a ball but silent. Tanner passed the baby to Beckett.

"Congrats, Alpha. A girl. Rub her back vigorously and she'll—" The baby let out a wail, her whole face screwed up. "She'll do that. Corvin, come over and cut the umbilical cord. Then someone needs to wrap her up and keep her close."

He looked up at me and Darius. "You're doing great, Omegas. One down, two to go." He looked over at Beckett, who was gazing at the baby with wide-eyed wonder. "Hand the baby to Darius, Alpha, we've got work to do. You too, Corvin."

Beckett laid the tiny, fluid-soaked baby on Darius's chest, tucking a blanket around her body. Her eyes were screwed closed, but as soon as her skin touched Darius's, her whole body relaxed, like she recognized his heartbeat.

Tears splashed down onto her damp head, and I realized they were mine. "She's beautiful," I whispered, my voice choked and rough. "So perfect."

"Another girl," Tanner announced proudly, handing a second baby to Corvin, but this baby didn't need any careful rubbing. She came out squawking, and it was the greatest sound I'd ever heard.

Corvin wrapped her up like a messy burrito, and moved her to his chest as if she was made of glass. As soon as the baby's cheek touched Corvin's chest, she stopped crying. God, she was so tiny. Smaller than one of Corvin's hands, but just perfect.

The final baby came out, and Tanner grinned. "A boy. He's tiny, but look at those bright eyes, Papa," he said to Beckett. Corvin cut the clamped umbilical cord one-handed, and then Beckett wrapped the baby quickly and held him to his chest.

"He's not crying. Should he be crying?"

Tanner frowned. "Bring him over here." He unwrapped the baby a little and looked at his chest and skin, before smiling. "He's fine, just a quiet one. That's okay, little one. Your sisters sound like they'll be loud enough for you as well." Beckett moved away, and Tanner looked over at a pale-faced Cooper. "You're doing a great job. Just the placenta still to go." He pulled out what I could only assume was a sea monster. "A couple more stitches here, ah, okay. Now you can let go, Alpha."

Cooper released the clamps and stood up. "Thank the Goddess." Then he passed the hell out with a thump. No one could catch him, and his head thudded against the floorboards. He'd be fine, of course, but my poor, traumatized Alpha.

Tanner actually laughed. "I'm surprised he lasted that long." He looked up at Darius. "Just a little more, Omega, and you can rest with your cubs."

He worked so fast that it was hard to follow, but soon enough, there was a neat row of stitches up Darius's stomach, and a cheerful-looking doctor was checking his vitals. Darius had fallen asleep almost immediately, even while the blood pressure cuff was still expanding, so I took the baby from his chest and held her to mine.

How could something be this small and fragile, then grow into a huge, fearsome Manix? It seemed impossible, but as I felt the warm press of the baby's cheek against my chest, I swore that I would protect her and her siblings with everything I had.

Tanner grinned from ear to ear. "I'm so chuffed at how that went. My first Manix delivery was a success, wouldn't you agree?" He looked so proud, you'd almost think one of the babies belonged to him.

"We own you one, Tanner," Corvin murmured, but didn't look up from the small, swaddled baby in his arms.

Tanner waved a dismissive hand. "All part of the job. The best part, I think." He looked longingly at the babies, and for the first time, I saw a flash of the human Tanner had been before his turning. Did he have kids? A family who thought he was fish food at the bottom of the ocean? Though it might just be a rumor that he'd been turned after being mauled by a great white shark.

He packed up silently, then whispered some instructions on caring for Darius to Beckett before leaving. Then the only people left in the house were the five of us and the three newest members of the family. I just prayed to the Goddess I didn't fuck this up.

46

CORVIN

I stood guard and watched my entire Pack sleep in the nursery their first night. The babies fussed if they weren't all together in the one bassinet, and I had this overwhelming fear that they'd bump into each other or roll onto each other and cause irreparable damage. So I sat close and counted all their breaths.

One. Two. Three.

Cooper and Beckett were bracketed around Kitten and Darius. Kitten was protective of Darius, even with us. She was basically guarding his wounds against our clumsy hands, because anytime one of the others went to put a hand over him in their sleep, she was like a narcoleptic ninja, her arm there blocking them while never fully waking up. It was actually kind of impressive.

I'd never been more happy or more terrified than I was right now. During the birth, I'd just been straight up terrified. If anything had happened to Darius or the cubs... God, I didn't even want to think about it.

But now? I was still scared, but it was outweighed by the absolute love I felt when I looked at the three tiny, wrapped bundles next to me. We hadn't even picked names—with the whole insanity of Maxton burning, and whether we stayed in Moonburst or left, we hadn't had a chance.

Cooper had eventually woken up when I'd dead-lifted him into the nursery too. Poor guy. I'd only seen flashes of the procedure and that was more than enough for me. I wasn't sure he'd ever recover.

"Can't sleep?" The soft voice of Kitten was a caress on my skin, and I shivered. I wanted to crawl across the bodies to her and wrap her up in my arms, just hold her to me. As if she read my mind, she extracted herself from the puppy pile. She stood up as she reached me by the door, leaning down to kiss me softly, before walking over to the bassinet. "They are so small."

They were tiny, a lot smaller than human babies, or even Beta-born Manix babies, who had the same gestation as a regular pregnancy. No, it was an effect of the male Omega pregnancy that they were born this young, but developed enough to be healthy. Eventually, they'd be the same size as normal kids, and you'd never know that once I could've held one in a single hand.

"They are, but not for long. They'll start doubling in size soon enough." I was secretly looking forward to it, even though as a parent I was meant to want them to stay small and cute forever. Not me though; I wanted them infinitely less breakable ASAP. They even had to have special baby bottles right now because they were so small. It was crazy.

They stirred, and we both stilled. "Let's go to the kitchen," Kitten whispered, and I followed her out into the main room, holding my breath at every squeaking floorboard, waiting for everyone to wake. But they didn't.

I breathed easier as we stepped into the kitchen, turning on the small light over the stove. I grabbed the milk from the fridge, while Kitten reached up to pull down two glasses. Someone had pushed them right to the back, and she huffed, hiking up a T-shirt that belonged to Cooper as she scaled the bench like a monkey. It reminded me of the girl she'd once been, wild and independent. Plus, it gave me a wonderful view of her perfect ass.

"Would you have ever predicted that we'd be here right now?" I asked softly, and she spun from where she was standing on the bench.

She shook her head. "Maybe once. When I was young and dreamed of a life together where we'd roam in the woods and hunt and you'd give me kisses in front of the fire." She laughed to herself. "That was because you guys started sneaking me romance novels in my care packages."

I snorted. We'd done that on purpose. Well, Beckett had. I was pretty sure he'd read each one first too, just so he could talk to her about them. He was a hopeless romantic like that, though he'd never admit it.

She looked down at me from up there, a teasing smile on her lips, her hair framing her face like a shadow. She just stole my breath.

"I wanted to kiss you, Kitten. Especially that last year. It was a physical ache to keep us in the friend zone. But we both wanted you to make the first move."

She reached down and stroked her fingers through my hair. This kitchen had been made for humans, so the countertops only came up to my groin. Which meant that even while standing on the bench, I could have comfortably buried my face between her thighs. Actually...

"Silly Alphas. I never would have made the first move. I'm not that brave."

I gripped her ankle and lifted it slightly, spreading her legs and baring her delicious pussy to my eyes. "Kitten, you're the bravest person I know. Now hang onto those cabinets—I've decided I want something sweet with my glass of milk."

I dragged my tongue through her folds, and her

knees went weak. I put her foot on my shoulder, leaning in close so I was pressing her against the cupboards, holding her steady with a hand on her hip.

"Corvin!" she whisper-shouted, which made me grin. Instead of answering, I just swirled my tongue against her clit faster, until she had both her hands buried in my hair and was holding on for dear life. Fuck yeah. She ground against my face, coating my cheeks in her juices, and then it was my turn to moan. I thrummed loudly on her clit, and she exploded over my mouth with a hiss of pleasure.

I whipped both of her legs out from beneath her, catching her even as she gave an adorable squeak. As I dropped her onto the countertop, she hissed again, but this time it was at the cold laminate against her asscheeks. I pushed down my boxers, and my dick was at the perfect height to nudge between her folds.

Hell yeah. I didn't care if we got chronic back pain from stooping down to cook dinner, I was never changing these benchtops. Ever. I folded her legs up until they wrapped around my waist. Then I slammed inside her, and she couldn't contain her high-pitched moan. I covered her mouth with my hand, my grin so wide it hurt my cheeks.

"Oh baby, I love it when you scream my name, but we wouldn't want to wake the rest of the house, would we?" I slid myself out all the way, and then pushed back inside again. Slow this time. Torturously slow. And again. Slow and steady I moved, until she was panting with the strain of keeping silent against my lips.

She wasn't the only one under strain though, as her pretty little cunt gripped me sweetly. God, it was like she was made for me, which sounded corny as fuck, but it was how I felt. There'd never been another female for me. There never would be.

Pulling back from the kiss, I whispered, "Love you, Kitten."

"Love you. Now harder," she commanded, and I laughed. See, she was perfect.

"Your wish is my command, Omega," my Beast growled back, the sappy fuck. Then I pounded into her like she was my own personal fuck toy, spreading her knees to go deeper as well as harder.

She clawed at my shoulders, her little muffled screams telling me everything I needed to know. Capturing her lips with mine, I switched angles, making her emit a long, low whine like she was a dying cow. Who knew I'd find that so fucking attractive?

Then she came around my dick, and it sucked me in like the greedy little pussy it was. I knew what she wanted though. The base of my cock was already starting to swell in response to her need.

"You want my knot, Omega?"

"Yes!" she whisper-shouted, and I chuckled low in my throat. I spread her thighs wider, pushing her back a little until her head hit the cabinets, then I eased my knot inside her.

It was still growing, and I nudged it in further with tiny thrusts until it popped past the tight circle of her entrance. My eyes rolled back into my head. She was gripping me tight like a fist. I continued to swell, making her writhe against me, and I gritted my teeth so I didn't blow inside her in an instant. I wanted her to come again, come wrapped around my cock, before I filled her with my seed.

I wrapped her in my arms and pulled her close, curling my body so I could suck her pretty pink nipples into my mouth. That was all it took. Covering her own mouth, she clenched around me as she screamed her pleasure, pushing me over the edge with her. Shooting my load deep inside her, I hoped her birth control still held, because I wasn't ready to do that whole pregnancy/birth thing again anytime soon. The Beast grumbled his disagreement, but he could suck it. If he had his way, both of our Omegas would be pregnant all the time. He wanted to see cum dripping from her every opportunity he could.

I'd stay locked inside her for a little while longer, so I lifted her up and walked her a few steps to the couch. I fell backwards, holding her close so it didn't tug painfully, and lay down. She fell onto my chest, her eyes already closing.

She blinked up at me one last time though. "How could I have ever predicted this?" she mumbled, and then fell asleep, and I even chased after her in our dreams.

47

KITTEN

Now the cubs had been born, we made the decision to go back to Maxton and see what was left. We knew from others that it wasn't much, but it was worth a try to recover something that hadn't been destroyed by fire, smoke, or the rain that had occurred after. I also needed to see that the cabin was gone with my own eyes. Needed the closure.

We'd traded in the car we'd fled from Maxton in for something new, with more safety features than a rocketship, eight seats and the ability to go off-road. The amount of seats had been the important part, since no one could agree on who should go in a separate car. The fire had given everyone some serious PTSD, because none of the Alphas could bear to let us out of their sight. Not me, or Darius, or the cubs.

So we'd forked out for the big SUV, and everyone

was happy. Well, I'd forked out for the car. It was the least I could do, and honestly, I had the money. Lorso would've been happy if I spent it on my family.

I looked at the tiny babies secured safely in the center row. They were asleep, but already twice as big as they'd been when they were born. Baby Lorso was by far the calmest of the three, content to sit back and watch the world. Sunny, the firstborn, was full of character, and was the first one to smile. Zena, right there in the middle, had already worked out that if she so much as grumbled a little cry, someone would appear to pick her up and cuddle her until she went back to sleep.

I loved them more than I'd ever thought possible, given they hadn't been born from my body. It didn't matter though, because when I looked at them, I saw myself. Sure, at this age, it was mostly wishful thinking —because they were more squish than features—but it didn't mean that Sunny wasn't looking back at me with my own eyes.

"How are they doing back there?" Cooper said from the driver's seat.

All three of them were sleeping like perfect angels. "Like a dream," I called back, and then leaned back between Beckett and Darius in the back seat.

"That's good. We're almost at the turnoff."

We'd settled into Moonburst now, the Alphas each with their own jobs, though neither Darius or I had decided what we'd do eventually, now that the Sanctum was no more. The Sanctum kids had all been adopted by the De Léon Pack, and the Alpha General had *strongly* emphasized that the knowing creation and abandonment of illegitimate Manix children would be considered a grievous offense, so the males had to wrap it up or step up.

About damn time too.

Three babies kept both Darius and I busy though, so I was just going to enjoy it before going through an existential crisis about what I wanted to do with the rest of my long life. I had started a community garden in the backyard, which I was enjoying.

As happy as I was in Moonburst, as soon as we hit the woods on the outside of Maxton, something settled in my chest. These woods had been my home for so long, and it was hard to let them go.

Not that they looked anything like they had before. The fire had eaten up every ounce of green, so the trees looked like charred sticks as they reached toward the sky. If I searched hard enough though, I could see the sprouts of green starting around the bottom of the trunks. Regrowth. Rebirth.

"Be careful of falling trees, Coop. I don't trust them. They should have cleared the ones closest to the road," Corvin grumbled.

Legion General Joshua, Raiden's dad, had been elected by the other Legion Generals to be interim

Alpha General of Maxton, and I think everyone was relieved. I'd met him once. He seemed nice. Now wasn't the time for big Alpha fights to work out who should be in charge.

I saw someone had dropped hay and what looked like large quantities of carrots along the edge of the forest too, and something eased in my chest. They were worried about the wildlife as well, and I hadn't realized how much that had been weighing on me until now. I'd told Courtland that's what needed to happen, of course, but I didn't know if he'd passed on the message to the Maxton Alpha General.

It wasn't just the Manix whose home had been decimated.

Beckett's hand wrapped around my thigh, and I looked up at him. "Are you okay?" he mouthed, and I nodded. I leaned into his body, not that there was much choice, since he was so huge that he took up most of the back seat. Honestly, we probably needed a bus because there was hardly any room back here for me, squished between Darius and Beckett's giant frames. It was kind of comforting though, and being pressed between them was one of my favorite positions —though usually we were naked and one of them was inside me.

My core tightened at the thought, and four sets of eyes whipped toward me. Whoops.

Darius leaned in so his lips were beside my ear.

"What are you thinking about, my love?" He gave my earlobe a teasing nip, making me shudder.

"The Stock Exchange," I tossed back, and Beckett laughed.

"Want to see my... portfolio?" he said, waggling his eyebrows, and I wondered if I'd ever stop feeling these overwhelmingly huge emotions for each of them. Love, of course, but joy and admiration, sometimes frustration. Everything within the Pack was always so much, that I thought maybe one day I would explode with these feelings they elicited in me.

"Keep your portfolio in your pants back there. We've arrived," Corvin grouched.

There was nothing but rubble left. A few low walls, but basically nothing. Except the mailbox, which was the only reason we knew we were at the right house. Sadness flooded the car, replacing the mirth that had been there only moments earlier.

We climbed out, which was kind of like watching a bunch of clowns unfold themselves from a tiny car, since Beckett had to turn his shoulder just right to squish through the seats.

For a moment, we all stood silently and looked at the wreckage. It was a home I'd only lived in for months, but for these guys, they'd been here for nearly a decade. This had been the place where their Pack had been formed.

Corvin went in first, though there wasn't much to

see. Melted metal, a few charred support beams. It was heartbreaking.

I leaned close to Cooper. "I just want to go and see the cabin. I'll be back."

He shook his head, not dragging his eyes from the mess in front of him. "I'll come with you. It's not safe out there. Besides, I don't think I can..." He waved a hand, and I understood. I nodded, and he quickly went and kissed a devastated-looking Darius, and told Beckett where we were going.

We decided to run, because it had been awhile since both Cooper had shifted and I'd really stretched myself. There were still signs of life out here—a deer leaping through the forest to escape us, rabbits who'd survived in their burrows. I even saw two damn goats just wandering around the undergrowth. All the goats had originally come wethered—which I'd had to hilariously explain to Corvin meant they had no balls—so I wasn't worried that they would overpopulate and destroy the ecosystem. They'd just have free range now, and if the growth ever came back, maybe they'd prevent this from happening again.

It was hard to navigate the way to the cabin with most of my markers gone, but after a little looping around, I realized we'd reached it. Or where it used to be. The cabin had been built by Lorso a century ago, out of materials he'd found in the woods around him, which meant it had all gone up in flames. There was nothing left but the stone hearth, and even that had crumbled a little. The tree I'd buried Lorso under had survived though, even if it was singed at the edges. But it still stood, and something about that made me feel better, even if the home I'd been raised in was now ash.

"Are you okay?" Cooper asked, his voice rough in his Manix form. I nodded as he dragged me into his arms. I rested my cheek against his stomach, the scales hard but warm. His words were a little muffled from the fangs that now rested on his lip, and his ears twitched at the sounds around us.

"Cute ears," I teased, and he tightened his arms around my body.

"You don't seem to mind them when you use them like a steering wheel, while appreciating the length of my tongue between your thighs."

Okay, so fucking them in Manix form was becoming a weird kink for me, but honestly, who knew their tongues doubled in length too? The possibilities were endless.

I grinned up at him. "Touché, Mr. Wiley."

I looked around the site once more, committing it to memory. I would never return, this much I knew. I put one hand over the stone that marked Lorso's grave. "I'll be seeing you again, Old Man."

Then I laid my past to rest right alongside him.

The guys had managed to salvage a small box of stuff from their home. Silly things had survived the fire: a single plate from the set they got as a mating gift from Cooper's parents, a trophy from when Corvin was in high school and won a wrestling competition, a picture of the four of them when they'd gone hiking.

It wasn't much, but it was enough. We stopped by the temporary Legion offices to give them permission to clear the land. We'd keep it, for now, not choosing to sell it back to the Maxton Manix just yet, but maybe one day.

The new Legion office was just a temporary building plonked on the cleared space where the Legion building had once stood. Surprisingly—or not so surprisingly, I guess—the cells at the bottom of the Legion building, where they'd stored all the files and paperwork they hadn't wanted to burn, had survived. Including my father's journals, which I had no urge to go back and read more of. Maybe I could use them to pin my mother's death on him, but what would that achieve? Nothing but more heartache. No, I would leave the past where it belonged now.

Soon enough, we were leaving Maxton. Maybe not forever, but definitely for the foreseeable future. But we had one more stop to make before we headed home.

I PROBABLY SHOULD HAVE ASKED for better directions, but the small rural cemetery wasn't so large that I couldn't find what I needed with a bit of searching.

"Over here," Darius called, Zena cradled in his arms. Honestly, he took my breath away as he stood there, the sun hitting his hair just right to make it more chestnut than its normal warm brown. His body had almost metamorphosed back to its original shape, and I knew there would be women in the world who'd hate him for the fact he had abs again four weeks after giving birth.

I drifted toward him, with Sunny in my arms. I could sense my Alphas converging toward us too. Darius leaned over and kissed my temple. "We'll give you a minute. Want me to take the baby?"

I shook my head and listened to his steps as he quietly moved away. Squatting down next to the head-stone, I read the rough-hewn words.

Here lies Leandra Adler.
A damn fine woman.
Too good for this world. May she rest in peace.

I LAUGHED, because it sounded exactly like Ol' Sam. I'd have to thank him, though I wasn't in any way responsible for my mother. I shouldn't have to thank someone for being a decent human being, but I would anyway.

I realized I wouldn't have been much bigger than Sunny when I was left on the border of Packlands, and I would never know if she meant to save me or kill me, or why she did that instead of running. But I chose, for my own mental health, to assume that she knew Lorso was out there and that he'd rescue me in time.

"I grew up. I was happy. I think that's what you wanted, and I hope it helps you rest easier. You live on, in Sunny and her siblings, and in my future children, and I hope that's what you wanted too. I'm sorry that I never got to know you, that I'll never understand your story, but at least mine has a happy ending."

I sat in silence a little longer, contemplating how hard it would be to give up Sunny at this age. It must have been heartbreaking for my mother, unless she was a monster. I had to hold onto the belief that both of my parents hadn't been evil.

Finally, a shadow blocked out the sun, and I looked up to see Beckett. "The other babies are getting fussy and it's still a long drive home. But we can stay if you need more time."

My ass and my arms—because babies were heavy —were dead anyway. I offered up Sunny, and Beck took her easily. "No, I'm done here."

With that, I climbed to my feet and walked to the car that was filled with the people I loved. The violence of my past might always be a mystery to me, but I knew in my soul that my future held nothing but love.

ABOUT THE AUTHOR

Grace McGinty is eclectic. She has worked as a chocolatier, a librarian, a forensic accountant and finally a writer. Like her professional career, the genres she writes are also eclectic. She writes romance, reverse harem romance, fantasy, contemporary young adult and new adult books.

She lives in rural Australia with her crazy family, an entire menagerie of pets, and will one day be crushed by the giant piles of books that litter every room.

Head over to www.gracemcginty.com and join my mailing list for sneak previews into what I am working on and to stay up-to-date with new releases and giveaways!

Want more of the Manix? Keep an eye out for the Preorder for CRAVE: SHADOW BRED BOOK 4, coming soon!

Skip to the back to meet Raine and her guys in the first chapter of Newly Undead in Dark River!

INTERCONNECTED SERIES LIST AND SUGGESTED READING ORDER
ALL SERIES CAN BE READ STANDALONE

Hell's Redemption Trilogy

A deal between omnipotent forces puts a dying woman in the path of the Seven Deadly Sins. The only way she can save herself is to save them all.

Damnation MC Duet

What do you do when the Angels are the demons and the Four Horsemen are your protectors?

The Azar Nazemi Trilogy

Azar just wanted to hide from the supernatural world, helping humans with her djinn fire powers. However, when the two worlds collide in the deadliest way possible, only Azar can help save them all.

Dark River Days Series

What happens when you wake up Undead in a town filled with reformed Vampires and your murderer is a citizen who is willing to kill you permanently to keep you from talking?

Black Mountain Mates

Years ago, a knock at her window sent Isla running from her home and the boys she loved. But they never gave up on finding her, and when they do, they are never going to let her go again.

Eden Academy Series

Welcome to Eden. A safe haven for the preternatural, for the lost and for the hunted. An Academy where young supes can learn who they are and grow into their powers safely. Well... almost safely.

Shadow Bred Series

The Manix have been hiding for a century, and now they were nearly extinct. Their female Omegas were all but a myth, and even female Betas were rare. That is until an impossible scent on the wind gives the entire species hope.

COMING SUMMER 2022

SHADOW BRED

CRAVE

BOOK FOUR

USA TODAY BESTSELLING AUTHOR

GRACE MCGINTY

NEWLY UNDEAD IN DARK RIVER

I woke to a rat scuttling across my chest, its tiny nose twitching as it paused to stare at me before scurrying off. Damn, I was hungry.

The fact that my initial reaction to a rat was hunger and not disgust was the first sign that something was very, very wrong. The second clue was that I was lying in a drainpipe in the middle of the night. Although it was hard to concentrate on anything but the hunger clawing at my stomach, I could hear the nocturnal animals shuffling around in the silence and smell the stale water that now soaked my clothes.

I tried to sit up and banged my head on the slimy concrete. Groaning, I rolled over and crawled my way out into the open. My body felt like I'd climbed Everest. Twice. I couldn't see my backpack anywhere. Panic began to fill my chest. Everything was in that pack. But it was pitch black, the moon not even visible behind the clouds. I became acutely aware that I was standing in the middle of the wilderness, at night, alone. I was a serial killer's wet dream right now.

I stared down the road, looking for the oncoming lights of a car or truck or something. Maybe I could hitch a ride into the nearest town. It was probably hitchhiking that had put me in this predicament to start with. My mom was going to be pissed that I'd been so irresponsible.

I felt dazed like I'd been tranquilized, but I patted down my clothing with sluggish movements. Nothing was torn, and all my clothes were still on. I didn't feel violated in any way. My brain was cloudy, and I tried to sift through the fog to remember why I was lying in a ditch, outside of...

I looked up at the road sign. *Welcome to Dark River.* Where the hell was Dark River?

Hunger tore at my belly again, a burning ache so painful I moaned into the darkness like a wounded animal. First, I needed to eat something. Maybe then I'd be able to work out what the hell was going on.

I stumbled down the side of the road, and I could see the muted glow of the town lights once I was over the small rise.

Electricity surged up through my chest, and the edges of my vision dimmed. The last thing I felt when my body buckled was the rough gravel scraping my cheek.

I snapped back to consciousness all at once, like when you dream you're falling. My head felt too full, and panic was beginning to mingle with the overwhelming hunger.

I was now in town, beneath the striped awning of Bert and Beatrice's Old Fashioned Diner. How the fuck did I get here? Everything was completely blank as if someone had plucked the memory from my brain like a bad apple. A clock tower sat in the middle of town, proclaiming it to be almost midnight.

I pushed through the glass door, and a little bell tinkled above my head. The place was filled to the brim, which was unusual seeing how it was basically the middle of the night.

Every set of eyes turned to look at me, and the old guy behind the counter dropped the soda glass he was drying, the smashing sound shooting pain into my skull. I must've really looked like hell. An elderly woman bustled out of the swinging doors, which probably led to the kitchen.

"What's goin' on out..." she trailed off when she saw me standing in the doorway. She nudged the old man out of the way.

"Lass, are you feelin' alright? Bertie, get the girl a drink. The house special," she said slowly, her accent a thick Scottish brogue. "Tilda, call the Sheriff, please. Get him down here, quick smart." She was rounding the counter now. "Here, Lass, take a seat."

I obediently took the stool she indicated. She had a no-nonsense, matronly tone that soothed my panicked nerves.

"I lost my money and my passport." My voice sounded so weak that I hardly recognized it as my own.

The elderly lady just patted my shoulder.

"Not to worry, Sweet. It's on the house."

I could hear the sound of Tilda murmuring quietly into the phone down the other end of the diner.

"Yes Sheriff, just stumbled in the door. Looking like death, if you know what I mean."

The old man, Bertie I guess, slid a cardboard milkshake cup in front of me, complete with red and white straw. It smelled so good that I fell on it like a half-starved animal. When I'd sucked down the last drop, I looked up, embarrassed.

"Sorry. I was really hungry." Bertie just took away my empty cup and put a fresh one in front of me.

"Don't worry about it, Darlin'. Have another one." I was struggling to concentrate on her words. I found it hard to concentrate on anything but the milkshake in front of me.

The bell over the door tinkled, and everyone's eyes shifted in that direction again, even mine. A tall man in a chocolate brown uniform walked into the place, and everyone started talking at once. The cacophony after the complete absence of noise was hell on my eardrums. I pushed my palms over my ears to try and muffle some of the sounds.

"Quiet!" The guy was obviously the Sheriff, judging by the way that everyone's flapping jaws snapped shut with almost perfect synchronization. Silence again. The man strode over, his every movement elegant, to where I was sitting and gaping in his direction.

The man was hot. Like, spontaneous combustion, three-alarm, call in the National Guard, hot. He had sandy brown hair and deep green eyes. The uniform hugged his muscular body. He was so attractive it made my teeth hurt. Literally.

"Ma'am, my name is Sheriff Walker Walton. Do you need some help?" His deep voice was gentle, almost as if he didn't want to startle me.

"I don't know how I got here," I whispered. It was all a blank.

I'd been backpacking my way through Canada with my friends, but they had gone home last week, while I continued to travel up through Alberta by myself. I'd missed my bus to Yukon, so had decided to hitchhike my way through the last stretch to the border of British Columbia. After all, what's life without a little adventure? I'd been picked up by a family with teenage sons, but they'd let me off near Grande Prairie. I'd walked down the highway a bit more, and then poof, every-thing else was blank.

"Do you remember your name?" the Sheriff asked in the same soft voice.

"Mika McKellan. From Boston."

"That's good, Mika. I'd like you to come down to the station with me, so we can get this all sorted out. The town doctor will meet us there, just to check you over."

I nodded absently, and followed Sheriff Walton out of the diner, clutching my cardboard cup to my chest like a lifebuoy. He walked me over to the squad car, and let me sit in the passenger seat, instead of the back.

We drove in silence around the block, and I took the town in. It was actually quite beautiful. Not the cemetery stillness of most small towns after dark. Fairy lights were strung around the town square, and people milled about. The lights were on in all the shops, and small clumps of people were talking to each other on well-lit sidewalks.

"Is there a festival going on or something?" I asked Sheriff Walton.

"Or something," he replied, letting silence fill the car.

Within a minute, we'd pulled up in front of a skinny brick building. There were shiny bars on the windows, and a Police sign hanging over the front lawn.

Sheriff Walton moved around the front of the car and opened the passenger door. I heaved myself out of the seat. Moving wasn't as painful as it had been when I first woke up, but I still felt sluggish.

A plain woman with sparkling eyes met us at the front door. She looked me over and then sent a pointed expression to Sheriff Walton.

"Mika, this is Doctor Alice Sommer. I'm gonna get the Doc to check you for any signs of, uh, injury."

He held open the door of the station for me, and I gave him a polite smile.

"Let's go into the conference room. We need to have a chat after the Doc has looked you over. I'll be out here doing some paperwork."

He opened the door to an interrogation room. No windows, just a metal table with two chairs. Conference room, my ass.

"Thanks, Walker. I'll give you a shout when we're done," the doctor said softly.

The door closed with a click. The doctor sat a leather doctor's bag on the metal table. "Have a seat, Miss McKellan."

"Mika."

"Okay, Mika it is. But you have to call me Alice. Now, let me have a look at you." She shone one of those penlights in my eyes, and I let out a little squeal.

"Ouch."

"Hmm, light sensitivity. You have a little bruising

on your throat too." She got out a measuring instrument and measured the width of the bruise. "Anything else feel off to you?"

"Except for the starving feeling, the aching muscles, the weird blank spots and the passing out?" My sarcasm was obnoxious, but I couldn't seem to help it. "Other than all that, I'm as healthy as a horse."

The doctor clicked her tongue and wrote down the measurements. "Walker, can you get the cooler from the backseat of my car and come in here please?" She barely raised her voice, but the Sheriff must have heard because the front door of the station slammed.

"Don't worry, Mika. Your symptoms should lessen in a few days."

"Lessen?"

But the Sheriff was striding into the room, cooler in hand. Damn, he was fast.

"It's confirmed, Walker. Though let's face it, it was obvious to everyone as soon as she walked through the door of the diner. You can smell it just as well as I can."

The Sheriff ran a hand down his face and sighed. "I know, but I didn't want to believe it. I didn't want to think someone we know could have done this."

What the hell were they talking about? I sniffed my armpit stealthily. I didn't think I smelled that bad, considering I'd been sleeping in a ditch. My nose twitched. A tangy metallic smell was coming from the cooler. A smell that was so familiar, but I couldn't quite put my finger on what it was.

"You know, I'm still in the room. Do you think someone could take me out to the ditch and see if I can find my wallet and my backpack? Everything I have is in that pack."

"Ditch?"

"The one I woke up in. Under the welcome sign."

The Sheriff's eyebrows knitted together, and I could basically see the cogs turning. "Sure. We'll go take a look out there first thing tomorrow night."

"Why can't we go in the morning?"

Alice laid a hand on my arm and rested her butt on the table. She was looking down at me sympathetically. In my experience, that was never a good sign.

"Mika, we have something to tell you. This is going to sound outrageous and frightening, but I want you to know that we're here for you."

My heart started to race. Something in the back of my mind screamed that in a minute, nothing was ever going to be the same.

"Did my pet goldfish die? Are you two getting a divorce?" I deflected awkward situations with sarcasm. My therapist and I were working through it back home.

It was the Sheriff that answered. "No. Well, maybe, I don't know. I've never seen your pet goldfish, but I understand they die quite frequently." Walker ran his hand through his hair, and my hands itched to follow suit. "Look, Mika, I know this is going to sound strange, but it's our opinion that last night, you, well uh, you died."

I laughed. Maybe I'd stumbled into one of those reality TV shows. The producer was going to jump out any minute and make me sign a media release and a Non-Disclosure Agreement.

But the door never opened, and the two people opposite me never cracked a smile. "In case you guys didn't notice, I'm sitting right here, conversing with you. I haven't seen many dead people in my life, but I went to Great-Aunt Milly's funeral when I was twelve, and she didn't talk back to me from the coffin."

Alice gripped my hand. There was something off-putting about a doctor holding your hand like you were about to get really bad news.

"What Walker is trying to say, Mika"—they kept saying my name over and over like I'd suddenly forgotten it—"is that you are the undead. We believe you have been turned into a vampire. I should say, we *know* you've been turned into a vampire. It's the *how* that we don't understand yet."

I blinked. And then blinked again. They were actually serious. They thought I was a vampire. I'd definitely stumbled onto a TV set. It sounded like something the SyFy channel would come up with. But my heart was thudding, and I felt like I was going to throw up. It was like my body knew they weren't kidding, and it was just waiting for my mind to catch up.

"A vampire?"

Walker nodded sympathetically. "The hunger, the light sensitivity, even the blank spots, are all symptoms of the Turning."

"And you guys know this because..." No, this couldn't be right. My mind rebelled.

"Because we are vampires. The whole town is populated by vampires."

I stared at them dumbly, expecting something, I wasn't sure what. For them to turn into bats, or broodingly sparkle in the overhead fluorescent lights. But nothing happened. They just looked like ordinary people. Not overly pale, their eyes weren't glowing red, they didn't have crooked, needle-like teeth. Nothing.

Alice had mocha-colored skin and smooth blond hair that went all the way down her back. She wasn't extraordinarily attractive by any means. She was pleasant and professional; exactly what you'd want in a physician. Okay, so Walker was hot, but from what I remembered of the diner, it wasn't like I'd stepped onto the stage at Milan Fashion Week or anything out of the ordinary.

"Do you have any questions?" Walker asked. Uh, yeah, I had a few. Like could he pinch me so I would wake the hell up from this bad acid trip?

"So, I'm a vampire, and you're a vampire. And she's a vampire." He nodded. "Do you, I mean I, have fangs?"

Walker bared his teeth, and there, gleaming white against his pink lips, were two pointed fangs. They were actually quite sharp, and I wondered how he didn't cut his mouth up with them. I looked at Alice, and she too was baring her fangs, which weren't quite as long as Walker's and sat in her mouth with more ease. I eased my tongue over my own canines and found they'd elongated. I cut my tongue on them, and the blood dripped into my mouth.

Blood.

Hunger clawed at my stomach like a ravenous beast. Suddenly, I understood what the smell coming from the cooler was.

"Please." It was a half yell, half sob, as I dived for the cooler. Walker was around the table in a flash, his arms like iron bands around my body.

"Calm down. Alice is going to get you something to eat right now." As he said it, the Doc was getting a blood bag out of the cooler, like the ones you saw in hospitals. She unscrewed the cap on the tube and handed it to me.

Walker released me from his hold, and I closed off the part of my mind that was grossed out at the thought of drinking blood, and let my body take over. I sucked that baby like it was my first cocktail on spring break in Cabo. All that was missing was the little umbrella and the frat boys trying to convince me to come to a snow party.

All too soon, the bag was empty. "I want some more." My voice wasn't weak anymore, but it sounded slurred like I was drunk. Alice shook her head.

"With the two you had at the diner, and now this one, you've had enough. If you gorge yourself, you'll be vomiting for the rest of the night. I'll come see you tomorrow and we'll discuss how everything works. For the remainder of the night, you need to rest." She picked up the cooler and her doctor's bag. "Are you taking her to your place?" she asked Walker.

He nodded. "I'll find somewhere more permanent for her to live tomorrow." He walked the doctor out, leaving me alone in the windowless room.

The shock settled over me like a numbing cloak. My mind spun as I tried to process, well, everything. I placed my hand on my chest, and felt my heart slowly beating in there. Somehow, that made me feel better. I may have been dead, but my heart was still beating. The illogicality of that statement was something I'd deal with another day.

Walker was suddenly back, and his warm hand was on my shoulder. "There are a lot of things we have to discuss. We can do it here, or back at my place. I know that sounds almost creepy, but I promise you'll be safe." He shifted from foot to foot, almost uncomfortably. "You are new to this world, and I wouldn't feel right about leaving you on your own. There are rules, life or death rules that you need to know. But, if you'd like, we could do it somewhere a bit more comfortable."

I nodded absently, every warning my mother uttered about going home with strange men now defunct. What was the worst that could happen? I was already dead. Plus the guy was the Sheriff of a vampire town. If I couldn't trust him, who could a girl, err vampire, trust?

We hopped back into the squad car. I looked at the town through the window in a new light. I really studied the people, their inhuman grace, the fact that there were no children around. A guy stood on the pavement waiting to cross the road, and then magically was on the other side. I didn't even see him move in front of the car.

"Did that guy just teleport? Can we do that?" The thought was exciting. To just close my eyes and picture anywhere I wanted to be in the world, it would be amazing. Such freedom!

"I'm afraid not. He just moved really fast. As your vampirism settles into your body, you'll see him move as slow as a human. We can all move that quickly."

I was disappointed, though moving at super-speed was still pretty cool. "If we can move that fast, why the hell are we driving? Wouldn't we be wherever we are going almost instantly? Unless your house is in Alaska."

"Two reasons. Firstly, I didn't want to freak you out, plus you'll need a bit of time to get used to moving at that speed. Secondly, I enjoy the slower pace that a vehicle has to offer. Just because you can go at break-neck speed, doesn't mean you should." He sounded like my dad teaching me to drive. Thoughts of my parents made me feel homesick.

"I need to call my parents and tell them I'm okay. Sort of."

Walker looked uncomfortable. "If you want, but just wait until tomorrow. Give everything you'll learn tonight time to process first."

He pulled up in front of a cute little whitewashed cottage, with a wrap-around porch and a perfectly manicured hedge. I looked at the man in the driver's seat and then back at the house. I saw him as the log cabin type of guy, not the gingerbread vibe that this place had going on.

I followed Walker up to the front door. I don't know when I started to think of him as Walker instead of Sheriff Walton, but it was probably around my third dirty fantasy.

When we walked in, the space had a bit more of a masculine feel. Leather couches, a big-screen TV, and a scarred wooden coffee table occupied the living room. A large breakfast bar separated the living area from the kitchen, with three old diner stools tucked under the overhang.

Walker went over to the kitchen counter and poured two glasses of scotch into crystal tumblers.

"I can still drink?"

"Sure. You won't get drunk, but sometimes it's nice just to indulge in the nostalgia. You can also eat and go out in the sun. Though I wouldn't suggest going out in the daytime just yet. The increased sensitivity to light makes daylight extremely painful. It's something to work up to over time. Please, have a seat."

I walked over to the big scarred leather armchair. There was a burgundy throw rug over the arm, and I pulled it over my lap, even though I wasn't cold. The softness of the mohair was amazing. I could see the intricate pattern of the weave, the tiny flyaway fibers on each of the strands of wool. It was like my sight had become microscopic.

Walker handed me my drink and sat across from me, his elbows on his knees.

"I know this has been a lot to take in, but you have some serious decisions to make, Mika. This is a whole new world, with all new rules. Especially Dark River. We aren't your average community, as you know."

"Because everyone is the undead."

"Right, because we're all vampires. But it's not just that. Even within our own race, Dark River is rather unique. I'll explain the rules, and then it's up to you if you stay or you go. We can't keep you here against your will."

Well, that sounded ominous.

"Rule number one, there is absolutely no drinking from humans. Blood is delivered and distributed around the town by the Town Council, and no one goes hungry. The penalty is banishment from Dark River, forever."

That didn't sound so bad. It's not like I wanted to go around munching on people, giving them the hickeys from hell. I nodded for him to continue.

"Rule number two, you can never, ever, turn a human. The Town Council has decreed that the penalty for disobeying this rule is death. Because, in our eyes, turning a human is essentially murder." He looked at me imploringly. "This is what has happened to you, Mika. Someone has murdered you, and it's my job to find out who and bring them to justice. You are young, beautiful, and full of life. You should have had the opportunity to do everything you wanted to do. The opportunity to have children, get married, grow old with a loved one, live out in the light. You deserve retribution." His eyes lit up, and I don't mean sparkled with fervor, I mean literally started to glow.

"Uh, Walker, what's going on with your eyes?"

"Sorry. I didn't mean to freak you out. That some-times happens when I get worked up. Plus I need to feed."

He walked over to the fridge and pulled out a bag of O positive. I knew it was O positive because there was a huge sticker on the side. He poured it into his tumbler on top of his Scotch. Ew.

He sat back down in front of me.

"Okay, the third rule is usually the most problematic for new vampires who want to join our community. You must cut all ties with your old life, both for our safety and the safety of the people from before. You wouldn't know this yet, but being around humans is..."—he let out a shaky sigh—"an overwhelming temptation. Especially when you are only just learning to control your new body."

I collapsed back on the couch. I'd have to cut ties with my family? Never see my mom smile again, or hear my dad tell a lame joke? Never watch my youngest brother graduate high school? Tears welled in my eyes as my death sunk in. My mind was in the denial stage of grief, apparently. I mean, I felt fine now that I'd drank that blood bag. Maybe I could go home and become a goth or something. I lived alone in my apartment, so I could keep the blood hidden.

"I know what you're thinking. Really, I do. But think about it. You will never look older than you do today. You will live hundreds, if not thousands of years. If you go home, you'll watch your parents die, and your siblings, and their children, and then their children's children. Trust me when I say that it is a soul-shattering experience to watch everyone you have ever loved wither and die." The level of pain in his eyes told me that he knew from experience.

I couldn't decide this now; I needed time to think it over.

"What if I choose to leave?"

Walker bit his lip, his fangs pressing into his full lower lip. "If you choose to leave, then you are subject to the rules of the Vampire Nation. No telling humans what you are, or revealing your nature in a way that could bring vampires as a whole into the limelight. If you feed on humans, you must do it in a way that they do not suspect your true nature. Which basically means that unless you have the ability to wipe memories—which some vampires do—you'll have to kill them and dispose of their bodies discreetly. If you break these rules, Enforcers will come, and you will die. Trust me when I say that Vampire Nation always finds out if you break the rules."

Well, okay then.

Walker's shaggy hair slipped over his eyes, and he combed it back with his fingers. The move made his shirt pull taut against his chest, and a completely different kind of hunger overtook me. The need to lean over and rip open his shirt was almost impossible to resist.

Walker's eyes met mine, and whatever he saw in

them made him look nervous all of a sudden. He stood quickly and took a step away.

"Okay, I'll let you think it over. The guest room is the second door on the left, and the bathroom is right next door. Make yourself at home. If you need anything, just give me a yell." With that, Sheriff Walker Walton hot-footed it out of the room, faster than my eyes could follow.